More praise for
"Brilliantly Original" (*R...*
New York Times **bestsellin...**

"Readers will love Chet's ruminations on steak, bacon, chew toys and cats. Adorable describes this character-driven novel, which is also well-written and nicely paced. . . . Even cat lovers will howl with delight." —*USA Today*

"Sit and stay! You're going to love *Dog on It* as much as I did, because it confirms what every dog fan has long suspected—that our dogs are not only more fun than we are, they're smarter!"
—Lisa Scottoline, *New York Times* bestselling author of *Look Again*

"I'm not a dog fancier, but I had a great time reading this book. . . . Chet is a hoot—or should I say a howl." —*Boston Globe*

"Try to imagine the personality of Jim Rockford or Philip Marlowe somehow fused with one of Edgar Sawtelle's dogs and you get a clear picture of Chet's outlook. . . . [*Dog on It* is] sweetly engaging . . . and wonderfully entertaining." —*The Denver Post*

"Features the most winning narrator I've come across in a long time . . . [and] manages to ratchet up some real suspense."
—*Christian Science Monitor*

"I love this book. I devoured it in one night. It was so much fun. It was like Philip Marlowe working for Mma Ramotswe from *The No. 1 Ladies' Detective Agency* spun out by Charlotte on her beautiful web." —Cathleen Schine, internationally bestselling author of *The New Yorkers*

"Nothing short of masterful. . . . Sequels are a given, and a must."
—*Los Angeles Times*

"Grab your snacks, find a shady spot outside and curl up for a good time reading *Dog on It*." —*Sacramento Book Review*

"Spencer Quinn speaks two languages—suspense and dog—very fluently. Sometimes funny, sometimes touching, and in a few places terrifying, *Dog on It* has got more going for it than fifty of those cat-cozies. The best thing about the book is Chet, a canine Sam Spade full of joie de vivre. He's a great character because he sums up what we all love in dogs: how they love life, and how they love us. My sincere advice to you is to rush to your nearest bookstore and put your paws on this enchanting one-of-a-kind novel. Except maybe it isn't! I'm already howling for Bernie and Chet's encore."

—Stephen King

"A winning debut . . . that fans of classic mysteries are sure to appreciate." —*Publishers Weekly* (starred review)

"Bernie and Chet may be the most appealing detective duo since Watson and Holmes." —Sharon Kay Penman, *New York Times* bestselling author of *Devil's Brood*

"Stalwart, often mischievous narrator Chet's amusing, perceptive canine take on [the novel's] human characters should appeal to hard-boiled fans and canine fanciers alike." —*Kirkus Reviews*

"I love this book. I love Chet. You don't have to be a dog lover, though, to find *Dog on It* an exciting, stylish page-turner and a true breath of fresh air. . . . Brilliant. . . . Spencer Quinn is a remarkable new talent."

—Joseph Finder, *New York Times* bestselling author of *Vanished*

"*Dog on It* will delight dog-loving mystery readers, but the book is also an excellent PI tale, dogs aside. . . . Chet may well be one of the most appealing new detectives on the block, but Bernie is a close runner-up. Excellent and fully fleshed primary and secondary characters, a consistently doggy view of the world, and a sprightly pace make this a not-to-be-missed debut." —*Booklist* (starred review)

"A detective, a dog, and some major-league prose. *Dog on It* is a genuine joy."
—Robert B. Parker

"At last, a dog lover's mystery that portrays dogs as they really are. . . . Quinn's characters are endearing, and his narrative is intriguing, fast-moving, and well written. Even cat lovers will find it entertaining."
—*Library Journal* (starred review)

"Paws up for Spencer Quinn. . . . With a brilliantly original concept, an engaging plot . . . and characters who'll bowl you over, Quinn has fashioned one of the most creative mysteries you'll find this year, or any other. *Dog on It* defies subgenre categorization, and that's fine. What it doesn't defy is likability." —*Richmond Times-Dispatch*

"Dog lovers are likely to lick their chops over *Dog on It,* the first in an unusual, funny new series. . . . Highly entertaining. . . . Satisfying action abounds. Chet's down-to-earth narration is superb in a hilarious book that offers great escapism." —*Lansing State Journal*

"Exudes dogged charm. . . . Chet's unique voice and his relationship with Bernie keep us turning the pages. Chet, long on common sense and short on attention span, is an engaging protagonist. . . . Here's hoping there are more adventures to come for the dauntless duo of detective and dog."
—*Deseret News*

This title is also available as an eBook

DOG ON IT

A CHET AND BERNIE MYSTERY

SPENCER QUINN

ATRIA PAPERBACK
New York London Toronto Sydney

ATRIA PAPERBACK
A Division of Simon & Schuster, Inc.
1230 Avenue of the Americas
New York, NY 10020

First Atria Paperback edition September 2009

ATRIA PAPERBACK and colophon are trademarks of Simon & Schuster, Inc.

For information about special discounts for bulk purchases, please contact Simon & Schuster Special Sales at 1-866-506-1949 or business@simonandschuster.com.

The Simon & Schuster Speakers Bureau can bring authors to your live event. For more information or to book an event contact the Simon & Schuster Speakers Bureau at 1-866-248-3049 or visit our website at www.simonspeakers.com.

Designed by Claudia Martinez

Manufactured in the United States of America

10   9   8   7   6   5   4   3   2   1

The Library of Congress has cataloged the hardcover edition as follows:

Quinn, Spencer.
   Dog on it : a Chet and Bernie mystery / Spencer Quinn.
      p. cm.
   1. Dogs—Fiction. 2. Missing persons—Investigation—Fiction. I. Title

PS3617.U584D64   2008
813'.6—dc22   2008015371

ISBN 978-1-4165-8583-1
ISBN 978-1-4165-8584-8 (pbk)
ISBN 978-1-4165-8592-3 (eBook)

For Bailey, Gansett, Charlie, Clem, and Audrey,
without whom this book would not
have been possible

DOG ON IT

ONE

I could smell him—or rather the booze on his breath—before he even opened the door, but my sense of smell is pretty good, probably better than yours. The key scratched against the lock, finally found the slot. The door opened and in, with a little stumble, came Bernie Little, founder and part owner (his ex-wife, Leda, walked off with the rest) of the Little Detective Agency. I'd seen him look worse, but not often.

He mustered a weak smile. "Hey, Chet."

I raised my tail and let it thump down on the rug, just so, sending a message.

"I'm a little late, sorry. Need to go out?"

Why would that be? Just because my back teeth were floating? But then I thought, What the hell, the poor guy, and I went over and pressed my head against the side of his leg. He scratched between my ears, really digging his fingers in, the way I like. Bliss. How about a little more, down the back of the neck? I hunched my shoulders a bit, giving him the idea. Ah, nice. Very nice.

We went outside, me and Bernie. There were three trees out front, my favorite being a big shady one just perfect for napping under. I lifted my leg against it. Wow. Hadn't realized I was that close to desperation. The night filled with splashing sounds and I zoned out a little, listening to them. I managed to stop the flow— not easy—and save some for dampening the rock at the end of the driveway and the wooden fence that separated our property from old man Heydrich's next door, plus a squirt or two between the slats. Only doing my job, but don't get me started on old man Heydrich.

Bernie was gazing up at the sky. A beautiful night—soft breeze, lots of stars, lights twinkling down the canyon, and what was this? A new tennis ball on the lawn. I went over and sniffed it. Not one of mine, not anyone's I knew.

"Wanna play fetch?"

I pawed the thing. How did it get here? Cooped up all day, but I'd kept an ear cocked; except for when I dozed off, of course.

"Bring it here, Chet."

I didn't want to, not with this stranger's smell on it.

"Come on."

But I never said no to Bernie. I gave the ball a lick or two, making it mine, then took it over to Bernie and dropped it at his feet. Bernie reared back and threw the ball up the canyon road.

"Uh-oh—where'd it go?"

Where'd it go? He really couldn't see it? That never failed to surprise me, how poorly he saw after the sun went down. I tore after the ball, bouncing up the middle of the road in plain sight, got my back feet way forward and sprang, totally airborne, snaring it on the short hop, the way I like, then wheeling around in one skidding motion and racing full speed, head low, ears flattened by the wind I was making, and dropped it at Bernie's feet, putting on the brakes at the last moment. If you know something more fun than this, let me in on the secret.

"Got it on the short hop? Couldn't tell from here."

I wagged my tail, that quick one-two wag meaning yes, not the over-the-top one that wags itself and can mean lots of things, some of which I'm not too clear on myself.

"Nice." He picked up the ball and was rearing back again when a car came slowly down the street and stopped in front of us.

The window slid down and a woman leaned out. "Is this thirteen-three-oh-nine?"

Bernie nodded.

"I'm looking for Bernie Little, the detective."

"You found him."

She opened the door, started to get out, then saw me. "Is the dog all right?"

Bernie stiffened. I felt it; he was standing right beside me. "Depends what you mean."

"You know, is he safe, does he bite? I'm not that comfortable around dogs."

"He won't bite you."

Of course I wouldn't. But the idea was planted in my head, for sure. I could tell by all the saliva suddenly pooling in my mouth.

"Thanks. You never know about dogs."

Bernie said something under his breath, too low for even me to hear; but I knew I liked it, whatever it was.

She got out of the car, a tall woman with long fair hair and a smell of flowers and lemons, plus a trace of another smell that reminded me of what happens only sometimes to the females in my world. What would that be like, having it turned on all the time? Probably drive you crazy. I glanced at Bernie, watching her, patting his hair into place. Oh, Bernie.

"I'm not sure where to begin. Nothing like this has ever happened to me."

"Nothing like what?"

She wrung her hands. Hands are the weirdest things about humans, and the best: you can find out just about everything you need to know by watching them. "I live over on El Presidente." She waved vaguely.

El Presidente: Was that the one where the sewer pipes were still going in? I was bad on street names—except our own, Mesquite Road—but why not? I didn't need them to find my way.

"My name's Cynthia Chambliss. I work with a woman you helped."

"Who?"

"Angela DiPesto."

Mercy. I remembered endless nights parked in front of motels up and down the state. We hated divorce work, me and Bernie, never even accepted any in the old days. But now we were having cash-flow problems, as Bernie put it. The truth was, I didn't really know what "cash-flow problems" meant, but whatever they were, they woke Bernie in the night, made him get up and pace around, sometimes lighting a cigarette, even though he'd worked so hard to stop.

Bernie didn't commit to anything about Angela DiPesto, just gave one of those little nods of his. Bernie was a great nodder. He had several different nods I could think of off the top of my head, all very readable once you knew what to look for. This particular nod meant: strike one.

"The fact is, Angie spoke of you highly—how you stuck it to that creep of a husband." She gave herself a little shake. I can do that way, way better. "So when this happened, and you being practically in the neighborhood and all . . . anyway, here I am." She rocked back and forth slightly, the way humans do when they're very nervous.

"When what happened?"

"This thing with Madison. She's disappeared."

"Madison is your daughter?"

"Didn't I say that? Sorry. I'm just so upset, I don't know what I'm . . ."

Her eyes glistened up. This was always pretty interesting, the crying thing; not the sound—I could relate to that—but the waterworks, as Bernie called them, especially when Leda was on the producing end. They get upset, humans, and then water comes out of their eyes, especially the women. What is that all about? Bernie gazed down at the ground, shuffled his feet; he didn't have a handle on it, either, although I'd once seen water seeping out of his own eyes, namely the day Leda had packed up all Charlie's things. Charlie was their kid—Bernie and Leda's—and now lived with Leda except for visits. We missed him, me and Bernie.

This woman—Cynthia? Chambliss? whatever her name was—the truth is, I have trouble catching names at first, sometimes miss other things, too, unless I have a real good view of the speaker's face—took a tissue from a little bag she carried and dabbed at her eyes. "Sorry."

"Nothing to be sorry for. How long has Madison been missing?"

The woman started to answer, but at that moment I heard something rustling in the bushes on the far side of the driveway. The next thing I knew, I was in the bushes myself, sniffing around, maybe even digging, but only the littlest bit. Some kind of smell was in the air, frog or toad, or . . . uh-oh: snake. I didn't like snakes, didn't like them at—

"Chet? You're not digging in there, are you?"

I backed out of the bushes, trotted over to Bernie. Oops—my

tail was down, tucked back in a guilty manner. I stuck it right up, high and innocent.

"Good boy." He patted my head. Thump thump. Ah.

The woman was tapping her foot on the ground. "So you're saying you won't help me?"

Bernie took a deep breath. His eyes looked tired. The booze was wearing off. He'd be sleepy very soon. I was feeling a bit sleepy myself. Plus a little taste of something might be nice. Were there any of those rawhide chew strips left in the top drawer by the kitchen sink, the ones with that Southwestern flav—

"That's not exactly what I said. Your daughter didn't come home from school today. That makes her gone, what, not yet eight hours? The police won't even open a missing-persons file till a full day's gone by."

Eight hours I had trouble with, but a full day I knew very well, from when the sun rose over the hills behind the garage to when it went down behind the hills on the other side.

"But you're not the police."

"True, and we don't always agree, but I agree on this. You say Madison's a sophomore in high school? So she's what? Sixteen?"

"Fifteen. She's in the gifted program."

"In my experience, fifteen-year olds sometimes forget to call home, especially when they're doing something impulsive, like going to the movies, or hanging out, or partying from time to time."

"It's a school night."

"Even on school nights."

"I told you—she's gifted."

"So was Billie Holiday."

"I'm sorry?" The woman looked confused; the confused human face is almost as ugly as the angry one. I didn't get the

Billie Holiday thing, either, but at least I knew who she was—this singer Bernie listened to, especially when he was in one of his brooding moods.

But even if no one got what he was talking about, Bernie seemed pleased with himself, like he'd scored some point. I could tell by the smile that crossed his face, a little one, quickly gone. "Tell you what. If you don't hear from her by morning, give me a call." He held out his card.

She gave the card a hostile look, didn't touch it. "By morning? Seventy-six percent of disappearances are solved in the first twelve hours, or they're not . . ." Her eyes got wet again, and her voice sounded like something was choking her throat. ". . . solved at all."

"Where'd you hear that?"

"I didn't *hear* it. I looked it up on the Internet before I drove over. What you don't seem to understand is that Madison has never done anything like this and never would. Maybe if you won't help, you can recommend someone who will."

Recommend another agency? Had this ever happened before? I couldn't read the look on Bernie's face at all.

"If it's money you're worried about, I'm prepared to pay whatever you charge, plus a big bonus the moment you find her." She reached into her bag, pulled out a roll, peeled off some bills. "How's five hundred in advance?"

Bernie's eyes shifted over to the money and stayed there, his face now readable to anyone from any distance, his mind on cash flow. "I'd like to see her room first." When Bernie caved, he did it quickly and all at once. I'd seen it with Leda a thousand times.

Cynthia handed over the money. "Follow me."

Bernie stuffed the bills deep in his pocket. I ran over to our car—an old Porsche convertible, the body sandblasted, waiting a long time now for a new coat of paint—and jumped over the passenger-side door and into my seat.

"Hey. Did you see what your dog just did?"

Bernie nodded, the proud, confident nod, my favorite. "They call him Chet the Jet." Well, Bernie does, anyway, although not often.

A coyote shrieked in the canyon, not far from the back of the house. I'd have to deal with that later. I no longer felt tired at all. And Bernie, turning the key in the ignition, looked the same: rarin' to go. We thrived on work, me and Bernie.

TWO

One thing about humans: They like to get high. This comes up over and over again in our work. They drink booze, they smoke this and that, they pop pills, even stick needles in their bodies—we've seen it all. But the actual getting-high part was something I never understood, puzzled over for a long time. What was that all about? And then one day it hit me. What was my favorite thing to do in the whole wide world? Riding shotgun in the Porsche, far and away. Sitting up high, wind pushing my face all out of shape, and sights and smells—especially smells—rushing by so fast I couldn't take them all in. Speed, rush, sensation: I knew about getting high, had been high lots of times.

Like now, for example, as we followed Cynthia Chambliss, mother of the possibly missing Madison, down our street. I saw things, real quick, zooming by: a man taking out the trash—was tomorrow trash day? Yes! Loved trash day; my pal Iggy, sipping from his bowl right inside his front door, turning, a little too late, toward the Porsche, just missing seeing me, typical Iggy; and then—

"Chet—what're you barking about?"

I'd barked? Oops. Must have been at Iggy. And then: a white-tailed rabbit, standing very still on someone's lawn, that white tail very white in the moonlight. Hair rose all down my back.

"Chet. Get down."

I got down. But I've chased rabbits in my time, let me tell you. And once—oh, yes: It can be done.

"What's with you right now?"

Nothing, nothing was with me: stoned out of my mind, that was all. I got my tongue back in my mouth; it was all dried up from the wind, felt more like one of those towels I sometimes found on the laundry-room floor. I liked burying those towels out in the backyard near the big rock, but burying towels was never easy. The chew strips—that was another matter, easy to bury and— Whoa! At that moment I had a very faint memory of burying one that I hadn't dug up yet, near the orange tree by old man Heydrich's fence. Maybe it was still there! I was gazing up at the moon and making plans when we turned in to a driveway and came to a stop behind Cynthia Chambliss's car.

I hopped out. The pavement was still warm from the heat of the day. I smelled water, the swimming-pool kind, close by. We followed Cynthia to the front door of a house that looked a lot like ours, a lot like most of the houses in the high valley, but bigger.

Cynthia turned to Bernie. "The dog is coming in?"

"Why not?"

The skin on her forehead, between the eyes, got pinched up. That didn't signal anything good. "There's never been a dog inside."

Bernie glanced up at the house. "It's not too late."

The pinched-up look got more extreme. "Excuse me?"

Bernie smiled. He had lots of different smiles. This particular one I thought of as just showing teeth. I did the same. Bernie has nice teeth for a human, but I'm only being realistic when I say they're nothing compared to mine. "Good chance we'll be needing him, Ms. Chambliss. Missing kids—that's Chet's specialty."

She gazed at me. "He looks too aggressive to be around kids."

Closing my mouth now was the right move. I knew that, of course, but for some reason it didn't close, maybe even opened wider, plus I started to pant a bit, getting pretty charged up.

"Never aggressive, not inappropriately." Bernie patted my head. Thump thump. I calmed down. "Chet is a trained police dog, after all."

"He is?"

"Graduated first in his class at K-9 school."

That was stretching it a little, since I hadn't actually graduated, which is how Bernie and I ended up together, a long story I'll go into later if I have a chance.

"In that case . . ." Cynthia opened the door.

We went inside.

Bird crap. I smelled it right off the bat, sour and disagreeable, just like birds themselves. If I could glide around in the wide blue sky, would I be disagreeable? No way.

We followed Cynthia through a big room with a tile floor that felt nice and cool, then down a hall to a closed door. On the way I spotted a potato chip, lying there in plain sight near the wall, and scarfed it up on the fly; ruffles-style, my favorite.

A sign with a lightning bolt hung on the door. Bernie read it. "'High voltage. Keep out.'"

"That's just Madison's sense of humor," Cynthia said. She opened the door, we went in, and there was the bird, perched in a cage that dangled from the ceiling.

"Che-et." Bernie spoke my name in the stretched-out way he used when he had a concern about what might be coming next. And sure, because of my leaping ability—I'd been the best leaper in K-9 class, which had led to all the trouble in a way I couldn't remember exactly, although blood was involved—how could I not wonder a bit about certain possibilities? But I wasn't about to find out now, was I? We were on the job. Thump thump. "Good boy."

The bird—green with scaly yellow legs and feet and a weird spiky comb on top of its head—made a horrible croaking noise.

"Hear that?" said Cynthia.

"What?"

"He said, 'Madison rocks.' She taught him. He can say other things, too."

Whoa. Cynthia was claiming that he—this beady-eyed inmate—could talk? I didn't buy it.

"His name's Cap'n Crunch."

Cap'n Crunch bobbed his head back and forth, an ugly lizard-like motion, and made the horrible croaking noise again. It ended in a high-pitched squeak that hurt my ears. One glance at Bernie and I knew he wasn't hearing that squeak. Bernie missed some things, true, but you had to admire him: He never let his handicaps get him down.

"What else can he say?"

Oh, Bernie, please.

Cynthia approached the cage. "Come on, baby."

Squawk squawk.

"Hear that?"

"What?"

"'Light my fire.' He said 'Light my fire' when I said 'Come on, baby.'"

Right.

But Bernie had one of those looks on his face, very still, eyes dark, meaning he was getting interested in something. "What else?"

Cynthia tapped the cage. Her fingernails were long and shiny. "Cap'n Crunch? Want a drink?"

Squawk squawk.

"'Make it a double'?" Bernie said.

"You got it," said Cynthia.

"Pretty impressive." It was? A bird that supposedly said 'Madison rocks', 'light my fire,' and 'make it a double'? Impressive how? What was I missing? Bernie turned to me. "Chet! What are you growling about?"

I wasn't growling. But I sidled away all the same, sat down by the TV. It rested on a little table. At that moment I smelled a smell familiar from my days in K-9 school, and there, under the table: a small plastic bag of marijuana.

Bernie shot me a quick look. "For God's sake, Chet. Stop barking." He turned to Cynthia. "Does Madison talk much to the bird?"

"All the time. She's had him, like, forever, really thinks he's human."

Bernie tapped the cage. His fingernails were short, bitten right down to practically nothing. "Where's Madison?" he said.

The bird was silent. The whole room was silent. Bernie and Cynthia were watching the bird. I watched Bernie. Sometimes he worried me. If we were relying on eyewitness testimony from Cap'n Crunch, the case was hopeless.

"What a brilliant idea," Cynthia said. She gazed up at Cap'n Crunch. "Where's Madison?" she said. When the bird remained silent, she added in a pleading tone, "Come on, baby."

"Light my fire," said Cap'n Crunch. This time I heard it myself.

"Let's back up a little," Bernie said. "I'd like to establish a chronology."

"What's that?"

I was curious, too. Bernie used big words sometimes. If he had his choice, he'd probably spend every day with his nose in a book; but what with alimony, child support, and the failed investment in a start-up that made pants with Hawaiian shirt patterns—he loved Hawaiian shirts—Bernie didn't have his choice.

"A time line," he said. "When did you last see Madison?"

Cynthia looked at her watch. It was big and gold. She had more gold around her wrists and neck, and in her ears. I'd licked gold a few times, didn't care for it, although silver was worse.

"Eight-fifteen," Cynthia said. "When I dropped her off at school."

"What school?"

"Heavenly Valley High."

"Don't know that one."

"It's pretty new, just north of Puma Wells. My ex is a developer up there."

"Your ex is Madison's father?"

"That's right. We've been divorced for five years."

"Did you call him?"

"Of course. He hasn't seen her."

"You have custody?"

Cynthia nodded. "She spends some weekends with Damon, every second Christmas, that kind of thing."

Bernie took out his notebook and pen. "Damon Chambliss?"

"Keefer. I've gone back to my maiden name."

Maiden name? What was that again? They kept changing

their names, all these people. I didn't get it. I was Chet, pure and simple.

"Madison goes by Chambliss?"

"Yes."

"And she was about ten at the time of the divorce?"

"Yes."

"How did she take it?"

Cynthia raised her shoulders, lowered them: the shrug. Sometimes it meant not caring—a hard one for me, right there—but was this one of those times? "You know what they say."

"What do they say?"

"Divorce is better for kids than a bad marriage," Cynthia said.

Bernie blinked. Just a tiny movement, easy to miss, but I knew what was on his mind: Charlie; and Bernie's own divorce. As for marriage and divorce, don't look at me. Complete unknowns, both of them, where I come from.

"But," said Cynthia, "I don't see what any of this has to do with Madison's disappearance."

Neither did I, exactly.

"Just filling in the blanks," said Bernie. One of his favorite lines, worked like a charm in most situations.

"Sorry," said Cynthia. "Didn't mean to tell you your business. It's just . . . " Her eyes got wet again. Once one of Leda's big fat tears had fallen to the floor and I'd had a taste. Salty; a big surprise. "It's just . . . Oh God, where is she?"

Bernie glanced around, spotted a box of tissues on the desk, gave her one. "When did you realize she might be missing?"

"When she didn't come home. She takes the bus. I'm here, but afternoons are my busy time—I run a small business out of the house."

"Doing what?"

"Designing e-cards."

"E-cards?"

"I can put you on my list if you're interested," Cynthia said. She took another tissue, blew her nose. Her nose was tiny, useless, so different from mine, but I couldn't help wondering: What would that be like, blowing it? All of a sudden my own nose got twitchy. Cynthia and Bernie went on for a while about the bus, Madison not getting off, various calls she'd made to the school, Madison's friends, the ex, but I wasn't really listening, caught up in all these strange feelings in my nose.

And then: "Why is he snarling like that?"

"I don't think he's snarling," Bernie said. "More like wriggling his nose. Chet? You all right?"

Humiliation. I gave myself a good shake, always a nice way of making a fresh start, and moved closer to Bernie, alert, tail high.

"He's all right," Bernie said.

Cynthia was looking at me funny. "I've never seen a dog like that before."

"Like what?"

"His ears. One's black and one's white."

Bad manners, commenting on someone's appearance like that. Wasn't it common knowledge? I decided then and there I didn't like Cynthia. One look at Bernie and I could tell he didn't, either.

"I'll need some things from you," he said, his voice cool, on the way to cold. "Contact information for your ex, Madison's friends, any special people in her life—coaches, teachers, et cetera. Plus a good photo of her."

"Right away," she said, and left the room.

Bernie turned to me and, in a low voice, got down to business. "Find something?"

I went over to the TV table, leaned forward pointer-style. Bernie knelt, fished out the bag of marijuana. He hefted it in his hand, slid it back under the table.

"Good man." Pat pat—and a quick scratch between the ears. Ah.

Cynthia returned, gave Bernie a sheet of paper and a framed photo of a girl with a ponytail. Horses I could do without, but I like ponytails. "Does Madison have a boyfriend?" Bernie said.

"No."

Bernie looked around the room. "Then that should do it," he said. "Except for something with Madison's smell."

"Her pillowcase?"

Bernie went to the bed, stripped off a pillowcase that looked pink to me, although I'm no judge of color, according to Bernie. I sniffed at it a couple times, got Madison's smell: young human female, with hints of honey, cherry, and a kind of sun-colored flower I sometimes saw along roadsides. Bernie folded the pillow-case and sealed it in a plastic bag.

"We'll be in touch," he said. "But if you hear anything, call right away, day or night."

"Thank you. I'm so grateful." Cynthia led us down the hall to the front door. "Angela DiPesto raved about you."

Bernie stopped, turned to her. "You said you worked with her."

"That's right."

"How is she involved with e-cards?"

"She wrote my software."

"Angela DiPesto?"

Cynthia nodded, and opened the door. A girl was coming up the walk, a ponytailed girl with a backpack. Her face was still in the night shadows, but I knew who it was right away from the smell.

"Madison?" said Cynthia. She covered her mouth, one of those things that human females did sometimes and human males never. "Oh my God—where have you been?"

Under his breath, to no one in particular, Bernie said, "I need a drink."

From back in the house came the harsh voice of Cap'n Crunch: "Make it a double."

THREE

Madison smelled just like her pillowcase, except now there was sweat mixed in; sweat and a little marijuana, too. Sweat, human sweat, is a big subject. There's a kind that comes from exercise and has a fresh tangy smell. Then there's the kind that comes from not showering enough, less fresh, with faint non-human elements mixed in. The kind that comes from fear—what I was smelling now—is somewhere in between.

Cynthia stepped outside, grabbed Madison's wrist. "Where were you? I've been out of my mind."

"I—" Madison began, then noticed Bernie and stopped.

"This is Mr. Little. He's a detective."

"A detective?"

"I was worried sick."

"For God's sake, Mom. You called a detective?"

"Where were you? Answer me!"

Madison bit her lip. They do that sometimes. What does it mean? Hard to tell, exactly, but I always notice. "It's not my fault. Mr. Rentner recommended it."

"Mr. Rentner? What are you talking about?"

"Come on, Mom—my history teacher. The one who liked my essay on—"

"Right, right, what about him?"

"He said we should see this movie about Russia."

"You were at the movies?"

"They had a special showing at the North Canyon Mall. Just today and tomorrow. I watched the movie and then hung out till I could get a ride home."

"From who?"

"This senior—you don't know him."

"What's his name?"

"Tim something-or-other. I don't really know him, either."

Cynthia gazed at Madison, upward a little, since her daughter was taller. "Why didn't you phone?"

"Sorry. I forgot."

"And I called your cell a million times."

"I turned it off, Mom. Like, at the movies, cell phones, you know?"

"Don't talk to me that way."

Madison looked down.

There was a silence. Then Cynthia said, "Let's get in the house." She turned to Bernie. "Thanks for your time."

"No problem," Bernie said. "Glad everything worked out." He looked at Madison. "Big fan of Russian movies, myself. Which one was this?"

"*Dr. Zhivago*," Madison said. "We're studying the Russian revolution."

"Love *Dr. Zhivago*," said Bernie. We watched a lot of movies, me and Bernie, although I had no recollection of this one. Truth was, I didn't pay close attention unless my own guys were involved, even in a small way, like in *As Good as It Gets*, for example, or *Ghostbusters II*. Bernie added one more comment: "My favorite part was the tennis-court scene."

"Yeah," said Madison. "That was cool." Then she did something that took me by surprise: She came closer and gave me a pat, very soft and gentle. "I love your dog," she said.

They went in the house. We went home.

It was late. Bernie found a leftover steak in the fridge. He smeared on A.1., cut it in half, and we had a little snack. Bernie cracked open a beer, sat at the table.

"I feel guilty, not even offering to return the five C's."

I chewed my steak. Loved steak, could eat it every day.

"Except for one thing, Chet. Know what that is?"

I looked up from my bowl, a piece of meat possibly sticking out of the side of my mouth.

"There is no tennis-court scene in *Dr. Zhivago*."

Bernie opened his laptop. I turned to the water bowl.

"Let me freshen that up."

Bernie refilled the water bowl at the sink, even threw in a few ice cubes. Ah. Love ice cubes. He went back to the laptop. "Yup. *Dr. Zhivago*'s playing at the North Canyon Mall, on that little screening room at the back. And Mr. Ted Rentner teaches history at Heavenly Valley High." He sighed. Yes, the sigh, also interesting: The younger the human, in my observation, the less they do it. "Two kinds of lies, Chet. The big lie, totally out there, and the tiny one slipped into a web of truth. The girl's damn good." He shook the A.1. bottle, poured some more on his steak. "Did Cynthia say she was on the gifted track?"

No idea. I crushed an ice cube. Made my teeth feel great, and then cold little chips were swirling through my mouth, cooling me down all over. Dinnertime—even a quick snack like this—was something we always looked forward to, me and Bernie.

He flipped his laptop shut. "On the other hand, she's back home, safe and sound. Big picture. But you see why I don't feel too bad about taking the money?"

Sure. We needed money in the worst way. Our finances were a mess—alimony, child support, Hawaiian pants, and almost no revenue except for divorce work. Bernie went over and over that, almost every night. An ant, one of those juicy black ones, appeared from under the stove and tried to run right by me. What was he thinking? I hardly had to move my tongue. Bernie always stressed the importance of protein in the diet.

Bernie's bedroom—pretty messy, clothes, books, newspapers all over the place—was at the back of the house, looking out on the canyon. He slept in the big bed he'd shared with Leda. In those days, I'd slept in the kitchen; now I was on the floor at the foot of the bed. There was a nice soft rug somewhere under all the debris.

"'Night, Chet."

I closed my eyes. The night was cooling down, and Bernie had the AC off, windows open. Lots of action in the canyon—coyote yips, rustling, a sharp cry suddenly interrupted. Bernie's breathing grew slow and regular. He groaned once or twice in his sleep, once muttered something that sounded like "Who knows?" A car went down the street and, from the sound, seemed to slow as it approached the house. I raised my head. The car kept going, engine noise fading into silence. I got up, walked around in a little circle, and lay back down, stretching my legs straight out. One white ear, one black? So what? Very soon I was roaming the canyon, chasing coyotes, lizards, and javelinas under the moonlight—in my dreams, of course. In real life, the canyon was out of bounds, unless I was with Bernie. But he trusted me. At least I didn't have an electric fence to deal with, like poor old Iggy.

I woke up to the sound of Bernie snoring. The room was dark except for a faint silvery band between the curtains. I got up—feeling good, appetite sharp, a bit thirsty—and went to the bedside. Bernie lay on his back, just his face showing, from the chin up. His forehead was all wrinkled, the way it got when he was thinking hard about some big problem. There were dark circles under his eyes; he looked more tired than he had going to bed. I lay my head on the blanket.

A car came down the street. This one didn't keep going but stopped with a little squeak. A door slammed shut. Just from that slamming sound, I was pretty sure who it was. I trotted out of the bedroom, through the kitchen, and into the TV room. The window looked out on the street, and yes, there was Leda, striding up the walk. Charlie sat in the car, staring out.

I ran into the bedroom.

"Chet, for God's sake." Bernie grabbed the blanket, tried to keep me from pulling it away. "Knock it off. I'm sleeping."

Ding-dong. The front door.

Bernie sat up. "Someone's here?"

Ding-dong.

"Chet! What the hell? Get off the bed."

I was on the bed? And kind of pawing at Bernie? Oops. I jumped off. Bernie rose, threw on his robe, the one with lots of holes and a missing belt. He hurried out of the room, hair all over the place, breath pretty strong. I followed.

Bernie opened the front door, blinked in the light. Leda had pale eyes, like the sky in winter. She looked at Bernie, his messy hair, his robe; then at me; and back to Bernie. Bernie just stood there, mouth open.

"Does it make you feel good to humiliate me like this?" she said.

"Huh?" said Bernie.

I didn't understand, either. I'd always had trouble understanding Leda, even from point-blank range like this, where I could see every movement of her lips, every expression on her face.

She whipped out a piece of paper, thrust it at him.

"What's this?" he said.

"A letter from the school, obviously."

Bernie gazed at the letter, his eyes going back and forth. "The tuition check?" he said. "But I'm sure there was enough money in the account. I even—"

Leda snatched the letter from him. "Don't worry—Malcolm covered it."

Malcolm was the boyfriend. I'd only seen him once. He wore flip-flops and had long skinny feet and long skinny toes.

"So now you owe him."

"But I don't see how—"

I trotted out to the car. Charlie opened the door. I jumped up, gave his face a nice big lick.

"Chet the Jet! How you doing, boy?"

Just great, never better. Charlie stroked my back.

"Hey, what's this?" He was picking at my coat. "You've got a tick." A tick? I hadn't been aware of it at all, but now I felt it coming out: a pinch and then a tiny soundless pop, very satisfying. Charlie held up the tick, a horrible bloated thing. "Gross," he said, and tossed it in the gutter.

There was a strong current of air in the car, very pleasant. I didn't realize at first that it was on account of my own tail wagging so hard. Charlie laughed: the best sound made by humans, bar none, and kid laughter is the best of the best. Charlie had a round face and a funny mixture of teeth, some big, some tiny.

"I just vacuumed that car." All of a sudden Leda was right behind me.

"Chet doesn't shed," said Charlie.

"All dogs shed."

I backed out of the car. Leda gave me an angry look. Things were happening fast, always did when Leda was around. Shedding is a big problem, I'm aware of that, but humans shed, too: Hairs and all of kinds of stuff are raining down all the time, I assure you.

Bernie approached, tugging his robe closed. "Hi, Charlie."

"Hi, Dad."

"He's going to be late for school," Leda said.

"See you on the weekend."

"Can we go camping?"

"Don't see why not."

"Because it's going to be ninety-five degrees," Leda said. She got in the car.

"Bye."

"Bye."

And they drove away, sunlight glaring off the back of the car, Bernie waving.

In all the commotion, I hadn't noticed that another car had pulled up. A woman had stepped out, was watching us. Bernie turned to her.

"Bernie Little?"

"Yes?"

"Hi, I'm Suzie Sanchez." She came closer, held out her hand. Bernie shook it, clutching the front of his robe with his other hand, eyebrows raised. He had dark, prominent eyebrows that had a whole language of their own. "From the *Valley Tribune*?" she said. "I hope I didn't get the day wrong."

"The day?"

"For that feature we discussed—a day in the life of a Valley PI. Lieutenant Stine of the Metro PD recommended you."

"Oh," said Bernie. "Right, right." Had I heard about this? Maybe, maybe not. Bernie glanced down at his bare feet. "Running a bit late, sorry," he said. "Due to . . . circumstances. I'll be right with you."

Suzie Sanchez's eyes shifted to the road, in the direction Leda had gone. "No rush, I've booked the day." She looked at me. Her eyes were bright, dark and shiny like the countertops in the kitchen. "What a cute dog! Is he yours?"

"That's Chet."

"Can I pat him?"

"You don't know what you're getting into."

Suzie Sanchez laughed; not quite as nice as Charlie's laugh, but pretty close. She walked over, showed me her hand—it smelled of soap and lemons—then scratched me between the ears, where it turned out I was itchy. Ah.

"Does he like treats?"

Do I like treats? Was that the question? She reached into her bag, pulled out a bone-shaped biscuit, size large.

"You carry dog biscuits around with you?"

"Reporters run into dogs all the time," she said, "not all of them as nice as Chet."

She lowered the biscuit in range. Wouldn't do to snap it up in a greedy way, might not be in keeping with my cute appearance. I was just telling myself that when— Snap!

Suzie Sanchez laughed again. I downed the biscuit in two

bites, maybe one. Some brand totally new to me and the best I'd ever tasted. What a world!

"Can he have another one?" she said. "I've got a whole box in the car."

Strong air currents blew all around me.

FOUR

Stakeouts: I've sat through a million. Okay, possibly not a million. Truth is, I'm not too sure about a million, what it means, exactly—or any other number, for that matter—but I get the drift from Bernie. A million means a lot, like "out the yingyang," another favorite number of Bernie's, maybe even bigger.

"This is exciting," Suzie said.

We sat there, me, Bernie, Suzie Sanchez. We had a pickup we used for stakeouts, old, black, inconspicuous. There was a bench seat in front, so I was in the middle; not so good, what with the mirror interfering with my view, but I'm not a complainer.

"Exciting how?" said Bernie.

"Just knowing that something dramatic could happen at any moment." Suzie gestured with her coffee cup to an office park across the street. We were in the Valley but don't ask me where. The Valley went on forever in all directions, and although I was pretty sure I could find my way home from any of them, it wouldn't be by a method you'd understand.

Bernie opened a little packet, dumped the contents in his coffee, stirred with a pencil. "I wouldn't say dramatic. Not necessarily."

"But divorce is a life-changing event, isn't it? I call that dramatic."

Bernie nodded, a slow nod with his eyes shifted, a nod that meant she'd caught his attention. His eyes shifted back, looked past me, at her, then away. "Ever been divorced yourself?"

"Oh, no," she said. "But my parents were, so I know about the life-changing part."

Bernie sipped his coffee. I'd tried coffee once or twice, didn't get what all the fuss was about. Water was my drink: delicious every time, never failed. "So you're, uh, married?" Bernie said.

People began coming out the doors of the office buildings. I knew what that meant: lunchtime. I was getting a little hungry myself, although strictly a breakfast-and-dinner type, don't ask me why—take it up with Bernie.

Now was when we had to watch extra hard, in case our guy got lost in the crowd. But Bernie wasn't watching hard, wasn't watching at all. In fact, he was gazing down at his hands—Bernie had big strong hands, one or two fingers bent a little out of shape—doing what, I had no idea. Waiting for Suzie's answer to his question? Could that have been it? And Suzie did say something, but whatever it was, I missed it because there stepped our guy, out from behind two women on the other side of the street. Bernie was much better with faces than me, especially from a distance, but we'd been tracking this guy off and on for days, and he had a mustache, a big black one that divided his face into two parts, making him easy to spot.

"Why is Chet growling like that?" Suzie said.

"I don't—" Bernie raised his head at last and glanced out the window. "That's him. Justin Anthony III."

"He even looks suspicious," Suzie said.

Bernie laughed. What was funny?

Justin Anthony III got into a huge SUV, possibly one of those Hummers that Bernie hated so much; or maybe not—car identification was another one of my weaknesses. They all smelled the same. He pulled in to traffic. We followed.

Bernie drove, always keeping a car or two between us and the subject, which was the word we used for anyone we tailed. I sat up straight, then stood so I could get my face right next to the windshield.

"Chet. Siddown, for God's sake. Look what you did to the mirror."

But— I sat down.

"And don't pant."

Nothing I could do about that.

Suzie took out a notebook. "So the background here is that your client, Mrs. Justin Anthony III—"

"You're not planning to use real names?"

"Just yours."

"And Chet. You can use his real name."

"Is it short for anything? Chester?"

Chester? That was a name? Don't tell me my real name was Chester.

"Just Chet," Bernie said.

Whew.

Suzie wrote in her notebook. "So your client suspects that her husband's cheating on her?"

"But can't prove it. The divorce will go much better for her if she can."

"Are they rich?"

"I wouldn't say rich. He's a stockbroker and she's a real estate appraiser."

"Typical Valley couple."

Bernie laughed again. Why? No idea, but it was nice to hear.

"And what's your gut feeling?" said Suzie. "Cheating or not?"

"Cheating," said Bernie.

"But you've been following him for a week with no result. What makes you so sure?"

"Ninety-nine percent of the time, if a wife suspects the husband of cheating, she's right."

"Why is that?"

"They sense something."

Suzie's pen was moving fast. "And the other way? Husbands suspecting wives?"

"They're right half the time, if that."

"Yeah?" said Suzie. "Why?"

"Maybe men have more active imaginations."

"You're pulling my leg."

I glanced at Suzie's leg. Bernie wasn't even touching it, had both hands on the wheel. No explanation came—not that I cared about this particular subject, or any of the back-and-forth when we were on the job—because at that moment the SUV turned onto a narrow street and parked in front of a long low building with lots of doors and a big cactus sign.

"The Saguaro Motor Inn?" Suzie said. "My sister and her girlfriends stayed here last year."

"A respectable place in a safe area," said Bernie, backing into a space on the opposite side of the lot. "He's a stockbroker, after all."

Justin Anthony III got out of his car, went through a door at the end of the building, returned with a key in his hand. He walked all the way to a door at the other end and let himself in.

Bernie took out his recorder, spoke low. "Twelve-twenty-two P.M., subject Justin Anthony III enters room thirty-seven at the Saguaro Motor Inn, sixty-three-seventy-one East Pico Road."

We waited. "Mind if I smoke?" Bernie said.

"You smoke?"

"No. Not really." He didn't light up. On one hand, as humans said—maybe if they had four paws, they'd think differently—I knew how hard he'd tried to quit; on the other, I liked the smell.

"How long have you known Lieutenant Stine?" Suzie said.

"A few years."

"He spoke highly of you."

Bernie nodded, a tiny movement. That tiny nod was my favorite: It meant Bernie was pleased.

"He mentioned you'd gone to West Point."

"Uh-huh."

"That's quite an accomplishment, just getting accepted."

Bernie was quiet. We watched the door—I could see the number, two little metal pieces, but I'd have to take Bernie's word that it was 37.

"How does baseball fit in? Lieutenant Stine said something about that."

"I played a little ball. They were short on pitching that year. Otherwise they'd never have taken me."

"You pitched for Army?"

Another nod, this one not so happy.

"I love baseball. Were you a power pitcher or the finesse type?"

"Power, if you want to call it that, until I blew my arm out. That's when I learned that finesse wasn't my—" He stopped talking. A little car pulled quickly into the lot and parked beside the SUV. A woman of the curvy type got out, went to the door of number 37, a little unsteady on pointy heels, and knocked. The door opened from the inside. I caught a glimpse of Justin Anthony III with no clothes on. At the same moment I heard a click from Bernie's camera. The door closed.

Bernie spoke into his recorder, described the woman, noted the time of arrival, make and license number of the car. He snapped a few more pictures. Then he opened his laptop, tapped at the keys. "Car's registered to a Ms. Cara Thorpe." Tap tap tap. "She has a condo in Copper City, works for an insurance company, never married, no kids, credit rating six-three-five."

"Are we getting out of the car?" Suzie said.

"What for?"

"Don't you want to try to take pictures through the window or something?"

Bernie didn't answer. I took my eyes off the motel door and looked at him. The color of his face was changing, getting darker. This, I knew, was called blushing. Blushing was something Bernie always watched for when questioning someone, very important, although I wasn't sure why, but I'd never seen him doing it himself. "The evidence we have already should be sufficient," he said.

I'll say. Full-frontal nudity was the kind of evidence that couldn't be beat, not in our work. Humans look so guilty without clothes on, case closed; so different from me, for example, or any of my buddies, even Iggy. We just don't need them, end of story. Shoes, for example—what would I do with shoes? A coat and tie? Please.

Suzie turned a page in her notebook. "Lieutenant Stine said you left Metro PD about six years ago."

"True."

"Why was that?"

Sometimes Bernie had a way of taking a deep breath in through his nose—making a faint whistling sound—then letting it out of his mouth, slow and silent. He did it now. "Time to move on."

"And what was the path that led you here from West Point?"

"Is that really part of your story?"

"Off the record, then."

"I like the desert," Bernie said. "The American desert."

"You've been to other deserts?"

"Yes."

"In combat?"

"Yes."

"What can you tell me about that?"

I perked up. This was something Bernie never talked about, not to anyone. Bernie reached over, adjusted my collar; the metal tags had gotten twisted inside. Ah. That felt better. "There's really not much to say."

Then came a long silence, except for the faint sounds of Suzie writing in her notebook. Time passed. My mind drifted to a kind of Portuguese sausage I'd had once; couldn't remember where or when, but I could taste it, right there at the stakeout.

"What about—" Suzie began, just as the motel door opened. Justin Anthony III appeared, fully dressed. He smoothed out his mustache, climbed into the SUV, drove off.

Bernie recorded the time.

"That's it, then?" said Suzie.

"We'll wait till she goes."

"Why?"

"No real reason. The room was empty when we got here."

"A full-circle kind of thing?"

Bernie smiled. "Exactly." He and Suzie exchanged a quick glance; if it had any meaning, I missed it.

We sat there, waiting for Ms. Cara Thorpe to appear. A car drove into the lot, slowed down, parked beside hers. A man wearing a cowboy hat got out. He walked to the door of number 37 and knocked. The door opened. The man went inside, but before the door closed, I caught a glimpse of Ms. Cara Thorpe with no clothes on.

Suzie's eyes were wide open. "She's two-timing the two-timer?"

"On the two-timer's tab," said Bernie. "Wonder if they're using the minibar."

Suzie laughed. "Are you going to report this part to the client?"

Bernie shook his head. "Wouldn't lead anywhere good." He turned the key. I thought I heard a tiny squealing sound from behind the door to number 37. Humans squeal, and sometimes pigs, like the javelinas, for example: I'd heard them squeal up close, more than once. Any others? None that I could think of.

I liked to sleep at the foot of Bernie's bed, but my favorite napping spot was in the breakfast nook, under the table with my back against the wall, all cool and shady, plus there was often good snacking around Bernie's chair. I took a nap every day, sometimes two, and had settled down for a long quiet one when Bernie came in. I opened one eye. The top half of him was out of view. He was wearing sneakers and shorts; the long curved scar on one of his legs looked very white on his skin.

"You asleep?"

I gave my tail a little thump.

"The article's in the paper. About that stakeout." Then came paper sounds, rustling and crinkling. Bernie cleared his throat; I did that only in emergencies, like the time a bone got stuck.

"'Gotcha! On the Job with a Leading Valley PI, by Suzie Sanchez. Ever see Robert Mitchum as Raymond Chandler's ace detective Philip Marlowe? Although their faces are very different, that's who Valley PI Bernie Little of the Little Detective Agency reminded me of—a big shambling guy, one of those athletic types a decade or maybe two past his prime.'" Bernie stopped reading. One of his feet tapped the floor a few times. "'Shambling?' What the hell's that?" His chair squeaked. He got up and left the room. An airplane flew overhead, very high, making a faint, soothing buzz. I closed my eye.

And was nodding off when Bernie returned. "'Shambling,' dictionary definition—'moving awkwardly, dragging the feet.' Where'd she get that? I don't drag my feet." Bernie walked around the kitchen in an experimental sort of way. I opened my eye again. From my angle, he didn't appear to be dragging his feet. Sometimes Bernie limped a bit, especially when he was tired, but that was from his wound.

He sat down. Paper rustled. "'Little, accompanied on a recent stakeout by this reporter as well as his lively mongrel dog, Chet, claims not to like divorce work but on this occasion proved . . .'"

I turned my back. Mongrel? What kind of rag would even print a word like that? I closed my eye, stretched my legs way out, got comfortable.

"Chet? C'mon, wake up. Time to get in shape."

Huh? Get in shape? Speaking for me, I was about one hundred percent pure muscle, as always. I squeezed out from under the table, leaned forward, loosening up my back, then had a nice shake, the kind that rippled my skin back and forth in waves. Bernie was standing there in shorts and a wife beater.

"We're going for a run."

Both of us? There were lots of outings where Bernie walked and I ran, but Bernie running would be a first. We went out the back door, through the yard, out the gate, into the canyon. Bernie started running, sort of, up the trail that led to the hill with the big flat rock on top. It was nice out, the sun hidden by the distant mountains but the sky still light, the air not too hot. I loped along beside Bernie, then ran circles around him, and when that got boring, took off for the hilltop.

And right away spotted a lizard, one of those green ones with the tiny eyes! He saw me, too, and darted toward higher ground. I tore after him, closed the distance fast, and sprang, my front paws outstretched, and came down right on him. Or not quite. What was this? He'd bolted down a hole, a small round hole in the dirt. I started digging right away, real fast, got a nice clawing rhythm going, all four paws involved, and soon had a big hole under way. But all of a sudden I caught a whiff of something, a nasty smell with a bit of bacon mixed in, that meant one thing and one thing only: javelina.

I raised my head, sniffed the air. No doubt, and it was coming from down the hill, closer to the trail. I glanced around, saw I'd dug a hole, although I wasn't sure why. I lowered my nose and trotted after the scent.

It got stronger and stronger. This was going to be cake! Nothing beat hunting, the absolute best. And when I caught up to the little squealer, just you—

"Chet! Chet!"

I looked down. Bernie was no longer running, no longer moving at all; he stood on the trail, hands on his hips, chest heaving.

"Come on. We're going home."

That was it? The getting-in-shape run was over? At that moment, just when the fun was ending, I spotted the javelina, a big fat one, so close. And then I was charging, flat out, the wind whipping by. The javelina bared his tusks—as if that would stop me!—and made a quick little sideways movement. I ducked sideways, too, the hair rising all down my back, feeling hot and cold at the same time, and—

Ow.

I ran right into one of those skinny cactuses, the kind with the needles.

Back in the kitchen, Bernie removed the needles with tweezers, one by one, starting with my nose. "I'm going to be running three or four times a week now, so you'll have to use better judgment if you want to come along."

Run without me? Oh no. Of course I'd use better judgment, whatever that was.

He pulled another needle. Ah. Much better. The pain was fading fast; I could hardly remember it.

"Shambling? I'll show her what—"

The phone rang. Bernie didn't answer, let the machine take it. The light started flashing and a woman spoke.

"Mr. Little? It's Cynthia Chambliss. Madison's disappeared again. She's been gone for over a day. I didn't do anything, on account of how things turned out last time, but now I'm really worried."

Bernie picked up the phone. He listened. His hands fumbled around, found cigarettes. He lit up.

FIVE

Bernie unzipped a plastic bag. "Remember this?" he said, removing a folded-up pillowcase and holding it out.

I took a quick sniff: young human female, hints of honey, cherry, and that roadside sun-colored flower. Of course I remembered; actually felt a little insulted he'd even ask.

"What's that look for?" Bernie said.

Look? What look? I strolled out onto the back patio with my tail high and stiff and had a cooling drink from the little fountain Leda had put in. Water flowed from the mouth of a stone swan. I'd never seen a real swan and was wondering how catchable they might be when I heard Iggy's bark. Iggy had a high-pitched bark, an irritated-sounding yip-yip-yip. I barked back. There was a brief silence, and then he barked again. I barked back. He barked. I barked. He barked. I barked. He barked. We got a good rhythm going, faster and faster. I barked. He barked. I—

A woman cried, "Iggy, for God's sake, what the hell's wrong with you?" A door slammed. Iggy was silent. I barked anyway. And what was that? From somewhere far in the distance came an answering bark, a bark I'd never heard before. It sounded female, although I couldn't be sure. A silence. And then—yes: She barked. A bark that sent a message, a she-message of the most exciting kind. I barked back. She barked. I barked. She barked. And then: yip yip yip. Iggy was back. He barked. She barked. I barked. He barked. She—

"Chet. What's all the racket? Let's get going."

Bernie had the gate open. I tore past him and hopped into the Porsche, riding shotgun.

Cap'n Crunch stood on his perch and watched us, but he didn't say a thing. We were back in Madison's bedroom. Bernie asked questions. Cynthia answered them, but not in a way that helped. I could see that from Bernie's face, how his eyebrows were pinching closer together. I sniffed around. Madison's room didn't smell quite the same as before. I looked under the TV table. The bag of marijuana was gone.

"Have you called the police?" Bernie said.

"Not yet. I was waiting to talk to you."

"Call them," Bernie said. He wrote something on his card. "Ask for this guy."

"Does that mean you're not going to help me?"

"May I speak frankly?"

"Of course." Cynthia's hands were shaking, only the tiniest bit, but for a moment or two that was all I could see.

"Why don't we sit down?" Bernie said.

Cynthia sat on Madison's bed. Bernie sat at the desk. I sat where I was, on a soft rug with a floral pattern.

"Your daughter seems very bright," Bernie said, "and I'm sure she's basically a good kid. But at some point they all start developing independent lives, lives they don't necessarily share with their parents."

"What are you saying?"

"The other night, when Madison came home late with the story about *Dr. Zhivago*?" Bernie said. "It was just that, a story."

Cynthia's face got pale. That meant the opposite of a blush, blood draining out. You can tell a lot from blood flow to the human face. "How do you know?" she said.

Bernie explained how he knew, something about tennis courts that I might have heard once but had forgotten. I tilted my head sideways a little and scratched behind my ear. Ah. That felt good. I gave my coat a lick or two, for no reason.

"Bottom line," said Bernie, "I think she'll show up soon, with another story."

Cynthia shook her head. "But she'd never stay out all night, no matter what. And if she did, it would be with a friend, and none of them have seen her—I called every single one."

"Including Tim?" Bernie said.

"Who's Tim?"

"The senior who supposedly drove her home from the North Canyon Mall."

Cynthia opened her mouth, closed it. I always liked seeing that one, no idea why.

"And what about Damon?" Bernie said. "Your ex."

"The bastard hasn't seen her."

Bernie scratched behind his own ear. "You, uh, seem a little annoyed with him."

"He disparaged my parenting skills," said Cynthia. "What right has he to do that?"

Bernie spread his hands, then brought them back together. It was one of his ways of saying nothing. Cynthia gazed at him and then burst into tears. Bernie's eyebrows rose. I got up and pawed at a dust ball.

"For God's sake," Cynthia sobbed, "just say you'll find her for me. Money's no object."

"But I'm trying to tell you she's really not missing," Bernie said. "She could walk in any moment, like the last time. And when she does, my advice would be that the three of you—you, Damon, and Madison—sit down together and—"

Cynthia only cried harder. "Do I have to get down on my knees and beg?"

"Oh no. No, no, no," said Bernie. "God no." I could tell he wanted to be out of there. Me, too. "I'll need those same things we talked about before—names and numbers of all her friends, anyone else important in her life. Does she play a sport?"

"Archery." Cynthia dabbed at her eyes. "She came third in the Upper Valley meet."

"Where's her bow?"

Cynthia's own eyebrows—two thin arcs darker than the hair on her head—rose in surprise. I'd seen Bernie's questions do that to people before. She opened the closet. The bow, long and black, hung from a hook, a quiver of white-feathered arrows beside it.

"Include her coach and any teammates she was close to," Bernie said.

Cynthia moved to the desk, wrote a list.

Bernie looked it over. "I don't see Damon here."

She snatched up the pen, wrote fast, pressing hard. "There."

Bernie folded the paper, stuck it in his pocket, got up to leave.

"Don't you want money?" Makeup was smeared in tracks down Cynthia's face, black and green, like a scary mask on Halloween, the very worst of all human holidays. For some reason, I started to like her.

"We're still on the five hundred," said Bernie. "I'll let you know if I need more."

Oh, Bernie.

We drove to the North Canyon Mall. Bernie circled round and round a huge lot, finally found a spot. He was muttering to himself. Bernie hated malls, hated shopping of any kind. We got out, walked toward the entrance. Bernie stopped in front of a sign. I couldn't read the words, but there was also a picture of one of my guys with a thick line drawn through him.

"Uh-oh," said Bernie.

We went back to the car. Bernie drove around again until he found just about the only space in the whole lot that lay in the shade of a tree.

"Stay here," he said, giving me a pat. "Be back as soon as I can."

I was steaming, but what could I do? It wasn't Bernie's fault. I growled a bit, then leaned down and gnawed at my paw for a while, felt a little better. Outside, people went back and forth.

"Hey, Mom. Look at the cute dog."

"Don't go too close."

"But can't I pat him?"

"Don't be ridiculous. I'm allergic."

A word I hated.

"And see the way he yawned like that? Means he's aggressive. Hurry up."

First of all, I wasn't yawning, only stretching my mouth, always nice and relaxing. Second, I wasn't feeling aggressive: She must have been confusing me with hippos, ugly brutes I'd seen on the Discovery Channel and wanted no part of. I watched the distant doors of the mall. Bernie didn't come out. I lay down. A nap? Why not? I closed my eyes.

* * *

I had some kind of good dream that all of a sudden went bad. It startled me. I opened my eyes and there, standing right by the car, stood a very big guy, taller and broader than Bernie. He had light hair, maybe even white, but he wasn't old, had no lines on his face. I didn't like that face at all, something about the massive cheekbones and the tiny ears. Then I was up on the seat and barking, my loudest bark, probably on account of being startled.

That made the man jump and step back, no surprise. But now, when most people would have kept backing away, he did not. Instead, his face got distorted and angry, teeth bared, and he said something I didn't understand—maybe in a language I didn't know—but I knew it was nasty. And then, from inside his shirt, he pulled a knife, a long one with a gleaming blade. Very quick, he bent down and stabbed at one of our tires. The air hissed out, and before I could move, he stepped forward and stabbed another.

Then I was airborne, my own teeth bared, you'd better believe it. One of my paws caught him on the shoulder. It spun him a little, and he kept spinning all the way around and slashed at me with the knife. I felt the blade skim my coat, but I got past it and sank my teeth into his leg. He grunted and lost the knife. It clattered to the pavement, bounced, and fell through one of those storm grates. I twisted around, tried to bring him down. He reached into his pocket, and when his hand came out, it wore something metal. The metal flashed down at me. Then everything got wobbly.

The next thing I knew he was running, farther down the row of cars. He jumped into one. I raced after it. The car rolled forward. I sprinted alongside, barking and barking, in a hot rage. He glanced out the window, turned the wheel sharply. I felt a tremendous blow and went flying.

* * *

"Chet? Chet?"

"Are you calling your dog, mister? I think this is him over here."

I was lying on the pavement, feeling not too good. A kid was gazing down at me. Bernie came running into view. I started to get up—no way I wanted him seeing me like this. It took some effort. One of my front legs was letting me down. I limped toward Bernie.

"Oh my God." Bernie knelt, took my head in his hands. "What happened to you?"

The kid came closer. "I think he got hit by a car."

"Hit by a car?" Bernie sounded shocked. He glanced around. "What car?"

"A blue one," said the kid. "Your dog was kind of chasing it."

"Chasing the car?"

"Yeah. Then they collided. The guy maybe didn't even seen him. I think it was a guy."

"What did he look like?"

"I'm not sure."

"Any idea of the make of the car?"

"Just that it was blue."

Bernie stroked my coat, very gentle. "Christ, he's bleeding." I could see from his eyes how upset he was.

I licked the blood off my shoulder. Not much, no big deal. It got the metallic taste of the nasty guy's blood out of my mouth.

"Did you see what happened to my car?" Bernie said.

"Your car?" said the kid.

"Over there." Bernie got to his feet, started to pick me up. Getting carried? Out of the question. I backed away. "Come on, then," he said.

We walked over to the Porsche, me, Bernie, the kid. I was hardly limping at all.

"Wow," said the kid. "Somebody slashed your tires." He glanced back toward the place where I got hit. "You think it's the same guy?"

Bernie nodded. He handed the kid his card. "If you remember anything else, give me a call."

"Hey," said the kid. "Are you a real private eye?"

The kid went away. Bernie made some calls—tow truck, insurance, vet. Vet? Uh-oh. I moved over to the storm grate and started barking.

"Come on, Chet."

I barked and barked.

"Knock that off. You're going to the vet, and that's that."

Bernie! Look in the grate!

But he didn't. When the tow truck came, Bernie held the cab door open for me. I climbed in, maybe not with my usual ease.

"You okay, boy?"

"Hey," said the tow-truck guy. "Nice dog."

"You bet," said Bernie.

We got new tires—part of the deductible, whatever that meant, but it didn't seem to make Bernie happy—and drove to the vet. Her name was Amy, a big round woman with a nice voice and careful hands, but I always start shaking the moment I enter the waiting room, and this time was no different.

"What happened to you, poor baby?" she said.

They laid me on a table. I felt a tiny jab and then not much. Amy worked away on me.

"Funny kind of cut for a car accident," she said.

"Yeah?" said Bernie.

"More of a slashing type of wound," Amy said. "Maybe some chrome got him."

Chrome? Did I know that word? Didn't think so. In fact, I was losing the thread. I just lay on the table, quiet. Their mouths moved, Bernie's and Amy's, and sound flowed back and forth over me. Soon the shaking went away. I felt not too bad.

SIX

We sat in the TV room, Bernie on the couch with his laptop, me in the La-Z-Boy, my bad leg resting on a pillow. *The Hound of the Baskervilles* was on the screen. I'd seen it more times than I could count—which was two in my case: me and Bernie, for example—but the way that hound's howl kept scaring the pants off all those people never got old. If I could only howl like that . . . Hey! maybe I could.

"Chet. Please. You do that every time at the exact same scene."

I do?

He tapped at the keyboard. "I'm trying to concentrate. Turns out there are three Tims or Timothys in the senior class at Heavenly Valley High." Tap tap. "And one of them's in the archery club. Tim Fletcher." He glanced at me over the lid of the laptop. "See where we're going with this?"

I had no clue.

Bernie picked up the phone. "Missing persons, please. Sergeant Torres." He looked at me again, and in a whisper said, "How're you doing?"

Me? Never better. The hound of the Baskervilles howled again and Sherlock Holmes made a thoughtful face. That howl!

"Chet, please, for God's sake! Oh, hi, Rick, no, no, just talking to my— What I called about is this woman, Cynthia Chambliss. Did she get in touch with you about her daughter?" He listened. "Rick? I believe it's Madison, not Meredith." He listened some more. "That's what I think, too—she'll turn up. There's just one little thing bothering me. Do you know about her first disappearance, the one that turned out not to be real?" More listening. Then Bernie started explaining about the first disappearance. On the screen, Sherlock Holmes smoked a pipe. What would that be like, pipe smoke? All of sudden I was in the mood for Bernie to light up a cigarette. Sure, that was bad of me, but the smell was so nice.

"The point is, Rick, Madison was seen at the mall that night, but she didn't go to the movie, although she was in the ticket line. According to my witness—a cashier who ID'd her off a photo— a young male appeared, and after a brief talk, they went away together. That part—leaving the line—doesn't sit right with me. I think we should find out who he was." I could hear the voice on the other end of the phone, a tiny voice, not cooperating. "I'll look into that part myself, then," Bernie said. "In the meantime, I recommend putting her on the wire. Yeah, I know that contradicts what I . . . but—"

Bernie hung up. He rose, opened the slider, went out on the patio. Under one of the chairs, he found a twisted-up cigarette pack. He dug around in it, came up with a cigarette, shot me a guilty look. Poor Bernie. Smoking was bad for him, although I wasn't sure why; at the same time, he enjoyed it. What was going on with that? He patted his pockets. I knew what that meant: matches. I spotted a book of them on the couch, jumped off the La-Z-Boy, and—

Oh. My leg. Forgot about it completely. But—not too terrible. I went over to the couch, snapped up the matches, brought them outside.

"Chet! You're not supposed to be— Hey. What've you got there?" He took the matches. "Good boy." He gave me a pat. We sat outside, Bernie smoking, me downwind with blue smoke winding its way to my nose, and night falling. He took a deep drag. "Want to know what I think?"

I did.

"We should reconstruct that first night, the nondisappearance, find out everything that happened, where she went, who with, why, the whole ball of wax." That was hard to follow, and I kind of gave up, but then the ending grabbed my attention. I knew what a ball was, of course, one of my favorite things, and wax I also knew, on account of Leda being a candle lover, but putting them together? A wax ball: I could almost taste it. And was salivating a bit when I grew aware that Bernie was still talking.

"So what have we got, hard facts?"

A wax ball would probably be kind of soft, unlike our lacrosse ball, say, which made my teeth feel great every time I gave it a good hard squeeze. Other than that, I had nothing to offer.

Bernie took a deep drag, let smoke drift out through his nostrils. Ah. This was nice and relaxing, out on the patio. And what was that, lying under the barbecue, with a tiny end sticking out? Could it be? A possible bonus to this fine, fine evening? Yes, a forgotten hot dog, burned almost black, just the way I like it, although the name "hot dog" itself had never made sense to me. When was our last cookout? No idea. Was there a fly or two already at work on the thing? Maybe, but not for long. I gobbled it up. Mmmm. We were living the dream, me and Bernie.

"Two hard facts, as far as I can see," said Bernie. "One—a

young male appears at the line to the movie, and Madison leaves with him. Two—she tells her mother she got a ride home with Tim, a senior at her high school. Notice, Chet, I don't state as a fact that was how she actually got home."

I noticed. But what, if anything, he was driving at remained unclear, and besides, I was suddenly feeling a little pukey.

Bernie took another drag, tapped some ashes off his cigarette. They made a tiny whirlwind in the breeze. And what a breeze, coming off the canyon. So many smells, I'd never be able to separate them all, but one thing was sure: The fat javelina was close by. That brought bacon thoughts to my mind, and the next thing I knew, I was in the corner of the patio, coughing up the hot dog.

Bernie ran over. "Chet. You all right, boy?" He ran his hand lightly over my stitches. "Not hurting inside, are you? Maybe we should go to the vet."

The vet? No way. Just look down, Bernie, you'll see the hot dog, figure it out. But when I looked down myself, I realized there was nothing hot dog–like left to see, so I wagged my tail extra hard, out of ideas.

Bernie got the point, or sort of. "Good man." He turned the tap on the garden hose, sprayed the corner of the patio. The garden hose always revved me up; Bernie sprayed me a bit, too, so refreshing. I shook off. He toweled me down. "What I'm trying to say," he said, "is let's start by testing the assumption that it was Tim the archer who approached Madison in the line at the movies."

Fine by me. We went inside. Bernie brewed some tea. I had a chew strip. He found a home number for Tim the archer and called it. No answer. I heard a car drive slowly by.

No school, Bernie said—it was Saturday. Okeydoke. They were all the same to me. First thing in the morning, we got on the freeway, drove past the North Canyon Mall, took an exit that led to a development a lot like ours, except there was no canyon in back, just more and more houses. We stopped in front of one. It had a basketball hoop by the driveway and a grass lawn. A quick frown passed over Bernie's face: He had a thing about grass lawns in the desert. We didn't have even a shred of grass on our lawn. Everything was brown and spiky, except in spring.

Bernie opened the door for me. I got out, felt only the slightest twinge in my shoulder, almost nothing. I was all better! We walked to the front door, me actually trotting a bit. Bernie knocked.

The door opened. A little girl in pajamas looked out. "I'm up," she said. She was holding a stuffed animal of some kind; in fact, could it possibly be a . . . ? Yes. This was something I never understood. I had no desire at all to pal around with a stuffed human.

"Is Tim at home?" Bernie said.

"Timmy sleeps till all hours," the girl said. "Your doggie's big." She stuck her thumb in her mouth. If I'd had one, I'd have done the same every chance I got.

"His name's Chet," Bernie said. "He likes kids."

"Can I pat him?"

"Sure."

She reached out, touched my nose, so lightly I could hardly feel it. "His nose is cold."

From inside the house came a woman's voice. "Kayleigh? What are you—" The woman appeared. She wore a robe and had curlers in her hair and some green stuff smeared all over her face.

"Chet!"

Oops. I caught myself growling. Very bad, but she was scary.

The woman grabbed Kayleigh, pulled her back. "What's going on?" she said.

"The name's Bernie Little." He handed her his card. "I'm a licensed private investigator, and I'd like to speak to Tim."

"A licensed private investigator? My son, Tim?"

"Yes, ma'am. Tim Fletcher, if I've got the right address. There's a little problem at Heavenly Valley High, and your son may have useful information."

"Problem? Tim hasn't mentioned any problems."

"He sleeps till all hours," said Kayleigh.

"Kayleigh," said her mother, "please go to your room for a few minutes."

"Don't wanna."

"I'm not suggesting this problem has any direct connection to Tim," Bernie said. "It relates to the archery club."

"Did someone get shot?" the woman said. "With an arrow?"

Kayleigh's eyes opened wide.

"Not to my knowledge," Bernie said. "Not yet. But we wouldn't want anything like that to happen, would we? Think of the liability."

The woman bit her lip. Bernie was great at making people do that, women especially. It always meant we were about to get somewhere. "I'll wake him," she said. "You can wait . . ." She glanced around, maybe about to tell us to wait outside, but at that moment a landscaper's truck parked across the street. ". . . in the kitchen." We started inside. "Just a minute. The dog's coming inside?"

"He's a trained police dog," Bernie said.

"Chet," said Kayleigh. "His nose is cold."

We waited in the kitchen, Bernie at the table, me by the window. I heard voices upstairs. Bernie rose, opened the fridge, took a quick peek inside. That was Bernie, filling in the blanks. He was back in his place when the woman returned, trailed by a tall kid wearing boxers and a T-shirt; he had rumpled hair and puffy eyes.

"My son, Tim," the woman said.

"Hi, Tim," said Bernie. "Take a seat."

Tim took a seat. We'd gone through a stage, me and Bernie, of watching zombie movies. Tim moved like that. He noticed me and looked puzzled.

"Mrs. Fletcher?" said Bernie. "It would be helpful if we could talk to Tim alone. It'll only be a few minutes."

"Alone? Why?"

"Standard procedure." As he said that, he made a helpless shrug, like: Stupid, I know, but what can I do? We're stuck in this together. Bernie could have been a great actor; at least his mother thought so. I'll get to her later if I have a chance.

The woman blinked, started backing out of the room. "Call if you need me, Tim."

Tim grunted something. He gave off strong smells. I kept my distance.

Bernie gave Tim a smile, the kind that looked friendly if you didn't know him. "I see your mom brewed coffee. Want some?"

Tim shook his head.

"That your Mustang in the driveway?"

Tim grunted.

"Cool car. I had one of those when I was about your age. What are you—a senior?"

Tim nodded.

"At Heavenly Valley High?"

Another nod.

"Got plans for next year?"

Tim shrugged.

"You must be sick of hearing that question."

Tim gazed at Bernie, then spoke his first words. "I got accepted early at U of A."

"Congratulations," Bernie said. "Fine school. You're looking at four of the best years of your life, I guarantee it—as long as you stay out of jail."

Tim's eyes, suddenly less sleepy, opened wide, just like his little sister's, and out came another word. "Huh?"

"And the only way you can get in trouble on that account would be by holding back now."

"Holding back, like . . . ?"

"Let's start with last Wednesday night, when you drove Madison Chambliss home."

Tim's mouth opened, stayed that way for a moment.

"That was in the Mustang, I assume."

Tim shook his head. He had sleepy seeds in the corners of his eyes. I get them, too.

"Some other car?" Bernie said.

"No," said Tim. "No car."

"You're losing me."

"Like, I didn't drive her home."

Bernie sighed. He was a great sigher, had different sighs for different occasions. "The problem is, she said you did."

"I didn't. What's going on? I thought this was about the archery club."

Bernie sat back in his chair. It creaked under him. "Early acceptance is the way to go with college these days, no question," he said. "The only drawback is that it's conditional, as you probably know, on keeping up your grades. And other things, too, such as good behavior. A letter to the admissions department about noncooperation in a missing-persons case might make them rethink."

"Missing-persons case?"

"That's what I said."

"Who's missing?"

"You tell me."

"I don't know."

"See if you can figure it out."

Tim's eyes moved sideways. Thoughts pulled at human eyes like that. Bernie waited. Me, too.

"Maddy?" Tim said.

"Got it in one," Bernie said. "She hasn't been home in almost two days now. Know anything about that?"

"No. I swear."

"Tell me about your relationship with her."

"We don't have a relationship. We're friends."

"Friends? What about the age difference?"

"She's a cool kid."

"In what way?"

"You know, different."

"Different how?"

"Smart. Funny."

His mother poked her head in the doorway. No more curlers, no more green stuff on her face, but there was still something scary about her. "Everything all right, Timmy?"

She didn't scare Tim. "Go away, Mom."

She shrank back, out of sight.

"And close the door."

The door closed.

Tim gazed at Bernie. Bernie tilted his head up and raised one eyebrow. That was his encouraging face. It meant: Go! Tim lowered his voice. "Maddy told me not to say anything. But if she's really missing . . ."

"Not to say anything about what?"

"Driving her home."

"So you did?"

Tim nodded.

"From the movies?"

Tim shook his head. "She didn't go to the movies—which was, you know, why her mom couldn't find out."

"Where did she go?"

Tim rubbed his face, started looking less like a zombie. "She ran into somebody, I think at the mall. Maybe she was planning to go to the movies, something like that."

"Who did she run into?"

Tim looked down at the floor. I did, too, and noticed a few Cheerios under the table.

"Tim?" said Bernie. "Look at me."

Tim looked at him.

"When people go missing, they usually get found quickly, or not at all."

Tim bit his lip, actually chewed on it.

"We're already getting past the quickly stage."

Tim took a deep breath. "Ruben Ramirez," he said.

"Who's he?"

"This kid."

"A student at Heavenly Valley?"

"Used to be. He dropped out. Has his own place."

"What does he do?"

Tim looked down again. "Not sure."

"But if you had to guess."

Tim didn't answer.

"How about I take a swing at it?" Bernie said. "He deals pot."

Tim looked up, surprise all over his face.

"Did he bring her to his place?"

"Yeah."

"Where is it?"

"Not sure. Over in Modena, past that racetrack."

"Not sure?" said Bernie. "Didn't you pick her up from there?"

"No. She called me, asked me to come get her at this convenience store on Almonte."

"Next to a Getty station?"

"That's the one."

"Was she alone?"

"Yeah."

"So you picked her up and drove her home?"

"Yeah."

"What did she say?"

"Not much."

"Did she explain why she left Ruben's?"

Tim took another deep breath. "He came on to her."

"And then?"

Tim shrugged. "She left. Went to the convenience store."

"On foot?"

"Must've been."

"That's a bad area."

"Yeah."

"What was her mood like?"

"Hard to tell."

"What else did she tell you?"

"Just not to say anything."

"How upset was she?"

"Not too much."

"Was she stoned?"

"Maybe a bit."

Bernie rose. Me, too. Enough of this chitchat. It was time to crack this case the way we usually do, with me sniffing out the perp. Bernie handed Tim his card. "Anything new comes up, anything you forgot, call me right away."

Tim nodded. "You think Ruben's like, um . . ."

"We're going to find out."

We left. On the way, I made a quick detour under the kitchen table, scarfed up the Cheerios. The honey-coated kind: my favorite.

SEVEN

N ow entering Modena," said Bernie, honking at a low-rider car that swerved in front of us. "What we've got here is wasteland, pure and simple."

Wasteland smelled good to me: grease and nothing but, all kinds of grease—pizza grease, car grease, french-fry grease, human-hair grease. I was sitting up as tall as I could in the shotgun seat, taking in everything, my nose quivering. We were in a great mood, me and Bernie, on the job—not some horrible divorce case but our specialty, missing persons. Bernie was wearing one of his best Hawaiian shirts, the one with the martini-glass pattern. I wore my brown leather collar with the silver tags; I've also got a black one for dress-up.

"You know what this used to be, Chet? And not so long ago? Ranchland, as far as the eye could see."

We'd gone to a ranch once, me, Bernie, Charlie, Leda. Don't get me started on horses—prima donnas, every one, dim and dangerous at the same time. I preferred Modena just like this, greasy and horseless.

We turned onto a side street, the pavement all cracked and

full of potholes, the houses on either side small and worn-down. Bernie stopped in front of one of them. He unlocked the glove box, took out the gun, a .38 special, stuck it in his pocket. That didn't happen often.

"Just a precaution," Bernie said. "Let's go."

I hopped out.

"All better, huh?" said Bernie.

All better? All better from what? What was he talking— Oh yeah. I gave myself a shake. Bernie opened the gate. We crossed a dirt yard with a dusty couch in the middle of it, rusty springs sticking out here and there. Bernie stepped up to the door and knocked.

A voice sounded inside. "That you, Decko?"

"Yeah," said Bernie.

The door opened. A guy looked out, a young guy, and huge. His eyes, narrow to begin with, narrowed some more. A real big guy with slitty eyes: I didn't like him, not one little bit.

"You're not Decko," he said.

"Very acute," said Bernie. I missed that one: He was calling this guy cute? That wasn't Bernie. "I'm a private investigator," Bernie was saying. He held out his card. The guy didn't even glance at it. "I'm looking for a former Heavenly Valley High student named Ruben Ramirez."

"Never heard of him." The guy started to close the door. Bernie stuck his foot inside. I'd seen that move before, one of Bernie's best.

"No?" Bernie said. "What's the RR stand for?"

"Huh?"

"On the gold chain around your neck," Bernie said. "That RR."

The guy fingered the chain, the thick, heavy kind. His lips moved, but he couldn't come up with anything.

"How about Roy Rogers?" Bernie said. "There's one right around the corner."

"Huh?" the guy said again. I was a little confused myself.

"Tell you what, Ruben," Bernie said. "Now we've got the introductions out of the way, how about we go inside, sit down, sort this all out?"

"Sort what out?" said Ruben.

"This case we're working on."

"Don't know nothin' about it."

"A missing-persons case," Bernie said. He had a way of just plowing forward, a way Leda had never liked. But I did. "Turns out the missing person's a friend of yours, a Heavenly Valley sophomore named Madison Chambliss."

"Never heard of her."

Bernie nodded, this nod of his that had nothing to do with agreement. "I'm getting a real funny feeling, Ruben, a funny feeling that she's inside your house right now."

To my surprise—and I'm pretty sure Bernie's, too—Ruben turned out to be one of those huge guys who could also move. I barely saw what happened, and I doubt Bernie even caught a glimpse. Ruben's fist, bigger than a softball—a kind of ball I had no use for at all—flashed up from under with a whoosh of air and caught Bernie right on the point of the chin. Bernie didn't go down—it took a lot to put Bernie down—but he staggered back. At that point I saw red, despite Bernie's belief that I'm incapable of seeing red. The next thing I knew, Ruben and I were in the house, rolling around on a sticky floor.

I got a real good grip on his pant leg. Ruben wore very wide pants—I had a whole mouthful. He grabbed something off the floor, a lamp, maybe, and started beating me on the head. "Gonna kill you," he said, and called me a lot of bad names. I growled at him and held on. And then Bernie was there, down on the floor with us. He got his arm around Ruben's thick neck, in one of those grips he knew, and Ruben went all floppy.

Bernie rose. "Okay, Chet, let him go. C'mon, boy, you did great, now let go. Chet?"

I let go, maybe not right away. Denim scraps hung from my mouth, snagged on my teeth.

Bernie picked them out. "Good man. You all right?"

Never better. I didn't feel a thing. Bernie turned, went quickly through the house. I stood over Ruben. His eyes fluttered open. I barked in his face. He flinched. You're not the first, buddy boy.

Bernie came back. "She's not here," he said. "But you've got some interesting weapons, Ruben." Bernie had an AK in one hand and a sawed-off shotgun in the other. "And all that dope—what do you think? Eight, nine pounds?"

Ruben sat up, rubbing his neck.

"It can stay our little secret," Bernie said, pulling up a chair and sitting next to Ruben, the shotgun pointed casually at his head, "the weed, the guns, but I'll need your cooperation about Madison."

"Get your fuckin' dog away from me."

"Language," said Bernie.

"Huh?"

"Can't talk to Chet that way."

Ruben blinked. "Get your dog fuckin' away from me."

"Good enough," Bernie said. "We're pretty reasonable, Chet and I."

Ruben gave me a funny look. Like what? Like I wasn't reasonable?

But I backed off, as Bernie wanted. And backing off, I noticed a half-eaten burger on the counter, a burger with the works. Didn't touch the thing. Made no sense, but I just didn't feel like it.

Bernie tapped Ruben's shoulder with the shotgun, not hard. "Madison Chambliss," he said. "Start talking."

"Like, whaddaya wanna know, man?"

"Take it from the movie line at the North Canyon Mall."

Ruben shrugged. "I was hanging out there, cruisin' around, and she goes, 'Hey, Ruben.'"

"So you knew her already."

"Yeah."

"From where?"

"Huh?"

"From school?" Bernie said. "Were you in any classes together?"

"Classes, man? Nah."

"Was she a customer?"

Ruben looked at Bernie, then at me. I had this sudden urge to give his leg a nip.

"Yeah," Ruben said. "A customer. She goes, 'Hey, Ruben,' and we talk a little, she's in the market kind of thing. So we swung by here."

"And?"

"I sold her a nickel bag."

"And then you drove her home?"

"Yeah."

"Where does she live?"

Ruben didn't answer. I inched closer to his leg, staying in the sit position but dragging my butt along the floor.

"Or did you drop her at the mall?" Bernie said.

"Yeah, the mall."

"Want to hear a prediction?" Bernie said. "Your future's not too bright."

"Huh?"

"Let's move on. When was the last time you saw her?"

"Say what? That was the last time."

"How about two days ago?"

"Two days ago?"

"Thursday," Bernie said. "When Madison disappeared."

"She disappeared?"

"Want a tip?" Bernie said. "Only smart people can pull off playing dumb."

"Don't get it, man."

I was one short lunge away now. My lips curled back from my teeth all by themselves.

"Account for your whereabouts," Bernie said, "starting from Thursday morning."

"Thursday morning?" said Ruben. "I was still at County."

"What are you talking about?"

"I was locked up, man. They got me for speeding Wednesday night, found some warrants. I didn't make bail till a few hours ago."

Bernie gave him a long look. Then he put the AK aside and took out his cell phone. "Damn, no service."

"Wanna use mine?" Ruben said.

Bernie used Ruben's. He dialed a number. "Gina? Bernie Little here. Trying to confirm processing times for a possible recent booking down at County, name of Ruben Ramirez."

We waited. Ruben gazed at my teeth. The biting urge—I hardly ever get it, but when I do, oh boy—grew stronger.

"Thanks, Gina." Bernie clicked off, handed Ruben his phone. "Your story checks out."

"You gonna apologize?"

Bernie laughed. I loved Bernie's laugh. There's this crazy run I do in the yard, zooming back and forth, that always works.

"What's funny?" Ruben said.

Bernie stopped laughing. He tapped Ruben's shoulder with the shotgun, this time much harder. Ruben winced. "Paying attention?" Bernie said.

"I was at County, man. Why the hell—"

"Forget that part," Bernie said. "How did Madison get home from your place?"

"Already told you," Ruben said. "I drove her." Or something like that. I didn't really hear because at that moment my jaws were suddenly clamping around Ruben's leg. Not hard, no blood drawn or anything dramatic, but the big baby let out a scream like he was being ripped in two. "All right, all right, I didn't drive her. Call off your damn dog."

"Language."

"Oh God, come on, man." Ruben wriggled around on the floor.

"Chet?"

I unclamped. It took everything I had.

"Maybe take a moment or two, Chet."

Bernie was right. I walked around a bit, snapping up the burger in an absentminded way.

"If you didn't drive her," Bernie was saying, "how did she get home?"

"She walked out, that's all I know."

"Into a bad area? Why would she do that?"

"Couldn't tell you."

"Think," Bernie said. "We really want to know, Chet and I."

Ruben glanced at me, fear in his eyes, no doubt about it. I was licking burger juices off my lips. "Nothin' happened," he said. "I was feelin' a little romantic. She wasn't in the mood."

"You don't look like the romantic type."

Ruben frowned in a thoughtful way, like maybe he was learning something about himself. "I didn't touch her," he said. "Or hardly. She just walked out."

"In what direction?"

"Toward Almonte."

"You watched?"

"I wasn't really watching her," Ruben said. "There was this strange car out front."

"What was strange about it?"

Ruben raised and lowered his heavy shoulders. "Not from around here." He looked toward the window; there was tape on one of the panes. "Maybe the dude offered her a ride."

"What dude?"

"This blond dude in the car. He opened the door as she went by, kind of held out his hand."

"Held out his hand?"

"You know," said Ruben. "To stop her. But she didn't stop. Maybe even started running, now I think of it. Up to Almonte, kind of thing."

"And the blond dude?"

"He got back in the car, drove off."

"After her?"

"Don't remember."

"Think."

Ruben squeezed his eyes shut. Time passed.

Bernie sighed. "What make was the car?"

"A Beamer," said Ruben. "Which was how come I noticed in the first place."

"Model?"

"Don't know the models."

"Color?"

"Blue."

When Bernie was worried about something, his eyebrows got closer together, and his eyes seemed to be looking inward. That was happening now. On the way back to the car, I sprayed markings on the gate and maybe one or two other spots.

We tried the convenience store on Almonte. No one there remembered Madison. I started worrying, too, about what I didn't know.

EIGHT

"Here's a scenario," Bernie said, starting to lose me right off the top. "It makes sense, but I kind of wish it didn't," he went on, finishing the job. We were driving up our street, Mesquite Road. I spotted Iggy, watching from the window at the front of his house. He spotted me, too, and barked, a bark I couldn't hear. Iggy ran back and forth behind the glass. I stood taller in the shotgun seat and turned toward him, ears cocked. Then he was out of sight.

"Suppose," Bernie was saying, "that someone tried to snatch her twice. Madison might not even have realized what was going on the first time outside Ruben's, maybe wrote it off to routine hassling from some creep. But even if it scared her—and I don't think it did—didn't Tim Fletcher say she hadn't seemed upset?"

Bernie paused, glanced over at me. Tim Fletcher? Who was he again?

"The point is, scared or not, she wasn't about to tell her mother, because that would have led to the unraveling of the *Dr. Zhivago* cover story. See where this leads?"

I didn't. How come Ruben Ramirez wasn't the perp? He looked and smelled like so many perps we'd taken down.

"It leads," Bernie said, "to the conclusion that this wasn't spur-of-the moment but a premeditated snatch. Whoever it was failed the first time, coming out of Ruben's, and got her the second, how and where to be determined. And if that's true, we're looking for a blond guy in a BMW. A blue BMW, according to Ruben—maybe not the most reliable witness." He paused. Car identification, colors: neither of them my strengths, although I knew blue, the color of the sky and also Charlie's eyes. Bernie turned in to the driveway. "And wasn't the car in the mall that—"

He cut himself off. All this talk of cars, and now here was another one in the driveway, big and black, unfamiliar to me.

Bernie parked on the street. A man got out of the big black car, came toward us. We got out, too. The man was about Bernie's height but not as broad; he had a goatee, which always caught my attention, and I was staring at it when his smell reached me, the very worst smell in the whole world: cat. The man in our driveway smelled of cat. It was all over him.

"I'm looking for Bernie Little," the man said. Some people—Suzie Sanchez, for example, or Charlie, of course—had friendly voices. This man did not.

"Present," said Bernie.

A frown crossed the man's face. "My name's Damon Keefer," he said. "I understand my ex-wife, without consulting me, hired you to look for my daughter, Madison."

"She hired us, yes," said Bernie.

"And?" said Damon Keefer.

"And what?" Bernie said.

Questions, questions. I had a question of my own. Was there a cat, or maybe more than one, in that black car? Not likely: Cats, unlike my guys, weren't big on riding around in cars, another one of those bewildering things about them. What beat riding around in cars? Maybe a few things—I thought of that distant she-bark not too long ago—but not many. Was it possible cats had no idea how to have fun? I didn't know. All I knew was that the chances of a cat being in that black car were slim but not none. And a cat in that black car meant a cat on our property. A cat on our property? I heard a powerful rumbling sound, had the vague impression it was coming from my own throat. The next thing I knew, I was on the move.

"And what?" Damon Keefer was saying. "I'd like a report on your investigation so far, that's what. I'm assuming you haven't found her or else you'd— Hey! what the hell's that dog doing?"

What was I doing? My job, amigo. And at that moment my job meant checking out this black car—parked in our driveway, by the way, while we were stuck out on the street—for the presence of cats. How do you do that without standing up on your back legs and planting your front paws on the door to get your face right up close to the window? That's basic.

"He's scratching the goddamn paint."

"Chet!"

Good news: no cats. I pushed off, at the same time hearing a sound I wouldn't call scratching, more like chalk on a blackboard. That sound always did things to me, starting at the back of my neck. I shivered. My lips smacked around loosely. I felt pretty good, so good I charged around the yard a bit, bursting out of one tight turn after another, clods of lawn flying all over the place.

"Chet, for God's sake!"

I skidded to a stiff-legged dead stop, one of the things I do best, and not easy—try it sometime. A twig happened to be in reach. I flopped down, front and back legs all stretched out, and started chewing on the twig. Ah, eucalyptus, probably blown over from old man Heydrich's tree. Very tasty.

Bernie and Keefer were standing by the black car, gazing at the door. "Send me a bill," Bernie said.

I chewed the stick. I could smell my own breath. It smelled nice.

"What would be the point of that?" Keefer said. "You'd just pad your own bill—I know how these things work."

Bernie gave him a look I'd hardly ever seen from him before. "I don't pad my bills," he said.

Keefer met his look, but not for long. "Suit yourself," he said. "I'll hear your report and be on my way."

"Ever dealt with a private investigator before?" Bernie said.

"No, thank God," said Keefer.

"Then you're probably not aware that I don't report to you. I report only to the client, except for certain information I'm compelled by law to pass on to the police."

"The client? What the hell are you talking about?"

"I'm on a retainer from Cynthia. That makes her the client."

Keefer's face swelled up: another blood-flow thing, but not a blush. This swelling up was a sign of human rage. In my world, rage and noise went together, but when Keefer spoke, his voice didn't get louder; in fact, he lowered the volume. Humans—not all, but some—have a way of putting you off balance.

"What that tells me," Keefer said, "is that you're a touch slow in the detection department. Any half-decent detective would have figured out that every cent Cynthia has comes right from me."

Bernie? A touch slow? I stopped chewing the stick, got my back legs up under me, ready.

Bernie stayed calm. "That doesn't change anything. But I know this is a tough time for you, and if Cynthia gives her permission, I'll fill you in."

"I don't need her permission for—"

"Maybe the three of us could meet at your place."

"My place? Why my place?"

"Does Madison have a room there?"

"Yes, but—"

"I'd like to see it."

"Why?"

"Standard procedure," Bernie said. "I'm trying to get your daughter back."

"She probably took off for Vegas."

"Vegas?"

"She's impulsive, just like her mother."

"Does Madison have a gambling problem?"

"I didn't mean Vegas per se," said Keefer.

"Has she ever run away before?"

"How would I know? Think I'm in the loop?"

"According to Cynthia, there's no history of running away."

"What do you expect her to say?"

"Meaning?" Bernie said.

"She's a terrible mother—isn't that obvious?"

"Did you try for custodial rights?"

"No," Keefer said. "A young girl needs her mother. At least that's what I thought at the time. But now—" He raised his hands, palms up. Humans did that when they didn't know what else to do. I knew the feeling. When I reached that point, I took a nap if I was indoors; outdoors, I marked territory, always a good fallback.

Bernie was gazing at Keefer in one of his thoughtful ways, his head tilted to the side. That meant he was changing his mind about something, making new plans. "Tell you what," he said, "why don't I call Cynthia now? We can meet right here."

* * *

We met in the office, Cynthia and Keefer in the client chairs, Bernie at the desk, me under it. From there, I could see Cynthia and Keefer from their waists down. He wore dark pants and dark shoes with tassels; she had sandals and bare legs. Their feet were pointing away from each other. My eyes felt heavy right away.

"First of all," Bernie said, "I want to start with a very important question." Feet started twitching, first a sandaled foot, then one with tassels. "Has either of you received a ransom demand?"

"Ransom demand?" They both said the words at the exact same time; something about their voices together sounded unpleasant.

"If you have, the caller almost certainly warned you against telling anyone." Bernie said. "I promise you that not telling us would be a bad mistake."

"Who is 'us'?" Keefer said.

Bernie tapped his foot lightly on my tail. "The agency, of course. But you haven't answered the question."

"There's been nothing like that," said Cynthia. "What are you saying?"

"Are you telling us this is definitely a kidnapping?" said Keefer.

Cynthia's hands squeezed tight together. "Oh my God," she said.

"There's nothing definite at this stage," Bernie said. "Do you have any enemies?"

"Me?" said Cynthia.

"Or business rivals?"

Now she was wringing her hands. "I don't think of them as rivals, but—"

"For Christ's sake," Keefer said. "You design e-cards. He's talking about real business."

Cynthia's hands separated, balled into fists. There was a silence. Then Bernie spoke. "And you're a developer, Mr. Keefer?"

"I own Pinnacle Peak Homes at Puma Wells," Keefer said. "Competitors come with the territory. But we don't kidnap each other's kids. And if all you've got is speculation, you have no right to alarm us like this."

"This is just speculation?" said Cynthia.

"You can call it that," Bernie said. "But it's based on information we've developed, mostly concerning Madison's movements last Wednesday—the night she supposedly went to the movies." He started telling the whole story. The sound of his voice grew fainter. I got all warm and fuzzy, right on the edge of dozing off. I heard Keefer say, as though from a great distance, "Have you run this theory past the police?" Bernie answered from even farther away, "Not yet. She's already on the wire anyway, and besides . . ." Then I was over the edge, sinking into dreamland.

When I awoke, Bernie and I were alone. He was sitting at the desk, holding a check. I squeezed out from under, stretched my front legs way forward, bringing my jaw almost down to the floor, butt up high. That felt great.

Bernie looked down at me. "That didn't go so well," he said. He waved the check. "Two grand." What was wrong with that? A grand was always nice, and two grand was nicer. "The problem is Keefer wrote it. They're co-clients now. I would have preferred sticking with her. He's so . . ."

Whatever Bernie was planning to say about Keefer, I wanted to know, but at that moment the doorbell rang. We went and opened up. There stood Charlie, wearing his backpack.

"Hi, Daddy. Hey, Chet."

The window of a car parked on the street slid down, and

Leda looked out. "Have him back by two tomorrow," she said. "No later." Looking past her, I could see Malcolm the boyfriend behind the wheel, talking on a cell phone. I barked. Why the hell not? It was good to see the boyfriend glance over. He was scared of me and my kind, I could tell right away.

Charlie came in. I gave his face a nice lick. He said, "Oooo," and made a funny twisted smile. "I'm ready for camping," he said.

"Camping?" said Bernie.

"You promised."

"Then let's get packed."

We packed the tent, the sleeping bags, the air mattresses, the air pump, the pegs, the wooden mallet, a cooler full of food and drinks.

"Anything we're forgetting?" Bernie said.

"Matches," said Charlie.

Bernie laughed. My tail knocked something off the coffee table. I tried to slow it down.

It was getting dark by the time we left the house. Bernie opened the slider, and we carried all the gear—the mallet was my responsibility—into the backyard. There we set up the tent, pounded in the pegs, pumped up the mattresses, unrolled the sleeping bags. We had two kinds of camping: the kind where we got into the car and drove into the desert, and this kind. Charlie liked this kind better, especially when he missed a real bed in the middle of the night.

Bernie piled rocks in a circle, threw on some wood, made a fire. Charlie grilled sausages on the end of a stick, his face glowing from the flames. Bernie had two, Charlie one, me two, and later the third, right out of the package when no one was looking, because it was there. Then came roasted marshmallows, which I didn't touch. Love the skins, but there's some trick to swallowing the gooey insides that I've never mastered.

The fire burned low. Bernie sang a song called "Rawhide." Charlie joined in. Me, too, with the high-pitched woo-woo I can do if I get my nose pointed right up at the sky.

"Time to turn in, pardners," Bernie said.

He and Charlie went into the tent. I curled up by the dying fire, gazing at the coals. There was a bit of talking in the tent, then silence. Ah, camping. I closed my eyes.

And was almost asleep when I heard barking far away. I'd heard that bark before, the distant she-bark from the other night. This time it went on and on. Suddenly, I wasn't so sleepy anymore, more like wide awake. On my feet, in fact, and standing by the back gate, the entry to the canyon. Locked, of course, and high, maybe Bernie's height or taller. But did I mention my leaping ability? A moment later, or possibly less, I found myself on the other side of the gate.

Bark bark. I followed the sound. I was on high alert, had never felt so strong in my life. This was going to be great! The barking led me not into the open canyon but around the house, onto our street and down the hill, away from Iggy's place.

I'd only passed a few houses when I noticed a parked car with two men sitting in the front seat. It was dark, the nearest streetlight at the corner, but I can see at night, no problem. And what did I see? The man in the passenger seat had fair hair, massive cheekbones, tiny ears. I knew this man, oh but yes. What else? His window was open, and his arm rested on the door frame. I couldn't remember everything Bernie had said, but I knew one thing: the perp.

I charged, sprang, clamped down on his elbow.

The perp cried out. The man behind the wheel said, "Boris?

What the—" The driver saw me, reached down, came up with a gun, a fat gun of a kind I'd seen before, back in K-9 school: Taser. Then came a little popping sound, and something light hit my neck. The instant it did, a fiery pain went jolting back and forth through my body.

I fell on the ground, twitching. I wanted to bark, bark for Bernie, camping so close by, but I couldn't. The car doors opened. The trunk popped up. Boris and the driver—a dark little guy with eyebrows that joined in the middle—jumped out, picked me up, threw me in the trunk.

Thud. The lid slammed shut. I couldn't see a thing. The car started moving. I went crazy in that tiny space, crashing around. I couldn't even stand up! Bernie! Bernie!

The car was going fast now. I heard a whimpering sound, realized it was me. Very bad. I wasn't even hurting anymore.

I lay down and tried to be quiet. After a while I detected a smell I knew, very faint, almost at the limit of what I could do: a smell of young human female, with hints of honey, cherry, and a kind of sun-colored flower I sometimes saw along roadsides. Madison had been here before me.

NINE

My night vision is good, so good that whether it's day or night doesn't make much difference, but now, for the first time in my life, I couldn't see a thing. I didn't like it at all. There were plenty of smells beside Madison's: oily smells, rubbery smells, rotting-garbage smells. And sounds, too, high-pitched and whimpering. After a while, I realized that was me. Again? I got that to stop. Then came quivering, and I stopped that, too. I just lay there in total darkness. But what good would that do, just lying there, waiting?

I stuck out a front paw, touched one side of the trunk. Was scratching at it a good idea? Scratching at things was pretty much always a good idea, to my way of thinking. I scratched, felt some kind of carpet-type material. I scratched some more, soon had all four paws involved, digging my claws in deep, ripping out all kinds of stuff—hard stuff, soft stuff, maybe even some wires. A tiny spark flew by; then everything went dark again. I didn't know why, but the tiny spark seemed like a good thing to me. I scratched harder.

The brakes squealed. The car stopped, so suddenly I went

crashing into the front wall of the trunk. A door slammed, and another. Then I heard footsteps, coming close. The car made popping metallic sounds. Above them, I could also hear the wind, a high whine.

A man spoke. "What in hell this is?"

"Well, Boris, looks like the taillights went blooey," said another man. I recognized his voice: the little driver whose eyebrows met in the middle.

"Blooey?" said Boris.

"You know. In the crapper."

"This I am seeing," Boris said. "I am questioning why—maintenance of car is your responsibility." Or something like that. Boris was hard to understand.

"They were workin' this morning," the driver said. I heard a tap-tap, maybe the driver's hand on a taillight cover. "Dog must of done it."

"The dog broke the lights, you are asking me to believe?"

"You heard 'im bangin' around in there."

"Dogs breaking taillights, Harold?" said Boris. "Is not logic."

"Huh?" said Harold.

I didn't get it, either.

"Wan' me to pop the trunk?" Harold said.

That I got. I squirmed over onto my belly, pressed my paws down under me, crouched, all ready. This was my chance! There was going to be a moment when the lid went up and—

"No," said Boris. "Not now. At ranch, we pop."

"Your call," said Harold. "But what are we gonna do about the damn dog?"

"I am not knowing," said Boris. "This dog is trouble."

"Then why don't we shoot him right now, leave him by the side of the road?"

"Hmmm," said Boris. There was a pause. Then he continued, "Mr. Gulagov is master of logic. He will make decision."

Their footsteps moved away, crunch crunch. The doors opened and closed. And then we were on the move again. I scratched around for a little bit, but nothing happened. I lay down. The ride got bumpy.

Time passed, a long time, it seemed to me, a bumpy time of total darkness with no new sounds or smells. I kept my eyes open even though there was nothing to see. Important to stay alert, to be ready at all times. Bernie had a saying: something—couldn't remember exactly what—depended on preparation. My mind wandered over to Bernie. Did I mention his smell? The very nicest of any human I'd ever come across—actually, a bit doglike in some ways. Yes, that good. Nothing like mine, of course. Mine is the best. Hard to describe my smell: a mix of old leather, salt and pepper, mink coats—I know about mink coats on account of Bernie had one, his grandma's, that he gave to Leda—and a soupçon—a favorite word of Bernie's, meaning, I think, a tiny drop of soup: in my case, cream of tomato. I remembered the first time I smelled Bernie, back in K-9 school. This was just before the unfortunate—

The car came to a stop. The doors opened and closed. I got in my crouch, ready to spring. But nothing happened. Yes, there were footsteps, but they moved away. After that, silence except for the wind, very faint.

What was going on? I was ready, all set to spring, to attack, to fight my way out, but there'd be none of that until the trunk popped open. What could I do? Nothing came to mind. Except: Bernie.

I waited, and waited some more. Had to be prepared, had to

stay alert. Bernie would have been proud of me, how long I stayed prepared and alert before my eyelids got very heavy.

Squeak. Thump. Where was I? What was—

The trunk was open, the lid still vibrating. They'd popped it! I could hear it going sprong-sprong but couldn't see—all this blinding daylight was flooding in. But I could smell, and smell plenty: men, all nasty. Now! I sprang toward the light.

Then came confusion: metallic gleams, human faces, a hard landing. I bounded forward and thudded right into something solid. What was this? I'd leaped into a—

Clang.

A cage? A cage. Oh no.

I wheeled around, my eyes adjusting, too late. Boris slid the bolt into place, locking the door. I hurled myself against the bars, barking in fury, shaking the cage, but for nothing. After a while I just stood there, growling, looking out.

Three men were looking in: Boris, Harold the driver, and a short but very powerful guy with a thick neck, thick arms and legs, and a shaved head.

The third man spoke. "A fine animal," he said. The way he talked reminded me a little of Boris, but less strange.

"You think so, boss?" said Harold.

"He has given me lots of troubles, Mr. Gulagov," said Boris. "Even he was biting my arm." He held up his arm. "Look— Band-Aids."

Mr. Gulagov didn't look at Boris's arm. He was looking at me. His eyes were small and colorless, also in shadow under his heavy brow. "Perhaps we could train him."

"To do what?" said Harold.

"Fight other dogs, what else?" Mr. Gulagov said. "There is

good dogfighting in Mexico, I believe. I have contemplated investing."

"Is money in that?" said Boris.

"Where you find gambling, you find money," said Mr. Gulagov. "Remember this lesson, Boris."

"Yes, sir."

"I'll remember, too," said Harold.

Mr. Gulagov paid Harold no attention. He was gazing at me. "Yes, a fine animal. Get him some bones."

"Bones?" said Harold.

"For rewarding."

"Rewarding?" said Boris. "He is enemy."

Mr. Gulagov smiled. He had huge teeth for a human, and bright, the brightest I'd ever seen. "You watch, Boris. I will make him friend."

"With bones?"

"Sure, bones, but not only bones. We have reward, we have punishment. This is math, Boris. Reward plus punishment equals loyalty."

"The dog's going to be loyal to you?"

"One hundred percent," said Mr. Gulagov. "He will live and die for me. But first we must give him a name."

"I think he already has one," said Harold, "there, stamped on his coll—"

Mr. Gulagov gave the driver a look; the driver went silent. "We will call him Stalin."

"Stalin? Like the guy who—"

"This name sends a message," said Mr. Gulagov. He lit a fat cigar, talked around it. "Bring Stalin around to the barn."

All that went by quickly, hard to understand. But loyal to that guy? Never. And my name was Chet, pure and simple.

They all walked away, toward some buildings. We'd gone to a ranch once, me, Bernie, Charlie, Leda—did I already mention that? This place reminded me a little of the ranch, except everything was all run-down, and there were no horses around; I knew that right away from the lack of horse smell. Beyond the buildings rose a steep rocky hill, very high, with cactuses poking up here and there. And other than the hill, nothing: just desert all around, plus the wind, making a high-pitched sound like it was blowing hard, even though I couldn't feel any wind on my coat.

A motor started up, and out from behind one of the buildings came Harold at the wheel of a yellow forklift. I knew forklifts from a case of warehouse theft Bernie and I had cracked a while back. The forklift came close up and stopped. Then, with a little whine, the forks slid down. The truck moved even closer, getting the forks right under the cage. Harold's face was very near. I didn't like that face with its single heavy eyebrow, not one bit.

"Easy there, Stalin," Harold said.

I didn't think for a moment, just took off and flew at him. I forgot all about the cage until I crashed into it and fell to the floor. After that, I was a little woozy, barely aware of Harold's laughter.

We rolled slowly toward the buildings—a long, low house, a barn, some sheds—their wooden sides cracked, the paint peeled off, a broken window or two. Harold headed around the barn, lowered the cage, backed away, drove off.

It was very quiet. The sun rose higher. The heat rose, too. I couldn't smell water, not in the cage, not anywhere. I was pretty thirsty. I paced back and forth. Saliva started leaking out of my mouth, even foaming a little. I lay down. That was when I noticed a big black hole at the base of the rocky hill across the way, with a pair of rusty train tracks leading in. I knew what that was: a mine. Bernie had a thing about old abandoned mines in the desert. We'd explored lots, and one thing I knew—how cool they were inside. That stayed on my mind as the day grew hotter and hotter.

The sun sank behind the hill. The air cooled down, but that didn't help my thirst. My tongue felt thick and dry, a strange thing, like it wasn't part of me. Long shadows appeared. The sky grew dimmer.

All at once I smelled water, a clean, lovely smell with hints of rock and metal. Then I heard footsteps. I rose.

Mr. Gulagov appeared from around the corner of the barn. He carried a big bowl. Water slopped over the sides. He stopped in front of the cage, set the bowl on the ground. I almost could have stuck my tongue through the bars and lapped some up; it was the tiniest bit too far away.

He looked down at me. "Hello, Stalin. How is life treating you?"

I didn't do anything, didn't move a muscle, didn't make a sound. My name wasn't Stalin.

"You and I will be good friends, Stalin," Mr. Gulagov said. "It's a little warm out here. Are you thirsty?"

I stayed still.

"Here is water. We have well water at this old mine, nice and cold." He toed the bowl; a tiny wave of water broke over the side. "Want some nice cold water? I can move it closer, no problem. All you have to do is one simple thing—sit." He paused. "Ready? Stalin, sit."

I remained standing.

"Sit."

I stood a little taller.

"Don't disappoint me, Stalin. You must have been trained. You must know 'sit.'"

What I knew was between me and Bernie.

"There's something you will soon learn from me—I do not tolerate disobedience. And I always win." His voice rose, and his face got flushed. "Sit! Sit! Sit, you stupid cur."

No chance.

Mr. Gulagov kicked over the water bowl and stomped away. When he was out of sight, I stuck my tongue through the bars and licked up some of the moist dirt.

TEN

I was lying down, my tongue hanging out. I started to pant, couldn't stop. My mind drifted back to the one time I'd seen snow. This was on a hike Bernie and I had taken in some mountains, not exactly sure where. First there'd been a long ride in the car. Then we'd started walking, up and up, and all of a sudden, white stuff covered the ground. What a surprise! White stuff, everywhere. I zigzagged around.

"Snow, Chet," Bernie said. "This is snow."

I'd never even heard of snow. I sniffed it, tasted it, rolled around in it. Whooo—it gave me the shivers. Bernie threw snowballs. I caught them in midair. They went splat against my nose. I skidded all over the place, on my side, back to front, every which way. We had fun like you wouldn't believe, and after, on the way down, we came to a spot where the snow melted into water between some rocks and ran—burbled, that was how Bernie put it—into a stream. I lowered my face right in the flow. That was the best water I ever drank in my life. I thought of it now—couldn't think about anything else, really—in the cage behind Mr. Gulagov's barn, and stopped panting.

It was still light out, but just barely, when I heard them coming back. I got up, feeling a bit funny, not quite myself. This time there were only Boris and Mr. Gulagov, neither of them carrying water.

"Wow," said Boris. "The tongue is looking like a block of wood."

"A minor matter," said Mr. Gulagov, waving his hand. Big rings on his fingers caught what was left of the light. "Dogs can go for many days without water."

"I was thinking that was camels," Boris said.

Mr. Gulagov went very still. "Is this a joke?"

"Oh no, sir. No joke."

"Excellent," said Mr. Gulagov. "Humor is tricky."

"I will remember."

"Tricky and not for everyone."

"Never again," said Boris.

"I will handle the joking," Mr. Gulagov said. "Let us get started."

They walked up to the cage. Boris reached out. "Now?"

"Now."

Boris slid the bolt, opened the cage door. Big mistake, my friend. In a flash I was up and charging, right through that open—

But no. I heard a jingling sound; saw a metallic flash; felt something tight squeeze around my neck. I lost my balance, and then I was down flat in the dirt, my neck getting squeezed tighter and tighter. Looking up, I saw Mr. Gulagov planted right in front of me, leaning back, pulling hard on the end of a choke chain, gritting those huge teeth of his. I knew choke chains, had seen them being used once or twice on new puppies in the neighborhood, but not like this, and no one had ever used a choke chain on me, not even in the time before Bernie. I fought against the hard metal links, squirming and struggling, but that only made things worse.

"That will only make things worse," said Mr. Gulagov, pulling tighter, dragging me upright. I couldn't breathe. I strained and strained to suck in air but couldn't get any. "Do I have your attention now, Stalin?" He paused. Everything began turning white. "Sit," he said.

He moved his hands. The chain loosened. I breathed in air, breathed and breathed. The chain was looser now, but not so loose that my breathing didn't make squeaky sounds.

"Sit."

I stood there, feeling not quite myself; but I stood.

"Maybe his hearing is bad," Boris said.

"No," said Mr. Gulagov. "That is not the bad part." He smiled, smiled right at me with those big bright teeth. That confused me, because the human smile always went with nice things, in my experience. And in that moment of confusion, Mr. Gulagov jerked the chain down with huge force. I sank back down on the ground, the chain digging deep in my neck.

"Now we try again, yes?" said Mr. Gulagov, still smiling. He loosened the chain enough for me to breathe a few more squeaky breaths. "Up," he said. I lay there. Mr. Gulagov sighed. "Boris?" he said. "The whip."

"Regular whip or horsewhip?" said Boris.

"Horsewhip, I think."

"Where is it?" said Boris.

"Must I do everything myself?" Mr. Gulagov said. "You will have to look."

Boris moved off.

I lay on the ground, my tongue in the dust, unsure what a

horsewhip was. Mr. Gulagov gazed down at me. There was something about his eyes that made me look away.

"You have spirit," he said. "You will make a good fighting dog after I break you."

Boris returned. I saw what a horsewhip was.

"Crack it for demonstration purposes," said Mr. Gulagov.

Boris flicked his hand. The whip cracked like lightning, not far above my head. Mr. Gulagov tugged at the chain, pulling me up. "Stalin," he said. "Sit."

I stood there. It was dark now. Lights went on in one of the barn windows, high up. I saw someone at the window—a girl, and not only that but a girl I recognized: Madison Chambliss. Hey! I'd found her.

"Boris?" said Mr. Gulagov. "Now show him how it feels on the flesh."

"The whip?"

"What else would I be talking about?"

Madison opened the window and stuck out her head. "Don't you hurt that dog," she said.

Mr. Gulagov and Boris looked up. "Where is Olga?" Mr. Gulagov's face swelled up, getting flushed again. "What is going on?"

A big woman with her hair in a bun rose up behind Madison, arms raised high like a witch in one of Bernie's old horror movies. She started pulling Madison away. Madison's eyes opened wide. "Hey. Is that the dog who—"

Then she got yanked out of sight. At that moment I realized there was almost no pressure around my neck. I gave Mr. Gulagov a sideways glance. No need to turn my head for sideways glancing, just another one of my advantages, not having my eyes bunched so close together, human-style. Mr. Gulagov's gaze was still on the window, his hand on the choke chain relaxed, half open.

I bolted.

"What the hell?" said Mr. Gulagov.

The choke chain tightened, but only for an instant, and then got ripped from his hand. Free! I ran, swerving toward the far end of the barn, the chain dragging behind me. A barn door opened, and Harold stepped out. I smelled something new on him, a smell Bernie and I had worked on a lot: the smell of a gun, recently fired. Harold's hand moved to his pocket. Had I seen what guns could do? Too many times. I cut the other way, but Boris was already on the move, horsewhip raised high. I turned again, going all out in the only other direction, toward the rocky hill. If only I could get up there, maybe—

"Kill him," Mr. Gulagov shouted.

A gunshot rang out, and then another; a bullet pinged against a rock right beside me. I reached the base of the hill and bounded into the mine without a second thought, or even a first one. Guns fired and fired again. I kept going; I'd seen what guns could do.

The faint light from outside penetrated a short way into the mine, then got swallowed up in darkness. I felt railroad ties under my paws, cool hard-packed dirt between them. After a while, I looked back. The mouth of the mine was a dark and fuzzy circle in the blackness. Beyond it, I could see lights shining in the barn. I listened with one of my front paws raised off the ground, the way I do when I'm listening my very hardest. Silence, except for the high desert wind. I crept back toward the opening.

Slow, very slow. I can be real quiet when I want to: quiet as a shadow, Bernie said. I moved like a shadow now, was only a few steps from the opening. And then? Zoom. I'd be flying out of there, melting into all the other night shadows, on the way home. But as I took my last slow step, the end of the choke chain—I'd forgotten all about it—clanked against one of the rails.

Lights flashed on, bright as the sun.

"There he is."

I wheeled around and sprinted back down the tunnel, the choke chain clinking and clanking behind me. A gun went off, and then came a high-pitched ping off one of the rails, so close I jumped right into the air, all four paws off the ground. Mr. Gulagov, not far away at all, called out, "After him, but use your brains—there is only one way out. You know that. The animal does not."

That was me? The animal? And there was something I didn't know? But what? I didn't understand. I just ran, deeper and deeper into the darkness of the mine. Glancing back, I saw a bright gleam on the track, chasing after me. My thirst, my tiredness—I forgot all about them, went flat out. Was there a man on earth I couldn't outrun? No.

I heard voices behind me, farther back now: "Follow the sound."

Sound? What sound? I was like a shadow. Then I remembered the choke chain, remembered it again. Why did I keep forgetting? I slowed down, twisted my head, bit at the cold metal, bit as hard as I could. Nothing happened. Cutting through the choke chain was beyond what I could do. I kept trying anyway. Then all at once, the gleam caught me, raced by. Can't slow down, Chet. Up ahead I glimpsed the tunnel, bending around a curve. Crack: another gunshot, very loud in the mine. Something buzzed right through the fur at the end of my tail, and then wood splintered nearby. I took off, darted around the curve, back into darkness.

I ran and ran, ran my very fastest, on and on, but the sound of the chain followed me all the way, and glancing back, I saw the light following me, too. This was bad. I needed something, but what? I needed, I needed . . . And then I knew: a hole, a place to lie quiet. But there was no hole, so I just ran, maybe not my fastest anymore. Another glance back: The gleam came closer and closer, was going to catch me again for sure. I tried to run harder, and maybe I was a little, but after not many more strides, I smelled something new: water.

Water.

I followed the smell, the best smell there was—second best, maybe—up the tunnel, then lost it almost right away. I stopped, sniffed around. Don't stop, Chet. Run. But I did stop. I needed water, just a taste. Voices sounded again, and the gleam of the lights was traveling fast on the rails. I took a few steps back, toward the voices and the light, and there it was, the water smell again. It seemed to come from the tunnel wall. I moved toward the wall, and the smell got stronger. I followed it; and what was this? I was following it right into the wall? Yes: The smell was coming out of an opening I could almost see, maybe another tunnel, but very narrow. As the gleam was about to hit me, light me up for all to see, I squeezed into the opening, scraping against a sharp rock or maybe a broken piece of wood. I moved inside a little way, silent now, no rails under me for the chain to clank against. Then I heard Harold, very near.

"Why don't we wait at the front? You said yourself there's only one way out."

I lay down, went still.

"Who does the thinking, Harold?"

"You, boss. But it's dangerous in here—these supports are all rotten."

At that moment I heard a cracking sound, faint and far away.

"Perhaps you have a point," said Mr. Gulagov.

Their footsteps moved away, slowly faded. I lay there, the smell of water stronger and stronger. After a while, I crawled toward it on my belly. I could hear it now, a faint trickle. I stuck out my tongue and licked the wall. And yes, water, ah, dripping down the rocky face. I lapped at the wall, lapped and lapped, filled myself up with cold water, saltier than I like, but lovely anyway. I drank until my tongue shrank back to normal, drank until I couldn't drink any more, and began to feel more like myself. I lay there in my hole, resting. It was quiet, the only sound the beating deep in my chest, slowing down. My eyelids got heavy.

ELEVEN

Water trickled, a soothing sound. That meant the kitchen sink was leaking again. These things happened: Bernie had a tool kit, did all the home repairs, some of them over and over. Once he got his hand stuck in the garbage disposal and then the whole fuse box started smoking and the fire department—

I opened my eyes. At home in the kitchen? No. Everything came back. I was in the mine, darkness all around. But what was this? Darkness, yes, but not complete. In the distance, I saw a narrow shaft of golden light. I rose, realizing that not quite everything had come back to me: I'd forgotten the choke chain. I rolled over, squirmed this way and that, tried to get rid of the thing. But the choke chain stayed where it was, twisted around my neck, the free end trailing on the ground.

I sat up, still and quiet—I could sit very nicely, thanks, Mr. Gulagov—and listened. There was nothing to hear except trickling water. I licked some off the wall and moved toward the light.

It turned out to be far away. The closer I got, the more I could see. I was in a narrow tunnel, and it was getting narrower, the walls and ceiling all closing in. I had to crouch low as I reached the source of the light, a narrow crack in the wall. I sniffed at it, smelled outside things: mesquite, flowers, and another scent that reminded me of cats. I pawed at the crack. A bit of the wall crumbled away, and the crack got bigger. I pawed some more. The crack grew into a hole. Through it I saw big rocks, a ball of tumbleweed rolling by, and in the distance a tall butte.

The next thing I knew, I was digging, digging harder than I'd ever dug. Dirt and rocks flew all over the place. Soon the hole was big enough to stick my head through. I stuck my head through, blinked away some dust, saw I was high up a steep slope, way above the desert floor. I tried to wriggle the rest of me through the opening, got nowhere. That made me a little panicky. My front paws were stuck but not my back ones; they started digging crazily. Then came a strange rumbling sound, and the whole mountain seemed to tremble. With all my strength, I wriggled and dug, trying to get free. The mountain made a boom and shot me right out of the hole—in fact, the hole wasn't even there anymore. I tumbled down the mountainside, rocks and clods of dirt bouncing all around me.

I came to rest at the top of a narrow ledge, the end of the choke chain slapping across my body, dust blowing everywhere. Did I feel any pain? No: wasn't thirsty, wasn't even tired, only a little bit hungry. I remembered that cold steak Bernie and I had shared, slathered with A.1. All right: I was very hungry.

I got up and had a good shake, raising clouds of dirt, like a little storm. When it cleared, I could see down below to the desert. It went on and on, with some mountains in the distance: no sign of Mr. Gulagov or his ranch, no buildings of any kind in sight, no people. I was free! My next thought was of home and Bernie.

But home—which way? I sniffed around. I'd gotten home from far away before, always by following my own smell; a very nice one, did I mention that? This time the only scent trail of me led back up the mountain, into the mine. The wrong direction, for sure. I walked along the ledge, looking for a path down. That strange cat smell was in the air again, not quite cat but somehow more so. I found a narrow gully, followed it off one side of the ledge and around a big rock, the size of a car. Fresh air, not too hot, lots of sunshine: This wasn't too bad. My tail was up, alert, wagging a bit. All in all, I was feeling pretty good, and if I did have any worries, I couldn't think what they were.

Then, with no warning except a slight rush of air behind me, I got hit by something big and strong with so much force I flew off the ground, landing hard way down the slope. I rolled over, looked up, and saw a huge catlike animal bounding toward me, an animal I knew from the Discovery Channel: mountain lion. Huge teeth, huge claws, huge yellow eyes—cat blown up to nightmare size. What had Bernie said that time in front of the TV? "If you ever meet up with one of these suckers, whatever you do, don't run. Run and you're done." He'd even—this was after a bourbon or two, not always a good idea for Bernie—done a lion imitation and come at me, making his fingers like claws, saying, "Stay, Chet, stay."

I trusted Bernie, believed every single thing he'd ever told me. I turned and ran.

My very fastest running, paws hardly touching down, ears flat back: and yet she pounced on me almost right away, claws digging into my back. We rolled together, down and down the mountain, our faces close together. Those eyes: a killer's eyes.

We crashed into the bottom of a saguaro, came to a stop. I was up right away, and so was she. She crouched, ready to spring. I faced her and growled, didn't know why, just did it. She paused, as if in doubt—Bernie was right!—and then, instead of springing, lashed out at me with a paw, so quick I didn't even have time to flinch. I felt pain on my side, but what was this? She'd caught a claw in one of links of the choke chain. That brought another pause, a pause I took advantage of, turning my head a little and biting her on the shoulder. She roared, a horrible roar that sounded like a thunderstorm. My hair stood on end. She tried to free her paw, yanking it back, and I felt her tremendous strength right through my skin. The chain snapped at once, and she roared again, crouching to spring. But in the next instant her roar turned into a gagging cough, the kind familiar to me from chicken-bone incidents. What was this? Behind those huge teeth, at the back of her throat, I glimpsed a chain link; it must have flown into her mouth. She backed away, bending over, trying to cough it up. I took off and didn't look back till I reached the desert floor. No sign of her.

I followed the sun: That seemed right. It led me toward those distant mountains. I went into my trot. So nice to be free of the chain! Once I got going, I could trot forever.

But by the time the sun sank behind the mountains, cooling the air right away, I was walking, and not very fast. Hungry, tired, thirsty, all at the same time. My tongue was dried out again, too big for my mouth. Panting spells came and went, plus I smelled blood from time to time, had to be mine. Once I saw a sign on a post in the middle of nowhere. I gazed at it for a while, then at the mountains. They didn't look any closer, but their shadows were, and moving toward me all the time.

Night fell. Stars came out, filling the sky. I knew my direction was right, kept going. In the distance, I spotted a light, an unsteady kind of light, yellow and flickering. Soon after that, I smelled smoke, and not just smoke but meat, meat on the grill. I picked up the pace, even trotted a bit. Slowly, the flickering yellow light became a fire, with human-shaped forms moving around it. I approached, staying in the shadows beyond the reach of the light.

Humans, yes, of the biker kind; we didn't like bikers, me and Bernie. They sat around a big open campfire, men and women, drinking, smoking, cooking burgers; their bikes stood by an old falling-down shack. How many bikers? That was the kind of thing I couldn't tell you.

"Hey, what's that?"

My ears perked up.

"Coyote?"

I drew back, not in the mood for insults.

"Nah. Looks like a dog."

"Way out here?"

"Must be hungry."

"Hey, pooch—wanna burger?"

Not long after that, I was sitting around the fire, working on a burger, not my first, and socializing with the bikers. I changed my mind about bikers, or at least these bikers. They were big, the women, too, with lots of tattoos and piercings—the sight of piercings always gave me this unpleasant feeling all over my skin—but friendly.

"He looks pretty wore out."

"Wonder where he came from."

"Check his tag."

"Got no tag," a biker lady said, coming closer, giving me a nice pat.

No tag? Uh-oh. Couldn't feel my collar. I'd lost it? How did that happen?

"There's something on his back," the biker lady said. "Maybe dried blood."

The biggest biker, a huge guy with a huge white beard, leaned over and had a look. "That's nothin'," he said. "You should see the other guy."

Everybody laughed and laughed.

"You thirsty, pooch?"

I was.

"Like beer?"

I really didn't. What I liked was water, but there didn't seem to be any around. Someone filled an old hubcap with beer. I took a sip. Not bad, not bad at all. I lapped up some more.

"Dude!" said a biker. He gave me a pat. The biker lady gave a pat. Then the big biker shoved them both away and took over the patting, chugging a beer at the same time. Soon the flames were dancing in all kinds of interesting ways. Another biker lady reached down her T-shirt and pulled out a harmonica. The moon came up. I did some howling at it. So did a biker or two. They were real good howlers, almost in my class. Someone refilled the hubcap.

In the morning I was first one up, feeling not too good. The bikers were sleeping all over the place, some of them wearing not much. Like other humans, almost every one of them looked better with clothes on. I went behind the falling-down shack and did what I had to do. When I got back, the bikers were stirring. I smelled all kinds of human smells, a few brand-new to me.

"Hungover again," one said. "Been hungover every morning of my grown-up life."

"That's not the record," said another.

The huge biker with the white beard scratched himself for a while—good idea: I scratched myself, too—and then said, "Let's roll."

"What about the pooch?"

The huge biker gazed at me. "Can't just leave 'im here," he said.

The huge biker had a huge bike, silver and gleaming. I ended up sitting behind him, strapped in with a bungee cord. First time on a bike! I felt all better right away, alert and rested, even hankering for a little more beer. We roared across the desert, my eyes watering from the wind, my ears blown straight back, weird rock formations whizzing by. The biker turned his head, shouted something to me that I didn't catch. I barked in his ear.

"'Born to be wild,'" he screamed into the wind. "'Like a true nature's child.'"

Couldn't have agreed more: I barked my head off. We did a few wheelies.

TWELVE

We rode across the desert. Oh, the noise we made! Sometimes the huge biker and I were in the lead, sometimes we dropped back—to pass around a tequila bottle, for example. The mountains came nearer and nearer, and soon we were riding on paved roads, narrow at first, then with lots of lanes and some traffic, but did we slow down? Not a bit! The opposite! Like a true nature's child, we were born to be wild!

A little later, we entered the foothills and came to a town. The whole gang stopped outside a bar—I could tell it was a bar from the neon martini glass in the window, but also from the smell of human puke in the air—and everyone went in, everyone except me and the huge guy, my biker buddy. We kept going, around a corner and up a side street lined only by a few buildings, some boarded up. We stopped in front of the last one. My biker buddy got off and unhitched me.

"Cool ridin', huh?" he said. "Come on, pooch, let's go."

I jumped down and followed him along a stone path and through a gate that led to the building; he closed the gate after me. Hey! I caught the scent of my guys, lots and lots of them. What kind of place—

The biker opened the door and we entered the building. We were in a small room with a counter, a woman behind it, and lots more smells, all from members of my nation. That was one of Bernie's ideas—we were a nation inside of a nation.

The woman looked up. Her smile faded quickly when she saw the biker. "Help you?" she said.

My biker buddy gestured at me with his thumb. He wore a wide silver thumb ring; the sight distracted me, and I maybe only caught part of what he said next. ". . . picked up a stray."

"Wearing any tags?" the woman said.

"Nope," said the biker. "Looks like he's been through a rough stretch, but he's a good ol' boy."

"Why don't you adopt him? We could handle the shots right here and—"

My biker buddy waved his hand. "Nah."

"Are you aware that only fifteen percent of dogs left at shelters get reunited with their owners?" the woman said.

What was this? A shelter? I'd been in a shelter once, but that was undercover, me and Bernie working on a stolen-goods case I never understood too well. But I'd learned about shelters: no space, no running free, and lots of mysterious comings and goings, mostly goings. I turned to the door. Closed, and there was no other way out.

"Nope," said the biker.

"And that only twenty-five percent get adopted?"

"Didn't know that, neither."

"But you do know what happens to the others?" said the shelter woman. She lowered her voice. "Here, for example, we have a three-day grace period, if you follow."

The biker gave me a long look. I wagged my tail but not much: I didn't understand "grace period," and even "three days" was a little hazy. I noticed again how big my biker buddy was, all except his eyes. "I'm outta here," he said.

He turned and started for the door. I trotted after him, sure of one thing only: I was outta there, too. The woman laughed. "Isn't he the clever one?" she said. Then somehow she was right behind me, slipping a leash around my neck before I realized what was happening. She didn't tug hard, just enough for me to feel the pressure. I glanced at her, taken by surprise. When I turned back to the door, it was swinging shut, and biker buddy was gone.

"Easy, boy," the woman said. She came around in front of me, knelt down to my level, stroked the top of my head. "You're the kind of dog someone cares about, I can tell. Where's your collar?"

Good question.

She scratched behind my ear, just perfectly. She was an expert. "What's your name?"

Chet. Chet was my name. I lived on Mesquite Road, had an important job and the best partner in the world.

She sighed. "Hungry? At least we can get you fed." She rose, led me around the counter to a back door. We went through, and a whole lot of barking started up right away.

A corridor. Little rooms on both sides, with chain-link fronts and one of my guys in each, small ones, big ones, male, female, purebreds and no-breds, all barking except for a pit bull. She stared at me with her dusty brown eyes. I remembered watching prison movies with Bernie.

"Knock it off," the woman said.

Everyone went silent. Why? I felt like barking myself, so I did. No one joined me. We came to an empty room. The woman led me in, removed the leash.

"Shh, shh," she said. "Shh. You're a good boy."

I quieted down. She went away. I paced around the little room. There was no wall at the far end, which opened into an outdoor cage. I went out there. I could smell who had been this way before, and before that. A dachshund lay sleeping in the next cage. Sausages, Bernie called them. I liked dachshunds—Bernie said Iggy had some dachshund in him. I pawed at the chain link between us. The dachshund didn't wake up. I turned to the cage on the other side. A spaniel lay there, a fat fly buzzing slowly over her nose. I liked spaniels, too: Bernie said that Iggy was also part spaniel. I went over, pawed at the cage. The spaniel opened her eyes, gazed at me for a moment, and closed them.

The shelter woman came back with a bowl of kibble and a bowl of water. "Here you go," she said. She left, closing the chain-link door. I drank water, left the kibble alone, not hungry. I paced some more, then went outside. The dachshund was no longer around. I lay down. The sun moved across the sky. Shadows lengthened. Night fell. Motorcycle sounds came faintly from far away.

I dreamed about the ocean. I'd actually been to the ocean once, after we'd wrapped up a case I no longer remember, except for the part where I grabbed the bad guy by his pant leg. But I remember the ocean, all right. Those waves! We'd bodysurfed, me and Bernie, rolling and tumbling, so much fun, especially after I'd stopped trying to steer him to shore all the time, and also stopped making myself sick by drinking the water. The surf pounded and pounded. Bernie laughed his head off. He met a woman on the beach and seemed to like her. The whole time he talked, the woman's eyes never left a long string of snot hanging from his nose; green snot, I thought, but Bernie always said I couldn't be trusted when it came to color.

I woke up, hungry but rested, feeling good, ready to start the day. Then I saw where I was. My tail sank right down. I made it stand up, left the room, went to the outdoor cage. The spaniel lay where she'd been the last time I'd seen her, eyes open. This time she flicked the end of her tail the tiniest bit. I wagged back. Flies buzzed around her.

I turned to the cage on the other side, the dachshund side, only the dachshund wasn't there. Instead, a mixed breed, about my size, was pacing back and forth. He saw me and charged right away, not even hesitating a moment. Maybe he hadn't seen the fence. He bounced off it, landed skidding on his side, scrambled up with a twisting motion, and stared at me, saliva dripping from his mouth. I went back inside my room, turned a few times in a tight circle, and lay down. I didn't like this place.

Food came—it tasted all right. My water bowl got topped up. Someone took me for a walk on a treeless patch out back, gave me plenty of time to do what I had to. Everyone at the shelter was nice, so: no complaints. I still didn't like it.

A man came by with a clipboard, looked in on me. "Hey," he called to someone. "Does that first day count?"

"Yup," someone called back.

"Even though it wasn't a full twenty-four-hour day?"

"New protocol."

"So that leaves him with . . ." The man made a mark with his pen and went away. He left behind a smell that made me uneasy. I closed my eyes and dozed off, not a good sleep, but the kind I hate, sleeping because there was nothing else to do.

"What about this one?"

I opened my eyes. Some people stood in the corridor outside my room, gazing in at me through the fencing: the shelter woman, plus what looked like a family—mom, dad, two kids.

"Too big. Think of what it would cost to feed him."

"I think he's cute. Look at his funny ears."

"I'll pay the extra food out of my allowance. Please, Daddy, can we take him, please?"

"I'll think about it."

"You have until tomorrow," said the shelter woman. "Nine A.M."

I don't do much in the way of planning, but a plan began to form in my mind. Step one was leaving with this nice little family. Then came lots of hazy steps, and after that the last one, running home to Bernie. I got up and went closer to them, wagging my tail and trying not to look like a big eater.

"See how friendly he is, Daddy? Oh, please. Mom, make Daddy say yes."

The plan was working, working well. I wagged harder, rose up on my back legs, pawed at the chain link in my friendliest way. But uh-oh—what was this? The nice little family jumping back in alarm?

"He looks too aggressive," the mom said.

Me? I backed off, found myself pawing air.

"We've got another possibility down at the end," said the shelter woman. "Part Australian terrier, I think."

"I've always wanted to go there," said the mom.

"This one's very gentle and much, much smaller. His name appears to be Boomerang, but you can change it to whatever you like."

They moved away, out of sight.

I came down on all fours.

Time passed very slowly, but I lost track of it anyway. Mostly I lay down, either in the room or in the outside cage. The big mixed breed next door stayed inside; I could smell him. Once I opened my eyes and saw a man in a white coat opening the cage on the other side. The spaniel rose slowly and followed him out, across the hard-packed dirt yard and into a small building with a metal door and a tall brick chimney. Her tail wasn't down or up, just sticking straight out in a way I liked: I knew she'd be a good pal.

I slept for a while, woke up to the smell of smoke. This wasn't a nice smoky smell, like burgers on an open fire. I looked out, noticed a thin white plume rising above the brick chimney across the way. I went back inside, lay in the farthest corner of my room, but couldn't get away from that smell.

When I woke again, it was morning. I felt hungry but pretty good, ready to start the day. Then I saw where I was. I went out to the cage. The big mixed breed was lying down, facing away from me, not moving; on the other side, the spaniel side, there was now a puppy. He raced to the fencing the moment he spotted me and stuck his nose through—most of his face, actually: He was very small. I went over and gave him a little push with my paw. He tumbled backward, bounced up, stuck his nose back through, ready to do the whole thing again. But at that moment I heard a woman's voice out in the yard, a voice I knew.

". . . and our readers love stories about dogs, so we turned it into a whole series." I knew that voice, but who was it?

"And one of the stories is going to be about shelters?" said the shelter woman.

I went to the end of the cage, looked out, and saw, down at the end of the yard, the shelter woman talking to someone else, my view of whoever it was blocked by a shed.

"Exactly," said this person, this woman whose voice I knew. "And you were highly recommended."

"Really? That's nice. Where do you want to start?"

"Maybe with some stats first, to get an overview. After that, I'd like to see the dogs, get a few pictures if I could."

"No problem." The shelter woman stepped behind the shed, and I couldn't see her, either. "We'll start in the office," she said, her voice growing fainter as they moved away.

"And don't let me forget," said the other woman, almost out of my hearing range, "I've brought some treats."

"Treats?"

And then, at the very edge of what I could pick up, maybe even beyond, the other woman said, "Dog biscuits. I've got a whole box in my car."

Dog biscuits? A whole box in her car? Suzie! Suzie Sanchez! I started barking, barking and barking with all my might, hurling myself against the cage, again and again.

But they didn't come. Instead, the metal door opened across the way. A man and a woman walked out, both in white coats. "What's with him?" the man said.

"I think some of them just know," said the woman.

"Get serious."

They moved toward my cage. I went still.

"I mean it," the woman said. "They know more than we give them credit for."

The man shook his head. "I like dogs as much as anybody," he said, "but that's sentimental crap."

The woman gave him an annoyed look, which he didn't catch because he was opening my door. "Hey, boy," he said, "Let's—"

I bolted out before he finished his proposal, bolted out to freedom and Suzie San—

But not quite. The woman slipped a loop of rope over my

head as I went by, and now held on as I pulled her across the yard. The man grabbed on, too, and I came to a dead stop.

"Wow," the woman said. "He's so strong." She reached out to give me a pat. I tried to bite her. She flinched and drew back, eyes wide. They led me—dragged me, actually—to the metal door, and through. It was very cold inside.

THIRTEEN

A cold place, with lights that were much too bright shining on machines I didn't understand. Don't get me started on machines. The lawn mower is one of the worst, and these, not much like lawn mowers, somehow looked as bad. I turned back toward the metal door: closed.

"Here you go, big fella," said the man. "Hop right up."

Up there? On the metal table? Why would I want to do that? I stayed where I was, four paws planted on the floor. The woman reached out, patted me. Like the other woman, the one at the front desk, she was an expert patter.

"Everything's all right," she said. Pat pat.

"Just need to take a quick look at you," said the man. "Then we'll be all done."

Their voices were gentle. And their hands, too: They lifted me up onto the table. It was cold, that metal table.

"Lie down, there's a good fella."

I stayed where I was, standing up, panting a little despite the cold.

"Lie down, you'll feel much better," the woman said.

"Have you out of here in no time," said the man.

The woman glared at him again. I didn't know why, didn't care. My mind was on something else: Did he mean have me out of this room or out of the whole place, the shelter? Getting out of the shelter: That was what I wanted. I was so busy thinking about getting out of the shelter that I didn't pay much attention to them nudging me over onto my side, oh so gently. Every move was gentle. They knew how to handle my sort of guy.

Then came more patting, and I was hardly aware of some kind of clamps, maybe made of rubber, swinging down over me and locking me into place on the tabletop; hardly aware until it was too late. I tried to struggle, get up, thrash around, just move my body somewhere, somehow, but I couldn't. I barked. All I could do, so I did it. Out of the corner of my eye, I saw the man wheeling a machine closer, a machine with a long tube that ended in a sharp needle. I barked with all my might, so loud I missed the sound of the door opening, almost missed the voice of the shelter woman.

". . . and this is where we— Oh, sorry, didn't know you were busy."

"No problem," said the man.

"We could come back later," the shelter woman said.

"No," said another woman. I went silent. "I really should witness this," she added. Suzie! Suzie Sanchez, and I couldn't see her, clamped down the way I was, back to the door.

"We use the most humane methods possible," said the shelter woman.

"State of the art," the man said. "And put that away, if you don't mind—no pictures."

"How long does it take?" said Suzie.

"From when we get the IV in?" the man said. "Thirty seconds, tops."

"Not even," said the shelter woman.

Then a new sound started up, low and wild. That was me, growling. The woman in the white coat patted me with her gentle hand. I growled some more.

"Is that normal?" Suzie said. "That resistance?"

"Wouldn't call it resistance," said the shelter woman. "It's just so unfamiliar in here, that's all." At that moment I felt a sharp jab high up on one of my back legs.

"Now we just turn this little valve over here and—"

"Hey," said Suzie. "He looks kind of familiar."

"The dog?" the man said.

"Yes, the dog," Suzie said. "Where did he come from?"

"Out in the desert somewhere, maybe as far as New Mexico," said the shelter woman. "A biker brought him in—no collar, no tags."

I heard footsteps, moving fast, and then Suzie came in sight. Suzie! She looked down at me, eyes narrowed, face worried. "Chet? Is that you?" What a question! Did I need a tag dangling from Suzie's neck to identify her?

I was all clamped in place, couldn't move a thing. Yes, yes, it's me, Chet, pure and simple. How was I going to—and then I realized: couldn't move a thing *except my tail*. I raised that tail of mine and thumped it down with the loudest thump I could make. It shook that cold metal table, shook that whole cold room from wall to wall.

"Don't touch that valve," Suzie said.

I rode shotgun in Suzie's car, a box of dog biscuits between us. Sometimes she reached in and gave me a biscuit; sometimes I leaned over and gave her a lick on the face.

"What were you doing way out here, Chet?" she said. And: "Where's Bernie?"

I gave her another lick, all I could think of doing. She laughed. "Stop it—you'll cause an accident." I stopped, sort of. Suzie smelled of fruit—apples and strawberries. I wasn't a big fruit eater, but I liked fruit smells. Suzie smelled very good for a human, among the best I'd ever come across. There were flower smells mixed in, too, those little yellow flowers that bees—don't get me started on bees, I've had more than enough—

And all of a sudden I thought of Madison, looking down at me from that building at the mine, and all those bad people. I turned my head, glanced out the rear window. Suzie checked the mirror.

"What's back there, Chet?" she said.

All I saw was traffic, moving along in the usual way.

"I could have sworn you had a thought just now," she said. "Give a lot to know what it was."

My ears went up all by themselves, no idea why. Suzie handed me another biscuit. Where did she get biscuits this good, so crunchy? I tried to take my time with it and couldn't, gobbling it right up. Then I stuck my nose out the side window. Great smells, zipping by so fast I could hardly keep up. A bird glided by, low to the ground. Didn't like birds, had never managed to catch a single one, although I'd seen cats do it, even make it look easy. I barked at this bird, but it didn't seem to hear, so I barked some more. Great to be right here, up and doing! Was there a better life than mine? You tell me.

"Chet! What's gotten into you?"

I pawed at the dashboard for no reason at all; oops, maybe ripping it the littlest bit.

"That's leather."

I knew that, of course, knew the feel, smell, taste of leather very well. I felt bad, but not for long. The feel, smell, taste of leather—all just great—took over my whole mind. I came very close to scratching the dashboard again. What a world!

The road curved back and forth up a mountainside. From the top, we looked down over flatland, built up as far as the eye could see—to more mountains, far away and hazy—with human stuff.

"The pollution's not too bad today," Suzie said. "You can actually see why they call it the Valley."

Because why? I didn't get it. But I knew the Valley was home, and sat forward a little bit. We drove down, turned onto a freeway, hit stop-and-go traffic. Bernie grew very frustrated in stop-and-go traffic, muttering to himself and sometimes pounding on the wheel, but Suzie didn't seem to mind at all. She whistled a soft little tune—I'd heard lots of men whistle, but never a woman before this—and sometimes flashed me a smile. Suzie and I got along great.

We were down to the last biscuit when I spotted a familiar sight: the big wooden cowboy statue outside the Dry Gulch Steak House and Saloon, one of Bernie's favorites. I liked it, too. They had a patio out back where my guys were welcome. The scraps on that patio—don't get me started.

At that moment I heard a funny swishing sound.

Suzie glanced over. "Getting close to home, huh?"

I realized the funny swishing sound came from my own tail, whipping back and forth against the seat.

"Don't worry," Suzie said, taking out her camera and snapping a photo of the wooden cowboy through her open window. "Won't be long now."

I knew worry, usually did my worrying sitting up, head tilted to one side, but I had no worries now. We got off the freeway, made a few turns, and then we were driving up Mesquite Road. There was Iggy's place, with Iggy in the window! He spotted me and started jumping up and down in that weird way of his, his fat jowls wobbling in the opposite direction of every leap. No room in the car for me to jump up and down, too, which was what I wanted to do, so I just pawed at the dashboard.

"Chet!"

We rolled up to our place, mine and Bernie's. Everything looked the same—the three trees in the front yard, the rock at the end of the driveway, the fence separating us from old man Heydrich. The only difference was a huge sign standing by the street with a picture of one of my guys on it, wearing a collar that looked a lot like mine, the one I'd lost. Hey, in fact, it was mine, the brown leather collar with the silver tags—meaning what? I couldn't quite figure it out.

Suzie read the sign. "'Have you seen Chet? Big reward. No questions asked.'" She parked in the driveway, opened her door. I flew out, right over her, raced around the yard, making hard cuts this way and that, earth clods flying, took brief stops to mark the big rock, all three trees, the fence, and what was this? The front door, too? Uh-oh. And then: It opened.

Bernie! But he looked terrible, face thinner and deep dark patches under his eyes.

"What's going—" he began. "Chet!" His whole face changed. In a flash, he looked his very best. Bernie reached out for me.

Things happened quickly after that. Somehow Bernie got knocked down, and so did lots of stuff, maybe including a lamp and the old hat stand with Bernie's baseball cap collection. We rolled around on the floor. Baseball caps rained down on us.

"Chet! Stop!"

A little later, we were relaxing in the TV room, Bernie and Suzie at opposite ends of the couch, me on the floor, front legs curled up under my chin, nice and comfortable. They were drinking wine and munching pretzels, the only snack available; as for me, I'd had all I could possibly consume and more.

"I'm serious about the reward," Bernie was saying.

"Don't be silly."

"I'm not being silly. I really want you to—"

"Not another word on the subject. I'm just so happy I was there."

"I insist."

"All right—you can take me out to dinner sometime."

"I can?"

They looked at each other, then away. Bernie's gaze fell on me. The expression in his eyes changed, the way it did when he was on the job and getting one of his ideas. That's how we divided the work: Bernie was the idea man, I did the digging. "Where was this again?" he said.

"Sierra Verde," said Suzie.

"Sierra Verde, Chet? What were you doing way out there?"

I wasn't saying. The details were fading fast. All I remembered clearly was the feel of the choke chain, Madison's smell, and zooming down the road on the motorcycle. Oh, yeah: and Mr. Gulagov and his gang.

". . . for this story on shelters," Suzie was saying. "I needed a rural place like Sierra Verde for balance. Total luck."

"Bikers?" Bernie said.

"That's what they told me. And something about finding him in New Mexico."

Bernie reached down, touched my back. "What happened here?"

"They didn't say." Suzie put on glasses. Always so strange to me, always a little scary, maybe because glasses made humans seem even more like machines than they already were. "Looks like it's healing nicely," she said.

Now I remembered that part, too.

"What're you growling about, boy?"

I raised my head and barked, one short, loud bark.

"What's bothering you?"

I gazed at Bernie. He was watching me closely. Mountain lions, Bernie. Ah, what the hell. I was home, safe and sound. I lowered my head, closed my eyes. Their talk flowed back and forth over me, very nice sounds. Suzie laughed. Whatever Bernie said next made her laugh some more. Bernie laughed, too—he had this quiet little laugh he did when he made someone laugh; I didn't hear it often. Was the distance between them on the couch shrinking a bit? I kind of thought so but was suddenly much too tired to open my eyes. The rug, so soft, my belly so full, and here I was, home. A delicious sleep was on the way, would be on me real—

The phone rang, a sound I hated. Sleep got pushed away. I opened my eyes. Bernie was talking into the phone. "Nothing new," he said. "I'm sorry." He hung up, turned to Suzie; yes, they were a little closer together, and she wasn't wearing her glasses. "A missing-persons case. We're getting nowhere."

"Who's the person?"

"A teenager named Madison Chambliss."

I got up, started barking.

"Chet?"

I hurried to the front door.

"Chet? What is it? Is something out there?"

Bernie got a flashlight and opened the door. I ran out, down the street. I remembered Mr. Gulagov's ranch, with the mine and the old barn across from it, Madison in the window. But where was it? I trotted this way and that, sniffing for a scent trail to lead me back—Mr. Gulagov's scent, Boris's, Harold the driver's, Madison's, my own. Nothing. I slowed down, walked in a circle, came to a halt.

"What's on your mind, boy?"

FOURTEEN

In the morning we got right to work on the Madison Chambliss case, me and Bernie. First off, we drove down to Donut Heaven, me riding shotgun, not a cloud in the sky, everything tip-top. A cruiser was waiting in the lot. Bernie parked beside it in typical cop style, driver's-side doors facing each other. The cruiser window slid down, and there was Rick Torres, Bernie's friend in Missing Persons. He handed Bernie coffee and a doughnut and said, "Hey, Chet, how ya doin'?"

No complaints.

"Got an extra cruller here," Rick said, holding it up.

I wagged my tail.

"Chet's had his breakfast," Bernie said. "And he's never been big on sweets."

Oh?

"Empty calories," Bernie said.

"Huh?" said Rick.

"It's true. I've been reading up on nutrition. Check out what's happening to this country."

Rick glanced around.

"I'm talking about the way we look now and the way we used to look," Bernie said.

"I get you," said Rick. "Like William Howard Taft."

Bernie gave Rick a long stare. Then he took a big bite of his doughnut and with his mouth full, said, "Where are we?"

Rick bit into his cruller. I could smell it from where I was, easy. "Don't know where you are," he said, also talking with his mouth full. "But we've got *nada*." He took out a notebook, flipped through the pages. "I interviewed the parents, Cynthia Chambliss and Damon . . ." Rick paused, squinted at the notebook. Squinting was one of those human expressions best kept to a minimum, in my opinion. ". . . can't read my own writing—looks like Keller."

"Keefer," Bernie said.

"Yeah?" Rick found a pen behind the visor, made a mark on the page. "A fun pair, Cynthia and Damon. He thinks the kid's run off to Vegas, and she thinks it's a snatch."

"Any evidence for either?"

"Nope. No ransom demand, no sightings. Checked the school, her teachers, friends—everybody says she was a normal kid, smarter than most."

"Was?" said Bernie.

Rick turned the page. "Oh yeah—there's just maybe one little thing here."

"What's that?"

"Some suggestion she was hanging out with a pothead or possibly pot dealer."

"Ruben Ramirez?"

Rick looked up; his eyebrows rose, too.

"Forget him," Bernie said. "He alibis out."

"Okeydoke. So what we've done is put her on the wire, sent

her picture and description to every department in the state, checked Valley hospitals, the usual."

Bernie nodded. "One other thing," he said, taking another bite. "We might be looking for a BMW, probably blue, with a blond male driver."

I barked. They both turned to me. "He wants that cruller," Rick said.

Bernie sighed. "All right."

The cruller went from Rick to Bernie to me. I used my two-bite technique for managing big things, jerking my head back on the second. All gone. Delicious. Rick Torres was growing on me. But I hadn't been barking about the cruller, had I? I'd barked about . . . What was it again?

"Year and model?" Rick said.

Bernie shook his head. "And even the BMW part isn't completely reliable, but I think you should add it to what you've got."

"Go public with the car stuff?"

Bernie thought. When he was thinking, really thinking hard like this, things always seemed to get quiet around him. "Not yet," he said.

"But you're betting it's a snatch?"

"Yes."

"A snatch and no ransom demand?" Rick said. "Bad news." He ate the last of the cruller, then licked the tips of his fingers. I licked around my whole mouth, found a few sweet crumbs.

"He's right about one thing," Bernie said. We were gassing up at pumps across the street from Donut Heaven. I started zoning out on the smell of gas. "No ransom demand is bad news." He screwed the gas cap back in place. I took one last big sniff, felt funny, in a good way. "You know what I'm wondering?"

Why we hadn't picked up a bag of crullers to take home?

"I'm wondering why Damon Keefer keeps saying she's run off to Vegas." He got in the car, turned the key. "Let's find out."

Fine with me. I forgot all about the crullers. We drove up into some hills, housing developments on both sides, one after the other, and lots of construction going on.

"Guess how many people move to the Valley each and every day," Bernie said. "And that's only counting the legal ones."

No clue. Plus who cared, anyway? Sometimes Bernie worried for no reason.

"For thousands of years, this was open country," he said. "Rivers flowed. Where's all that water now?"

I glanced to the side, spotted water right away, making beautiful rainbows over a putting green. What was the problem? Enjoy the day, Bernie. I gave him a nudge with the top of my head. He laughed and said, "Glad you're back."

Back, and on the job. We went past the golf course and turned at the next road. A big sign stood on the corner. "'Welcome to Pinnacle Peak Homes at Puma Wells,'" Bernie read. "'The Number One Gated Prestige Luxury Development in the North Valley.'" The road led up a winding canyon. "I prefer my prestige ungated," Bernie said, a remark that zipped by me in complete mystery. We followed a truck that was painting a yellow line down the middle. Was that fun to watch or what? I wanted to jump out and lick that glistening yellow line so bad I could hardly sit still.

"Chet, for God's sake, sit still."

Houses went by, not all of them finished, clustered together with tiny spaces in between. A big palm tree lay flat down beside a hole in someone's yard. "Funny," Bernie said. "Midmorning on a workday and no workers around." We parked in front of one of the finished houses. It had a sign in the window. "'Model home and office,'" Bernie read. We hopped out and went to the door. Bernie knocked.

"Come in," called a woman.

We went in, found ourselves in a room with a cool tile floor and a fountain in the middle, water splashing in a small pool. What was Bernie talking about? There was water out the yingyang.

A woman sat at a desk by the fountain, tapping at a computer keyboard. "Dr. Avery?" she said, rising. She was tall, Bernie's height, with long fair hair in a ponytail and tiny ears. And beautiful: I knew that from how Bernie stumbled the tiniest bit on his next step. "I wasn't expecting you so soon."

"Who's Dr. Avery?" said Bernie.

The woman blinked. Bernie was good at causing those confused blinks in people, did I mention that already? "You are not here to see the Phase Two Red Rock Garden Casita designs?" she said.

"Sure," said Bernie. "We'll take a look at them. But first I'd like to see Mr. Keefer."

"Is he expecting you?"

"Not exactly, Ms. . . ."

"Larapova. Elena Larapova, VP marketing."

". . . Ms. Larapova, but I know he'll see us."

Ms. Larapova's eyes went to me. She made a friendly clucking sound, a sound I liked. I wagged back. "Mr. Keefer is on site at the moment," she said.

"Can you call him?"

"Perhaps. Who shall I say . . . ?"

Bernie handed her our card. She read it, then looked at me again, quickly, her eyes widening. "Something the matter?" said Bernie.

"Oh, no, no, Mr. Little. It's just—I've never met a detective before."

Bernie smiled. "We don't bite," he said.

Speak for yourself, was my thought.

Ms. Larapova took a phone off the desk. "Hello, Da— Mr. Keefer," she said. "There's a Bernie Little to see you." She listened for a moment and hung up. "Come," she said.

We went outside, climbed into a golf cart, Ms. Larapova behind the wheel, Bernie beside her, me in back. I'd ridden in golf carts before, loved them.

"Your dog is coming?" she said.

"You object?"

"No. Well-behaved pets are always welcome at Puma Wells."

"Then please make an exception for Chet."

"Excuse me?"

"On both counts—well behaved and pet." Bernie laughed to himself. What the hell was he talking about?

"Explain, please?"

I was on her side, all the way.

"Sorry," Bernie said. "Just a joke."

Ms. Larapova gave him a quick glance, the corners of her mouth turned down, a look often appearing on women's faces after one of Bernie's jokes. She shifted away from him on the bench seat and drove onto a cart path.

We bumped up a fairway, headed toward a big building in the distance. I didn't see anyone playing, but all of a sudden a golf ball came soaring over a hill, hit the ground right beside us, and bounced up. I snatched it right out of the air before I even knew what I'd done. Looking back, I saw another golf cart topping the crest of the hill far behind us. I lay down on the backseat, chewing quietly.

"So," said Bernie, "what brings you here?"

The puzzled human face is one of my favorites. That was what Ms. Larapova showed Bernie now.

"Aren't you from Russia?" he went on.

She nodded. "But I have been in this country for many years, am now a citizen like you."

"Even better, I'm sure."

Russian? Wait a minute. That triggered something in my mind, but what? I mulled it over, meanwhile working my way through the golf-ball covering. Underneath lay all kinds of interesting stuff; I knew from experience.

". . . and I love the wide-open spaces," Ms. Larapova was saying.

"Aren't there wide-open spaces in Siberia?"

"You have such a sense of humor." But not enough to make Ms. Larapova laugh. She drove up to the big building. "The clubhouse," she said. "Gourmet restaurant and bar, indoor and outdoor pools with Jacuzzis, five-thousand-square-foot gym with personal-trainer service, Japanese steam and Finnish sauna, full-service spa."

"What's it cost?"

"Membership is restricted to residents only."

"And then it's free?"

For the first time, Ms. Larapova laughed. Human laughter: usually one of the best sounds there is, as I might have mentioned, but not Ms. Larapova's, which was booming and strange, kind of like an explosion. "Free?" she said. "Introductory-rate initiation is one hundred fifty K, and that is for three-bedroom units and above."

"Introductory-rate?" said Bernie.

"Until Labor Day. After that—two hundred. Plus greens fees, of course."

"Goes without saying," said Bernie.

We got off the cart, followed Ms. Larapova around the club-house. "What's in your mouth, Chet?" Bernie said.

I swallowed what was left, looked innocent. Way back on the fairway, two golfers were walking in little circles, heads down. Golf was a game I didn't get at all.

There was a big swimming pool behind the clubhouse. I trot-ted over to the edge. Hey. No water. Not that I'd have jumped in—almost certainly not—but I liked gazing at water. A man in a dark suit sat under an umbrella at a poolside table spread with a white cloth; I'd pulled on an overhanging end of one of those once, with bad results; but for some reason, my mouth suddenly wanted to get hold of this one. The man was talking on a phone. I smelled cat on him, saw his goatee, and recognized him: Damon Keefer. "It'll clear, for Christ's sake," he was saying. One of his feet was tapping under the table, very fast, out of sight, although not out of my sight, down here. "Don't be such a—" He saw us, said, "Gotta go," and clicked off.

Bernie and Ms. Larapova approached the table. I stayed where I was, poolside, hit by a surprising attack of indigestion. Keefer motioned with his hand, and Bernie and Ms. Larapova started to sit down.

"I'll take it from here, Elena," Keefer said.

Ms. Larapova, in the act of pulling out her chair, went still. "As you wish, Mr. Keefer," she said. She gave me a quick glance, then turned and walked away. I turned, too, and gagged what was left of the golf ball into the empty pool. Ah, much better: at the top of my game once more, and the slightest bit hungry, believe it or not. I sniffed the air in hope of scraps; poolsides were usually good for a potato chip or two, or even one of those mini hot dogs—had to be careful about the toothpicks they came on,

I'd learned that the hard way—but I smelled nothing except cat, the odor coming from Keefer. I thought of mountain lions right away, and then a faint memory of Madison in the window came and went.

Bernie sat opposite Keefer, hands folded on the table. I always got a good feeling when Bernie's hands were folded like that, couldn't say why.

"Any news?" Keefer said. Under the table, his foot was tapping away—in fact, his whole lower body was jittery, although the top part of him was still.

"I'm afraid not," Bernie said. "We followed up on one or two leads, but they ended nowhere."

"So what are you saying? Your involvement in this is over?"

"Far from it."

"Don't tell me you want more money."

"Money's not the issue now, Mr. Keefer. The retainer will take us through to the end, and we'll send you a bill then. But the point, what we've got to focus on, is making sure that end's a good end."

Keefer took a pack of cigarettes from his pocket and lit one. "Think I don't know that?" He blew smoke through his nostrils, something Bernie liked doing. In fact, Bernie's gaze was locked on those smoke trails. Keefer noticed. "Smoke?"

"No, thanks," Bernie said, even though I could tell he wanted one bad. "I've been in touch with Rick Torres over at Missing Persons. He says you told him you think Madison's run off to Las Vegas."

Keefer shrugged.

"You told me the same thing."

Keefer took a deep drag. All that lower-body twitchiness lessened a bit. "Vegas is just an example."

"Of what?"

"The kind of place she might have taken off for."

"But Cynthia says she's never taken off before."

"Cynthia. Christ."

"Do you have any reason to believe she's not telling the truth?"

"A dozen."

"A dozen?"

"That's how many years I put up with her." Keefer's lower body was back at full speed.

"In your experience, then," Bernie said. "Has Madison ever disappeared like this?"

"My experience with Madison is getting her every second weekend and alternating Christmases and Thanksgivings. Any idea what that's like?"

Bernie didn't answer, just gazed at Keefer. Keefer took one last drag, then spun the cigarette into the empty pool. "No," he said. "The answer's no. She's never done this before."

"That's helpful," Bernie said. "Because you wouldn't want us going off to Vegas on a wild-goose chase."

A wild-goose chase! I'd heard that expression so many times but never been on one. It sounded like the most exciting thing in the whole world. Yes, I wanted to go on a wild-goose chase, and if that meant Vegas, so be it.

Keefer gave Bernie a strange look, any meaning it might have had completely missing me. "No," he said, "we wouldn't want that."

"Ruling out the runaway scenario," Bernie said, "at least for now, that leaves us with accidents—"

"What kind of accidents?"

"All kinds—traffic, recreational, domestic—but Rick Torres

has checked all the hospitals in the Valley and come up empty. That means we're most probably dealing with kidnapping, of which there are two types: for ransom and not."

"I told you the other day—there's been no ransom demand."

"You've checked?"

"Checked what, for God's sake?"

"Your mail, e-mail, fax machines, voice mail."

"They're checked all the time. I'm running a business here."

Bernie glanced around. "It's impressive. One of the nicest I've seen."

Nicest what? Bernie could be hard to follow. But Keefer seemed to understand. He gave a slight nod.

"I asked you before about competitors."

"And I told you we don't kidnap each other's kids."

"I remember," Bernie said. "But how can you be sure all your competitors are legit?"

"What does that mean?"

"Some businesses act as fronts or are financed by criminal organizations."

"Not in real estate development, not in the Valley."

"How can you be sure?"

"The same way you'd be sure about key facts in your business, assuming you're any good."

Was that an insult? I didn't know and couldn't tell from Bernie's face, which didn't change a bit. "What about your suppliers?"

"What about them?"

"Or your contractors, your labor—do you ever have trouble with them?"

"I have nothing but trouble with them. That's what this business is about."

"How bad does it get?"

———

"Not kidnapping bad, if that's where you're going with this. We negotiate, we work things out, we keep building."

Bernie looked around again. "What about today?"

"Today?"

"I don't see anybody—is it a normal workday?"

Keefer didn't answer right away. He lit up another cigarette, breathed out more smoke. Poor Bernie got that craving look in his eye again. "Yeah, a normal workday, just an extended break, that's all."

"And how's the development going as a whole, Pinnacle Wells?"

Keefer's voice, already sharp, sharpened some more. "Pinnacle Peak Homes at Puma Wells," he said, "is going just fine."

"Are you the one hundred percent owner?"

"I am."

"Where do you get your financing?"

Below the table: lots of twitching.

"Various reputable Valley banks. They don't resort to kidnapping for outstanding accounts even if there were any, and there are not."

"I don't suppose Madison has any connection to the business."

"Correct."

"Any of these people—competitors, suppliers, bankers, workers—drive a BMW, possibly blue?"

"Dozens, probably. What kind of a question is that?" Under the table: still twitching, maybe even more.

"Not a good one," Bernie said. He took a deep breath, let it out slowly. That meant soon we'd be doing something different. "I'd like to see Madison's room as soon as possible."

"What room are you talking about?"

"Where she stays when she's with you."

"Why?"

"Because it's basic casework."

Under the table, Keefer's legs went still. "I'll take you there myself," he said. "Meet me at the office in fifteen minutes."

Bernie and I went back down the fairway on foot. Walks with Bernie were the best. I ran a few circles around him just for fun, hoping for a little chase, but he didn't seem to notice.

"Keefer's smart," he said. "Very."

He was? I'd missed that.

Some workers appeared, pushing wheelbarrows and carrying shovels, rakes, hoes, and other equipment I didn't know. When they got close, Bernie waved hello and said, "Coming off your break?"

One of the men laughed. "*Sí*, three days break."

"How come so long?"

The man made a gesture with his hand, rubbing finger and thumb together. What did that mean? A golf ball thwacked off a tree, bounded nearby. I sidled over toward it.

FIFTEEN

The dog's coming in?"

We were outside Damon Keefer's house, a real big one with walls around it and a metal sculpture out front, a strange sculpture, huge and gleaming, but the shape reminded me of a fire hydrant. I felt eyes on me; otherwise, I'd have gone right over and put my mark on it.

"Chet's his name," Bernie said. "He specializes in missing-persons cases."

Keefer looked down his nose at me; I've got a look like that, even better because of my longer nose. "You're referring to his sense of smell?"

"Among other things," Bernie said.

Keefer gazed at me. Did he realize what a leaper I am, that I could be right up there at face level with him in a flash, teeth bared? "All right," he said.

We went inside. Surprise: a big house with big open spaces and glowing tile floors, but only one piece of furniture, a leather couch. And perched on that couch, as I could have told you with my eyes closed: a cat. A cat who smelled like Keefer but way more so. The cat saw me at once, of course, and every hair on his body stood straight up, and he made a sound like the mountain lion's roar but much tinier. That's all cats are—midget lions. I'm nobody's midget, baby.

"Uh," said Keefer, "is your dog all right?"

"In what way?" said Bernie.

"In what way? Look at him—he's about to attack Prince."

"Prince?" Bernie said. He hadn't even noticed the cat? How was that possible? Keefer pointed Prince out. "Oh, Chet wouldn't do anything like that," Bernie said. He glanced at me. Something in that glance made me realize I had one of my front paws up in the air and was leaning forward, maybe in a way someone who didn't know me might interpret as aggressive. I lowered my paw to the floor, looked peaceful. Prince's coat went back to normal, and he regarded me in the usual snooty cat manner that always makes my blood boil, before rolling over on the couch and turning his back to the room. Cat moves like that get under my skin like you can't imagine. I wanted to take him and— But not now, not while we were on the job. Some other time, though, supposing ol' Prince and I happened to run into each other in a dark alley, say, or maybe—

"Nice place you've got here," Bernie said. "Just moving in?"

"Out, actually," said Keefer.

"Oh?"

"Correct," said Keefer. "Madison's room is this way."

He led us down a long hall, past some closed doors and into a room at the end. I smelled her right away—honey, cherry, sun-colored flowers—but faint. The room itself had a bed, desk, bureau, stuff like that: Bernie walked around, seeing the kinds of things he knew how to see. A framed photograph stood on the desk. Photographs often gave me trouble. Watching TV, that was more like it, the Discovery Channel and lots of movies, too—check out White Fang's fight with Cherokee! and once we caught this show called *When Good Animals Go Bad*—wow! that elephant scene!—but this one, this photo, I got with no problem: Keefer and Madison standing in front of a birdcage, his arm over her shoulder, both of them laughing.

"When was this taken?" Bernie said.

"Couple of years ago," said Keefer, not really looking at it.

"And that's Cap'n Crunch in the cage?"

Keefer nodded. "Stupid bird," he said, and I couldn't have agreed more. Then came another surprise, at least for me: Keefer's eyes filled with tears. Uh-oh, the crying thing. Water came out of human eyes sometimes—usually women, but not always, usually because of sadness, but not always—and whenever it happened, I got confused. And now Keefer, this dude I didn't much like, this dude with Prince's stink all over him, was having one of these floods inside. I knew men could cry—had seen Bernie tear up that time Leda came and packed up Charlie's stuff; did I mention that already? At that moment I came close to making— What would you call it? A connection, maybe, a connection between Bernie's situation and—

But it didn't happen. I spotted a Cheeto under the bed. Munch munch and it was gone. Not bad at all, if you didn't mind a little dust, and I'm not fussy about things like that. When I turned back to the room, Bernie was watching Keefer, a new look on his face.

"How would you describe your relationship with Madison?" Bernie said.

"What the hell kind of question is that?" Keefer said, his eyes drying up fast. "No way you have kids yourself, or you wouldn't ask it. She's the best thing in my life."

The expression on Bernie's face changed again, went cold for a moment, and then just nothing. I hated seeing that just-nothing look on Bernie's face. I went over and sat at his feet. He didn't seem to notice.

"I'm doing my best to get her back for you," Bernie said. "But I need the facts. If you're holding anything back, now is the time."

Their gazes met. There was a silence, at least for them. Myself, I heard distant barking, she-barking most likely, and possibly of the most interesting kind.

"The chance won't come again," Bernie said.

Keefer licked his lips. The human tongue doesn't appear that often, and when it does, I always notice. This time, in combination with that goatee, it didn't sit right with me, no idea why. At that moment a phone went off in Keefer's pocket. He checked the tiny screen, said, "Got to take this," and moved out of the room and into the hall. Bernie followed, soft on his feet, and stood behind the door, where Keefer couldn't see him. I followed Bernie, even quieter. We cocked our ears and listened in.

Keefer's voice was low and buzzing, the way human voices get under pressure. "I need more time." Then, after a silence: "Don't even say that—where are you? I'll . . . Hello? Hello?" We heard him coming back and moved deeper into the room, Bernie on tiptoes, me on those old reliables, silent padded paws.

"What was that about?" Bernie said.

"Business," said Keefer. "And none of yours."

"Did it have anything to do with Madison?"

"Of course not." Keefer's tongue flicked out again. "I just told you. We're in a little dispute with some suppliers."

"Which ones?"

Keefer's nostrils widened. What was that about? I had no idea, just felt uneasy. "Irrigation," he said. "But what's it to you?"

"I need you to be forthcoming."

"And I have been."

"Not entirely. Before that call, you were about to tell me something."

Keefer paused, his eyes on Bernie. "You seem pretty smart," he said. "How did you end up in law enforcement?"

"I wasn't actually smart enough for law enforcement," Bernie said. "That's why I'm a private eye."

Keefer blinked. Some kind of struggle was going on, but about what and who was winning: anybody's guess. And how was all this back-and-forth going to lead to me grabbing the perp by the pant leg? All I knew was that when Keefer spoke again, his voice was different, less unpleasant.

"You said there were two types of kidnapping, for ransom and . . ."

"And not," Bernie said.

"Meaning what?"

"Do I have to spell that out for you?"

Keefer shook his head. "I'm just wondering why your focus is on the ransom kind."

"You've got some other idea?"

"I hesitate to say."

"There's no time for hesitation."

Keefer nodded. "This is pure speculation."

"But you have a name for me."

Keefer blinked again. "Not based on any facts, you understand, just the odd . . . feeling or two."

"And the name is?"

"First off, you didn't hear it from me."

Bernie tilted his head to one side. Did Keefer take that for agreement? I knew it was one of Bernie's head tilts, not necessarily meaning anything, simply moving things along the way he wanted.

"And don't hold me to it," Keefer went on. "Pure speculation, as I said, and I would never—"

"The name." Bernie's voice rang through the empty house. That was thrilling.

Keefer licked his lips one more time. His tongue was stubby and stiff, pointed and pale, next to useless, in my opinion. "Simon Berg."

"Who's he?"

"I thought you might have run across him by now."

"Why?"

"Simon Berg is Cynthia's boyfriend."

"Ah," said Bernie.

"What does that mean—'ah'?" Keefer said.

I had no clue myself.

"Have you ever seen him around Madison?" Bernie said.

"Once or twice."

"And?"

Keefer shrugged—that raising and lowering of the shoulders, one of those human expressions I'd never liked. "I just got a feeling, that's all. Probably nothing."

"Did you ever mention this feeling to Madison?"

"No. Maybe I should have."

"Or Cynthia?"

"Think I'm nuts? I have enough trouble with Cynthia." He wrote on a piece of paper, gave it to Bernie. "Here's the address—he owns a business in Pedroia."

* * *

"Think he's nuts?" Bernie said when we were back in the car.

That was a tough one. Sometimes—like now, on the freeway, stuck in traffic stretching as far as I could see, everybody going slower than walking speed—I thought just about all humans were nuts.

"I don't," Bernie said.

In that case, I didn't, either.

"The expression 'crazy like a fox' comes to mind."

Not to mine. I knew foxes, had dealt with them more than once in the canyon. Cowards, each and every one, skulking around out there, sneaking up and backing down. What did "crazy like a fox" mean, anyway? I glanced at Bernie, hoped he didn't think foxes were smart, or even worse, smarter than my guys. Impossible. I stopped worrying about it, sat high in the shotgun seat, and enjoyed the ride.

A long ride. We drove away from the sun but still had many suns glaring off car windows ahead of us. Bernie put on his wraparound shades. I didn't like it when he wore them, maybe barked a little.

"For God's sake, Chet—it's me."

We got off at a ramp, were soon in an industrial area—I could tell from all the trucks, loading docks, chain-link fences.

"Pedroia," Bernie said. "Know what used to be here? The original Pedroia Ranch, very first cattle ranch in the whole Valley. And now look."

I laid a paw on Bernie's knee.

We parked in front of a long, low building. Bernie read the sign: "'Rover and Company.' Wonder what they do." He opened the door, and we went in. A security guard at a desk looked up.

"Looking for Simon Berg," Bernie said.

"He's expecting you?"

"No," said Bernie, handing over our card. "We're conducting an investigation. I think he'll see us."

The security guard glanced at me, didn't seem bothered that I was inside, not always the reaction we got. "Wait here," he said, leaving through a door at the back. Bernie went to the desk and read the writing on the guard's clipboard. I smelled around. Hey! The smells in here were really nice, even better than that.

The security guard returned with another man, much smaller than Bernie or the guard. He was dressed all in white, also wore a white hairnet.

"Bernie Little?" he said, coming forward, hand extended. "Simon Berg. Cynthia's told me a lot about you." They shook hands, one of the best human customs going, to my way of thinking, although in my world we do some cool meet-and-greet stuff, too. "Have you got any news?"

"No," Bernie said. "Can we talk for a minute?"

"Right now?"

"It's important."

"Sure." Simon Berg turned to the guard. "Do me a favor—tell them to hold number three?"

The guard hurried off.

"What goes on here?" Bernie said.

"At Rover and Company? We make high-end dog treats. One hundred percent organic, fresh ingredients, no additives. And tasty, too."

I knew one thing right then: This was not the perp.

Simon Berg looked at me and smiled. "And this must be Chet. I had one a lot like him when I was a kid—the original Rover." He got down on his knees, took my head in his hands in a way I didn't mind at all. "Oh, you're a good-looking boy, aren't you? This is a real stroke of luck."

"Why is that?" Bernie said.

Simon Berg rose. "We're testing a new rawhide chew today,

made from grade-A hides imported from Argentina. I wouldn't mind seeing Chet's reaction."

"Doesn't sound like his kind of thing," Bernie said.

Simon Berg gazed at Bernie, then burst out laughing. "And maybe you'll have time for a tour."

"Thanks," Bernie said. "But first—do you drive a BMW?"

"Me?" said Simon. "Oh, no—a Prius."

I tested the new rawhide chew. We toured the plant where the high-end treats got made and did some more testing. It didn't get better than this.

"I want to talk about Madison," Bernie said as we left the testing kitchen.

"Of course," Simon said. "Cynthia's worried to death about this, and so am I, although I try not to show it around her. Madison's a great kid, and not only because of how bright she is. If you need more money to pursue the investigation, let me know."

Bernie nodded. "Tell me about your relationship with Madison."

"It's a good one, I hope," Simon said. "We go to the movies sometimes, the three of us. I've been careful not to impose myself—I'm new in both their lives, and Cynthia's divorce is still a bit raw."

"What do you think of Damon?" Bernie said.

Simon paused. Just then some of my new friends from the testing kitchen came out with a number of fresh bowls, and I missed whatever Simon ended up saying. In fact, I missed everything until we were back in the car.

"Exactly what I was afraid of," Bernie said. "A wild-goose chase."

That was a wild-goose chase? No geese? But who cared? Even a goose or two couldn't have made it any better.

SIXTEEN

M aybe not a wild-goose chase," Bernie said, farther along the freeway. "Maybe more like a red herring."

Red herring? That was new. The truth is, I'm not a seafood fan. I've had more than one bad experience with fish bones; plus, there's a smell I detect, even with very fresh fish, that puts me off my feed, except for a piece of barbecued swordfish I took once at a party from a discarded—at least I thought it was discarded—plate. That was pretty good. But herring, of any color, I'd never tasted.

"There's a difference, Chet."

Between what and what? He'd lost me. I stuck my head out the side, felt the warm sun and the breeze, so strong it blew my ears back flat. And what did we have in the trunk? Bags and bags of samples from Rover and Company! Did I have a care in the world? You tell me.

Bernie glanced over. "Just between the two of us," he said, "I'm getting worried."

Uh-oh.

"Does it feel like a runaway case? No. Kidnapping by a sicko? No. Kidnapping for ransom—that's how it feels to me."

If that was how Bernie felt, I was on board.

"But you see the problem."

I waited.

"No ransom demand. Whoever heard of a ransom snatch with no demand?"

Not me.

"So what's going on?"

Did I have the faintest? Was this still about wild-goose chases and red herrings? Wait a minute. Not so fast, Chet. I actually did have the faintest, a weak and fading memory of Madison in a window.

"Why are you barking?" Not too sure, but I kept on. Bernie glanced around. "Because of where we are?"

Where were we? In traffic, hardly moving. Outside, I saw a huge mall, parking lots extending far into the distance, all of it vaguely familiar.

"The North Canyon Mall, Chet. Where you got hurt."

Yes, the North Canyon Mall—where I got hurt, you bet. That part was so clear, my first encounter with Boris, how he'd caught me napping, flattened our tires, then knifed me and run me down with his car. But I'd hurt him, too—don't forget about that. I barked louder.

"What's on your mind, boy?" Bernie took the turnoff to the mall. I went quiet.

We drove around the parking lot for a while. "Somewhere around here, wasn't it?" Bernie said. "In the shade of this tree, maybe?" He pulled in to a nearby slot. We got out, walked around. Bernie gazed up at the treetop. "What went on here, Chet? What's the story?"

The story? I'd napped in the shade of this tree and— I paused by the tree, sniffed at the trunk. Wow. Marks on top of marks on top of marks. Had I ever smelled anything this complicated? It made me dizzy. When the dizziness passed, I took a moment to lift my own leg. Why not?

The story, not a good one: caught napping. That was the main thing. I hung my head.

"What's wrong?" Bernie said. He came over, stroked my back. "What happened?" He took a few steps down the row of cars. "Why don't we try to reconstruct . . ." His voice trailed off. I followed him. "We were parked in this slot, or maybe here. Then what? When I came out, you were down over there." He pointed to a spot farther along the row. We moved toward it, side by side, and on the way, we came to a storm grate. I stopped right there, took a sniff, then stuck my nose through a gap in the metal bars.

"What is it, Chet?"

I smelled all kinds of things, but that wasn't the point. The point was those smells brought back a memory of this grate and what had fallen in: one of the sharpest memories I'd ever had, so sharp my side hurt.

"What are you barking about?" Bernie got down on his hands and knees, peered through the grate. "Can't see a goddamn thing. Can you?"

Nope. But I didn't have to: I knew what was down there. I pawed at the grate. Bernie gazed at me, then went to the car and came back with the flashlight. I loved the flashlight, how it poked holes in the dark, and always got a bit excited when we were using it.

"Stop charging around like that."

I stopped, returned to the grate. Bernie was kneeling again, shining the light down through.

"Give me some room, for God's sake."

But I just couldn't. I squeezed up against Bernie, peering down with him. Water glistened at the bottom, and I was pretty sure I saw one of those fast-food burger boxes. I preferred burgers the way Bernie made them on the grill but had no objection to the fast-food kind, none at all. Picky eaters exist—Leda, for example—but I'm not one of them.

"Hey, mister! Lose your car keys down the sewer?"

We turned, saw a big woman leaning on a shopping cart.

"Go see security—they got this thing."

"Excuse me?" said Bernie.

"For getting them out," the woman said, at the same time chewing on a big wad of gum; nothing but trouble, gum, I'd learned that lesson more than once. "Reason I know, I'm as dumb as you, did the same thing myself."

A little later, we had a big crowd around the grate: security guards, shoppers, skateboarders—I can ride one, by the way, might have time to go into that later—and a wino with blurry eyes swaying beside a cart full of dented cans, his smell strong enough to wipe out everything else, plus two small trucks with flashing lights.

The head security guard had a long pole. "Big-ass magnet on the end, my own invention," he told Bernie. "Fish those keys up in no time." He stuck the pole down through the grate. Everyone moved in closer, except for the wino, who saw me and smiled; a real big smile but no teeth. No teeth? How did that work?

"Stand back now," said the head guard. The pole was in deep, and he had his head cocked to the side, as though listening for something. People standing around the grate cocked their heads, too, like they were all doing imitations of one another. Once we'd watched a show about monkeys, me and Bernie. Great show: I haven't thought about humans the same way since.

"Think we got a bite," said the head guard. "Stand back."

"Stand back," said the other guards.

Everyone drew in closer instead. "Tricky part," said the head guard. "Landing the critter." He raised the pole, slow and careful. "Wouldn't want to—"

The end of the pole came up through the grate, and everyone gasped, all but Bernie and me—we don't gasp—and the wino. Stuck to the horseshoe magnet on the end of the pole was a knife, a long one with a gleaming blade. Then came silence, except for the tiny sound of water dripping off the sharp point.

Otis DeWayne was our weapons expert. He lived in Gila City, which was somewhere in the Valley or maybe not—I couldn't remember what Bernie had said—and had open country in the hills behind his house. I always liked visiting Otis. Couldn't beat open country, of course, and guns often got fired out back for testing purposes, which was always fun, but the best part was General Beauregard, the German shepherd who lived there, too.

Otis opened the front door. He had hair down to his shoulders and a beard down to his chest, was wearing a gray uniform—did I mention he did a lot of Civil War reenacting, had even talked us into trying it once? Civil War reenacting was a mystery to me then and still is. Never been so hot and dusty in my life—the Civil War's all yours. Bernie gave him the knife.

"Ah," said Otis, turning it in his hands, "interesting."

"How so?" said Bernie.

But I missed whatever made it interesting, because General Beauregard came bounding out, growling, mouth in biting position, huge fangs exposed, a bit on the aggressive side, as was the big guy's habit. Then he realized it was me, and his attitude changed right away. General Beauregard and I had had a tussle or two when we'd first met—just one, actually—and the general had been surprised, let's leave it at that. Now we got along great; not like Iggy and me, but with the electric fence, Iggy and I don't get to pal around like in the old days.

General Beauregard gave me a nip on the ear, saying hi. I gave him a nippier one on his, saying hi back. He charged around our car, came zooming back, knocked me on my butt. I charged around the car and knocked him down harder, General Beauregard being the type who needed constant reminding.

"Hey, you guys."

"There's blood already."

But by then we were out of there, sprinting around the house, neck and neck, dust rising above us. We stampeded up into the hills, birds taking flight all over the place, and then all of a sudden picked up a very interesting scent, kind of like our own, but gone sour: coyote! It led us over a rise, across an arroyo—water smells but no water—up another rise and across a wide flatland with a single big saguaro in the distance. The scent grew sharper. Was that a gray tail way up there, glistening in the sunshine? We picked up the pace as one, running flat out.

We were pretty thirsty when we returned, General Beauregard and I, and climbed onto the back porch, maybe limping a bit. The General's water bowl stood in the corner. We went to it, pushing and shoving, and lapped up every drop, butting heads at the same time. Bernie and Otis came outside.

"Christ," Otis said.

They took us in and started tweezing out all the cactus spines, me first. I was the guest.

After, General Beauregard and I lay on a nice soft rug while Bernie and Otis sat at a long table covered with knives from Otis's collection. Bernie reached for one, examined it beside the knife from the grate. "It looks like this one."

Otis peered over. There was something caught in his beard, possibly a bit of fried egg. I wanted it; loved fried eggs. "Excellent, Bernie," he said. "There's a resemblance, and why not? Master smiths from Solingen arrived in Zlatoust centuries ago. Iron mines all over the place in those parts."

"Lost me," said Bernie.

"I'm just saying my knife is German and yours is not."

"No?"

"But influenced by German methods—that was astute of you, spotting that."

"Total luck," said Bernie. "So where's my knife from?"

"I just told you," Otis said. "Zlatoust. It's almost the twin of this one." Otis rose, walked down the table, picked up another knife. "The Korsa—very nice, got it in last week. A mean-looking bastard—how sharp is this?" Otis rolled up his sleeve, drew the blade across his arm, shaving off a patch of hair. "But yours, just as sharp, same steel, forty X ten C two M—isn't a Korsa. Notice the deeper runnel."

"That groove?"

"Exactly. Lets the blood out faster. A fine piece of work, Bernie, and brand-new to me—thanks for bringing it over. Here. Stick out your arm."

"No, thanks," said Bernie. "Where's Zlatoust?"

"Near the iron mines, didn't I mention that?"

"What iron mines?"

"In the Urals, of course."

"Russia?"

"Are there other Urals?" Otis said. He started laughing. I loved Otis's laugh. It always went on and on in a loud crazy way until he ended up coughing and beating on his chest. "Any Russian connection to your case?" he said when the chest-beating part was over and he'd had a glass of water.

Bernie started to shake his head, then paused. "Not a connection in any way I can see, but there is Ms. Larapova."

"Who's she?"

"A receptionist, or maybe a real estate broker," Bernie said. "She looks like one of those Russian tennis players."

Otis rubbed his beard. I was hoping that the piece of fried egg would fall out but it didn't. "Think she'd be interested in the reenactment scene?" Otis said. "Could use some women—we're refighting the whole Chattanooga/Chickamauga campaign next weekend."

"I'll ask her," Bernie said.

"Could use some women," Otis repeated, this time softer and with a faraway look.

General Beauregard was snoring beside me. With no warning, my own eyes felt very heavy. I took a nice deep breath and let them close, and sank into dreamland at once, a dreamland where the General and I chased after all kinds of creatures big and small, scaring the hell out of each and every—

"Chet? Wakie-wakie. We're out of here."

I bounced right up, stretched, gave myself a shake, followed Bernie to the door. General Beauregard didn't open his eyes, but he gave his tail a single soft thump on the floor. The fun we'd had with those poor coyotes: our little secret.

SEVENTEEN

I had a lovely snooze in the car, maybe twisted around a bit with my head poking through to the backseat, but the gentle motion and the rumble of the engine zonked me right out. When I woke up, totally refreshed, rarin' to go, we were pulling in to Pinnacle Peak Homes at Puma Wells, don't ask me why. We parked in front of the model home and got out, Bernie carrying the knife in a manila envelope.

We entered and there we were, back in that room with the tile floor, so nice and cool against my paws, and the fountain, no longer splashing. Right away I wanted to amble over to the edge and lift my leg. Why? I didn't really need to go. A woman sat at the desk, a dark woman, not Ms. Larapova. She gave us a smile.

Bernie smiled back, not a real smile because his eyes weren't part of it, just showing teeth, although he had nice ones for a human—did I mention that already? "We're looking for Ms. Larapova," he said.

The woman stopped smiling. "Ms. Larapova is not here."

"When will she be back?"

"Ms. Larapova is no longer with the company."

"No longer with the company?" Bernie said. He picked up a card lying on the desk. "It says right here—'Elena Larapova, VP Marketing.'"

"I'm afraid that card is obsolete," the woman said. She took it from Bernie's hand and dropped it in the wastebasket.

"Chet!" Bernie said.

Oops. Did I hear growling, in fact, almost snarling? I made it stop, even though I didn't like how she'd grabbed the card from Bernie, not one little bit.

"Do you know how I can contact her?" he said.

"I'm afraid not."

"But suppose mail comes for her—she must have left a for-warding address."

"I'm afraid she didn't."

Bernie was still smiling, and now his smile seemed real, maybe actually was. Bernie was full of surprises. Sometimes I didn't understand him at all.

"Nothing to be afraid of," he said. "I'll just see Mr. Keefer for a moment."

"I'm af— Mr. Keefer is away on business."

"He was here this morning."

"Now he's gone."

"Is he at home?"

"He's away on business."

"Where?"

"I'm not sure."

"What's your best guess?"

The woman's mouth opened and closed, but no sound came out. I loved when Bernie made that happen. We walked outside feeling like winners, at least I did. Standing in the parking lot, Bernie tried Keefer's home and cell numbers, got no answer. He opened his laptop, searched for a number for Ms. Larapova, found only one listing—the Pinnacle Peak office we'd just come from.

"What's *our* best guess, Chet? Where's the girl? Where's Madison?"

Madison? Her face up in that barn window, across from the entrance to the old mine: I could see it. And how she'd tried to help me, actually did help me, making my escape possible: That I remembered. I started trotting around the parking lot, sniffing for my scent trail, the trail that would take me back to Mr. Gulagov's ranch. My scent was in the air, easy to find, but all it did was lead me round and round in circles.

"Chet?"

And then all at once, maybe because the man was on my mind, I picked up a scent by a spiky bush in a corner of the lot, a very faint scent that I knew. Human, male, musty and a bit nasty, with a hint of cooked beets: Mr. Gulagov. I trotted around the bush, followed the trail toward the office door, where it petered out. Then I backtracked to the spiky bush, tried to find a trail going some other way, and couldn't. I sat down and barked.

"Chet? What is it? Keefer? His scent will be all over the place around here."

I barked louder. Help me out, Bernie.

"Come on, boy. Nothing more we can do here."

No? There had to be, but I didn't know what. We drove home.

The phone was ringing when we went inside. Suzie's voice came over the answering machine. "Hi," she said. "Nothing important—just wondering how Chet was doing."

Bernie ran for the phone, sliding a bit on one of my toys—a favorite, actually, bone-shaped, made of a nicely chewy but firm rubber—and losing the manila envelope. As he skidded to a stop—a stiff-legged skid almost as good as one of mine—the knife flew out of the envelope and stuck point first in the floor, the handle quivering.

"Hello?" Bernie said. "Chet! Knock it off!" He listened for a moment, said, "He's, um, fine, his usual— Chet!"

But I couldn't help it. The knife—that knife!—sticking in the floor, vibrating in my ears with this throom throom throom: You'd be jumping up and down, too, count on it. Bernie grabbed the rubber bone and flung it through the open window. I dove out after the bone, raced across the backyard, snagged it, spun around, and jumped back inside. A new game, and what a game, indoors and outdoors, running and leaping—this one had it all.

"Chet!" Bernie grabbed my collar. "Calm down." I tried to calm down, tried to keep a grip on the rubber bone, tried to pant, all at the same time: way too much for me. I barely noticed that Bernie was no longer on the phone. "For God's sake, Chet—she's coming over for dinner. The place is a shambles."

Uh-oh. Shambles. I wasn't sure what that was, only knew it meant the vacuum cleaner, and I couldn't be in the house during vacuuming, we knew that from experience. Bernie got to work. I went into the backyard, checked the gate first thing—closed, too bad—and buried the rubber bone in the far corner. I sniffed around for a bit, detected the recent presence of a lizard, probably one of those tiny-eyed ones with a flickering tongue, but nothing else new, and dug up the rubber bone. I lay down and chewed it till my jaw got tired and buried it again, digging a real deep hole this time, one of my very deepest. It took a long time to shove the dirt all back in, get everything packed down the way I like, but it sure felt good, doing things right. That was one of Bernie's sayings: A job worth doing is worth doing well. I lay down for a spell, thought about nothing. The sun felt good. I decided to dig up the rubber bone again. I'd only scratched the surface when I heard Iggy barking next door.

I barked back. Iggy barked. I went over to the side fence, peered through a space between the slats. There was Iggy in a side window at his place, peering out. I barked. Iggy's head snapped around toward the fence. Could he see me? Why not? I could see him. He barked. I barked. And then, from far away, came that she-bark again. I got a funny feeling down my spine. We went quiet, Iggy and I, listening for that she-bark to come again. Iggy had his face right to the window, his flabby round ears as straight up as he could get them.

"Oh God," Suzie said when Bernie came in from the grill, a big smile on his face and two big steaks with those perfect cross-hatched marks burned into them, "I should have told you—I don't eat meat."

Bernie's smile did a funny thing, kind of lingering while his face moved on to other expressions. Suzie didn't eat meat? That was like saying she didn't eat. I was shocked, and Bernie, too: The steaks almost slid off the platter. But not quite. I sat back down.

"Oh, uh, it's, um, my fault," Bernie said. "Someone like you, I should have known."

Suzie smiled as though having fun—but how could this be fun, suddenly finding out you weren't getting dinner? "Someone like me?" she said.

Bernie made a few awkward—what was the word Suzie had used? shambling?—yes, shambling movements and said, "You know. Delicate."

Suzie's smile broadened; yes, she was having fun. "Delicate."

"And strong," Bernie said. "Strong and delicate. More strong than delicate, definitely."

Suzie laughed. A really nice laugh—did I mention that already?—so much more pleasing than Ms. Larapova's. "Mind if I check your fridge?"

"Oh no, you don't want to—"

But the door was already open. "I'll just freshen this up a bit," she said, removing something from way in the back.

"I couldn't let—"

"It'll be fine. You and Chet can have the steaks."

Suzie: a gem.

They sat at the kitchen table; I was over in the corner by my bowls. "You, uh, drink wine, yes? Or not?"

"Love wine," said Suzie.

"Red or white?"

"Red, please."

"Hey, me, too."

Easy on the wine, Bernie. That was my first thought—I'd seen things go wrong in this area before.

Bernie poured. "It's from Argentina," he said.

"I've always wanted to go there."

"Yeah? Me, too."

If he was going to keep saying "me, too," we were in for a long night. I spotted a layer of pure fat on one end of my steak and bit into that first.

"Mmm, delicious," said Suzie.

"You like the wine?"

"Very much."

"Oh, good. Great. I like it, too. A nice shade of red. And the taste, not too—what's the word?—but at the same time . . ." His voice trailed off. Often, maybe even usually, Bernie ended up being the smartest human in the room. Tonight was different.

They clinked glasses. I loved that, clinking glasses, the sight and the sound, but mostly how no glass got broken. How did they do it? My adventures with glass never turned out that way.

Under the table, their feet weren't very far apart. Bernie wore flip-flops. His feet were strong and wide; if you were reduced to spending your life on two feet, his might see you through. Suzie wore sandals; her feet looked strong, too, but skinnier and much smaller. Her toenails were painted some dark color, and she wore a silver ring around one toe. Suzie was interesting, no doubt about it. An urge came over me to sidestep my way under the table and give her toes a quick lick. I resisted it. She was the guest.

"Any progress on your case?" she said. "The missing girl?"

Bernie placed his glass on the table. He leaned forward, his back now stiff: the posture of tense Bernie. "Short answer or long?"

"Both," said Suzie.

Bernie's back, still straight, relaxed some. He wasn't all the way to laid-back Bernie, but closer. "No progress—that's the short answer," he said. "We may even be going in reverse."

"But isn't going in reverse what you do?" Suzie said, losing me right away.

Not Bernie, though. He gave her a sideways look and said, "Yeah." Then he went to the counter, got the manila envelope, took out the knife, and set it in front of Suzie.

"What's this?"

"Our only tangible clue," Bernie said. "It was used to attack Chet. The attacker drove a blue car. On the night Madison came home late, she was accosted by a blond man who stepped out of a blue BMW."

"And therefore?"

Bernie sipped his wine, actually more like a gulp. "Possibility one: The blond man tried once more, this time successfully. Possibility two: She escaped again and is now on the run."

"Why wouldn't she just come home? Or go to the police?"

"Sometimes family dynamics, in this case not too good, get in the way of logic. But the other problem with possibility two is this attack on Chet. If Madison was on the loose, no one would be coming after us."

"They came after you?"

"Maybe it was meant to be a warning—or maybe he was looking for me. Either way, the implication is that someone has Madison and doesn't want her found. And that adds up to kidnapping for ransom, except there's no demand."

Suzie pointed at the knife, not quite touching it. "What about tracing this?"

"Russian, that's all we know. Our knife guy is checking out the serial number, but it's not like guns—you don't need a license to own one."

Suzie took a bite of whatever she'd freshened up from the fridge, something brown and spongy. "Mmm," she said. Had to like Suzie. She drank some wine and said, "Are Madison's parents rich?"

"Damon Keefer's the dad. He's a developer in the North Valley, looks rich to me."

"What developments has he done?"

"In the past? I don't know, but right now he's finishing something called Pinnacle Peak Homes at Puma Wells. He's fussy about getting the name right."

"They're all like that," Suzie said. "I've done hundreds of developer stories." She shifted her feet under the table, came within a hair of brushing against one of Bernie's. "Maybe I could help in some way."

"Oh, no," Bernie said, "I'd never . . ." And then he paused.

"What?" said Suzie.

Bernie shook his head.

"I have this rule," Suzie said. "Once you start saying something, you have to finish."

Bernie laughed. His foot shot out and banged one of hers pretty hard. "Oh, sorry." He jerked his foot back.

"No problem," she said, rubbing her hurt foot with the other one. "Out with it, Bernie."

Bernie went still. This stillness—was it because she'd called him by name? Bernie is a very nice name, my second favorite. "Fair enough," he said. "It's probably nothing. Almost certainly. But in this business, you get into the habit of checking up."

"In mine, too," Suzie said. "Checking up on what?"

"Keefer took a phone call. I couldn't really hear, but it sounded unpleasant. He said it was his irrigation supplier, whatever that is."

"But you didn't believe him?"

"I wasn't sure."

"Who did you think it was?"

"No idea."

"Something to do with Madison?"

Bernie didn't answer.

"You don't want to say it out loud?" she said.

He grinned, for a moment looked like a kid—in fact, a lot like Charlie.

"Tell you what," Suzie said. "Why don't I do the checking up on the irrigation supplier?"

"Tell *you* what," Bernie said. "Why don't we do it together?"

"Deal," Suzie said.

"Great," said Bernie, making some gesture with his hand that ended up knocking over Suzie's glass, spilling wine all over her. I closed my eyes.

EIGHTEEN

Sometimes Bernie sang in the shower. Bernie singing in the shower meant things were going good. He had three shower songs, "Your Cheatin' Heart," "Born in the U.S.A.," and "Bompity Bompity Bompity Bomp Blue Moon Blue Blue Blue Blue Moon," my favorite, which was what he was singing now. The problem was things weren't going good, not with the Madison Chambliss case. That was our job, the Madison Chambliss case, finding her and bringing her back safe—so why was Bernie singing? I nosed the bathroom door open and went in.

Love bathrooms. I'll say that straight out. I've had a lot of fun in bathrooms. We've got two, one without a shower, by the front door, and the other in the hall between the two bedrooms. Water puddled the floor here and there, as always after Bernie's showers. I lapped some up and noticed that Bernie was standing in a strange way in front of the mirror, twisted around and peering over his shoulder.

"Christ," he said. "I'm getting back hair."

So? What was wrong with that? I've got back hair, lots of it, thick and glossy, and no one's ever done anything but praise it.

"Why now, out of the blue?" he said, reaching for a razor. "Women hate back hair."

They did? Females of my kind—well, let's just leave it this way—had no problems with my physical appearance. My mind wandered to the unknown she-barker somewhere across the canyon. Bernie, in an awkward position, reached down his back with the razor. I couldn't watch.

"Let's go in your car," Suzie said. "It's so cool."

"This old thing?" said Bernie, but I could tell he was pleased from the way his shoulders rose a little. We got in—Bernie behind the wheel, and then there was an odd moment when Suzie and I both went for the shotgun seat.

Suzie laughed and said, "I'll get in the back."

Not much of a backseat, really, in the old Porsche, impossible to get comfortable. Maybe I even felt the tiniest bit guilty, but bottom line—who always rode shotgun?

Bernie touched her arm. "No, no," he said. "C'mon, Chet, squeeze in back."

Squeeze in back? He was talking to me? I didn't move. In fact, a little more than that: I did this making-myself-immovable thing I can do, tensing all my muscles.

"Haven't seen that in a while," Bernie said. "When he goes all mulish."

Mulish? What a thing to say, a new low, no doubt about it. But in a standoff like this, didn't someone have to take the high road? I squeezed into the tiny space—me, a hundred-plus-pounder—and turned my attention to whatever was going on outside the back window, which was nothing.

Suzie got in front. Bernie turned the key.

"I just love the rumble of your engine," Suzie said. "The way it—"

I loved that, too, but engine rumble was not what we were hearing. Instead came a high-pitched whir-whir-whir, a noise that gave me this weird writhing feeling from deep inside my ears all down my neck, a noise we were hearing a bit too much lately in the Porsche, me and Bernie.

Bernie tried again and again, cranking that key harder and harder. Nothing happened except the whir-whir-whir got weaker and weaker. Machines and what went on inside them: a complete mystery to me—and to a lot of humans, too, a fact that kind of surprised me at first. Soon Bernie said, "Damn," which was not what he usually said at times like this, flung open his door, and popped the hood. From there, everything played out in the usual way—clanging, muttering, swearing, metal parts falling free and rolling under the car, wisps of rising smoke, hood slamming shut, smudge of grease on Bernie's face, call to AAA. We piled into Suzie's car, Suzie behind the wheel, me riding shotgun, Bernie steaming in the back, arms folded across his chest. Things have a way of turning out for the best: That's my core belief.

"That must be it," Suzie said. "Just past Home Depot." She pointed up ahead. Hey! I'd seen this place before—a huge water-fall in front of a low building—and always wanted to pay a visit. All of a sudden I was thirsty, needed to stick my tongue in that waterfall right away. Suzie read the sign: "'Water Water Every-where, One-Stop Shopping for All Your Irrigation Needs.' Cute name."

"Huh?" said Bernie.

"From the poem," Suzie said, losing me fast.

And maybe Bernie, too. "This is a goddamn desert," he said. "There's no water water everywhere, and there never was. Why is that so hard to remember?"

Suzie glanced at him in her mirror, a glance that made me uneasy, as though she thought there might be something a little not right with Bernie. But how could that be possible? I worried for a moment or two—I wanted Bernie to be happy, went without saying—but then we were parked and out of the car, all of this— poems, rearview glances—forgotten, and me on a fast trot to the base of the waterfall. Ah. Cold and frothy, simply delicious.

A man with a clipboard came out of the building, gave me a funny look—like what? he was afraid I was going to drink up his whole waterfall?—then turned to Bernie. "I'm Myron King, owner," he said. "Help you with something?"

"Ever sold one of these waterfalls, Myron?" Bernie said.

Bernie was a great interviewer. One of his best skills, a skill that had cracked a lot of cases for us—will I ever forget "then how do you explain that safe on your back?"—but I could tell from the expression on Myron's face that this interview was off to a bad start.

"You offering to buy?" Myron said.

Bernie blew air through his closed lips, making them flap in a way I always enjoyed, but it was never a good sign. I sensed things about to go off the rails, had a sudden urge to go off the rails, too, perhaps by lifting my leg right over Myron's tassel loafer—crazy, I know. At that moment Suzie stepped in.

"We're still in the research stage," she said.

"Researching what?"

"Irrigation requirements for a housing development centered around a golf course."

Bernie gave her a quick look, eyebrows rising.

"Whereabouts?" said Myron.

"Not at liberty to say just yet," Suzie told him.

Myron nodded, one of those nods that said: You're dealing

with a shrewd character. My guys were never shrewd, but I knew shrewdness: plenty of shrewdness out in the wild—take foxes, for example. According to Bernie, shrewd was smart's screwed-up brother, whatever that meant. "Haven't closed on the land yet?" Myron said.

"Something like that," said Suzie.

"Meaning you're looking at water supply from scratch, surveys, design, installation?"

"That's right."

"How many units?" Myron said.

Suzie hesitated. Bernie said, "We're thinking along the lines of this place we saw the other day."

Now it was Suzie giving Bernie a quick look—as though . . . as though they were getting their timing right, teaming up. Impossible, of course. The team was me and Bernie.

"What place was that?" Myron said.

"Remember the name?" said Bernie.

"Who could forget?" Suzie said. That made Bernie smile. "Pinnacle Peak Homes at Puma Wells," she said.

Myron's expression changed; he looked like he'd chewed on a lemon. I'd tried that *once*. "Good luck to you," he said.

"Oh?" said Bernie.

"You'll need it, if that's your model."

"Something wrong with Pinnacle Peak Homes at Puma Wells?" Suzie said.

Myron turned away and made a spitting sound with his mouth, although no spit came out. Spitting was something I liked a lot, could have made good use of myself, but dry spitting made no sense to me.

"Care to expand on that?" Bernie said.

"Huh?" said Myron.

"My partner means," said Suzie, "is the irrigation at Pinnacle Peak not up to your standards?"

"Hell, no," Myron said. "State-of-the-art—one of my own jobs, designed it personally, even ran a tunnel clear under the sixteenth fairway to tap in to those original wells, what's left of them. There'll be nothing greener than that golf course in the whole state."

Something I never want to see with Bernie is when this vein right in the middle of his forehead starts throbbing. The only times I've seen it, bad things happened soon after. And it was throbbing now. Suzie seemed to notice out of the corner of her eye. She said, "Sounds like a smart idea, Myron. So what was the problem?"

"The problem?" Bernie said, voice rising. "The problem with tunneling—" He cut himself off. I almost missed Suzie stepping on his foot, very quick.

"The problem?" Myron said. "My bills going unpaid—or isn't that a problem where you come from?"

"The worst," Bernie said, that blue vein settling down now, almost invisible.

Myron gazed at Bernie, gave another little nod, the kind indicating they were on the same page at last, could even become buddies. That meant he wasn't really on top of the situation. Didn't he know how close he'd come to ending up in that waterfall? I was still hoping.

"Damn straight," Myron said. "The worst. What am I supposed to do—rip all my pipes up out of the ground?"

Bernie was about to answer, but before he could, Suzie said, "Of course not. But isn't it like building a house—don't you get an advance and then partial payments along the way?"

"Yeah," said Myron. "Normally."

"But in this case?" said Bernie.

"Oh, I got the advance all right. And a couple of partials after that. But little glitches kept happening."

"Like?"

"Like with money quote due any day from a bank in Costa Rica. And the guy's one of those smooth talkers, very believable."

"The developer?" said Suzie.

"Name of Keefer," Myron said. "A smooth talker, but now he won't even take my calls. Never again, boys and girls."

Bernie and Suzie exchanged a quick glance. "Wow," said Suzie.

"Actually stopped taking your calls?" Bernie said.

"Haven't spoken to the jerk in three weeks," Myron said.

"Is that a fact?" Bernie said.

"Think I'd make this up?" said Myron. "My lawyer's slapping liens upside his head and down. Thank Christ it all blew up before we installed Splashorama."

"Splashorama?"

Myron pointed to the waterfall. "You're looking at two hundred and fifty grand. Plus tax. Makes a statement, boys and girls. But I can show you a scaled-down version if this baby's too rich for your blood."

"Fuck you," Bernie said when we were back in Suzie's car, same sitting arrangement as before, maybe because I'd hopped in first.

"I'm sorry?" said Suzie.

"That's the statement his waterfall makes," Bernie said. "The aquifer's almost dry. Rivers used to flow through the Valley, all the way to the Gulf. Now there's not even a trickle. And why?"

Silence. Bernie was upset, the water thing again. I didn't get it. We had waterfalls! "Too many goddamn people, that's why," he said. "And they keep coming, like . . . like a dry flood."

Too many people? I didn't get that, either. Except for perps, gangbangers, and other bad dudes, I liked people, the more the merrier. And they liked me!

"Can I quote you?" Suzie said.

"Quote me?"

"That dry-flood idea—might be useful in a piece someday."

"It's all yours," Bernie said.

Suzie gave Bernie a glance in the mirror. Human eyes had a way of looking foggy when thoughts were happening inside, complicated human thoughts that always seemed to stop the fun, in my opinion. "So where are we?" she said.

"We?" said Bernie.

"With the case."

"Oh," said Bernie. "The case." He took a deep breath through his nose; I loved that sound. "One of those obvious discrepancies. Keefer says he had a phone conversation with his irrigation guy yesterday. The irrigation guy says Keefer stopped taking his calls three weeks ago."

"And therefore, partner?"

Bernie laughed. Whoa. Partner? What was she talking about? I was the partner. I turned my head, nipped a little bit at the material on the inside of her door, stopped when I realized it was vinyl, not leather. How could that be? The dashboard was leather; I remembered from when I'd pawed at it before. I didn't understand the car business at all. And the taste of vinyl? Don't get me started.

"Therefore," Bernie said. "We look into it."

"How?"

"One of two ways," Bernie said. "We could—" His phone rang. The ring on Bernie's cell phone sounded like those old phones in black-and-white movies we often watched. I liked watching them because black and white was so easy for me to see; as for why Bernie liked them, I wasn't sure, just knew that if it came to a choice between black and white and color, he always chose black and white. He listened to the phone for a while, and for no reason I could explain, I knew something was up. Bernie said, "Okay, thanks," and clicked off. "That was Rick Torres in Missing Persons. Madison Chambliss has been spotted in Vegas. He's on his way to our place." Our place, meaning his and mine: home.

Suzie drove us there. They hardly talked the whole way. I was quiet, too. I'd never been to Vegas, only knew it was far away and hated by Bernie. Madison in a high-up window: That picture was very faint in my mind, almost gone. Was that old mine in Las Vegas? That didn't make sense, but I couldn't be sure.

We got off the freeway, drove up the canyon, turned onto Mesquite Road. Iggy wasn't in his window, but a man stood in our front yard, not Rick Torres. This man was tall with shoulder-length hair. He reminded me of a movie star Bernie didn't like, the name escaping me at the moment, but that wasn't the important thing. The important thing was that a stranger stood on our property.

"Who's the pretty boy?" Bernie said.

Suzie's hands tightened on the wheel. "Oh my God."

"You know him?" said Bernie.

Suzie nodded.

"Who is he?"

"Dylan McKnight," Suzie said. "He's my . . . my ex-boyfriend."

"Oh," said Bernie.

"But what's he doing out?" Suzie said.

"Out of where?"

"Northern State Correctional," said Suzie. "Eighteen months to two years on a drug violation."

"Oh?" said Bernie.

NINETEEN

"Call off your goddamn dog," said Dylan McKnight.

"He's territorial," Bernie said, running across the yard to where I had Dylan McKnight backed up against the tree, and making a grab for my collar. "It's nothing personal."

Territorial? Didn't know that word, a new one on me. But there was nothing complicated about this situation, and it couldn't have been more personal. Dylan McKnight, a stranger, uninvited— and if I hadn't missed something, also a jailbird—was on our land! And now he turned out to be one of those humans with a deep fear of me and my kind; always fun to bump up against one of those. No hiding fear like that from me—I could smell it. I bumped up against him again, not too hard.

"I don't give a shit whether it's personal," said Dylan McKnight, possibly trying to climb the tree backward, something I'd never seen.

"C'mon, now, Chet, take it easy," Bernie said.

I barked one of my most deep-throated barks, fierce and savage, a wonderful sound, even scared me a little bit, which made me do it again, even wilder, like to frighten myself back for frightening myself. From next door came Iggy's yip-yip-yip. Were we cooking or what? Iggy was a great pal.

"Chet? For God's sake! Chet! Sit."

I sat, quiet and still.

"Everything's all right," Bernie said. He patted my head—still a lot of swirling going on in there—and pointed with his chin. "Go on up to the house."

I went up to the house, watched from the front door. Bernie and Dylan McKnight were standing by the tree. Dylan was giving Bernie an unfriendly look; Bernie's face was unreadable. That was good, a sign Bernie was in charge. Suzie came toward them from her car. Dylan stepped away from the tree, straightening his clothes.

"Hi, Suze," he said. "How're you doing?"

"Me?" she said. "I'm fine. How about you?"

Dylan smiled—he had nice teeth for a human, big and bright, had to give him that—and said, "No complaints."

Suzie's whole body stiffened; she didn't look happy. "Dylan, this is Bernie. Bernie, Dylan." A human introduction—ours involved sniffing and got to the point much quicker—usually involved handshaking, as maybe I already mentioned, but not this time. Dylan gave Bernie a little nod; Bernie did nothing. Suzie turned to Dylan. "This is a bit of a surprise."

"Yeah, for me, too," Dylan said.

"I don't get you," said Suzie.

"Nothing new there, babe," Dylan said, giving her a smile, not big, but cool in the way movie actors smiled sometimes. I'd nailed this dude from the get-go.

Suzie blinked a few times, very fast, always a sign of confusion in humans. "What I was trying to say," she said, "is aren't you out a little early?"

"Don't seem too happy to see me, Suze."

"You're not answering the question," she said.

The smile left his face, but not quickly. Very interesting to watch—had I ever seen that before, a slow fading smile? Not that I remembered. For some reason, it made me want to bite him, bite him good. I glanced over at Bernie and stayed where I was.

"Yeah, I'm out early," Dylan said. He turned to Bernie. "Been a guest of this great state for a stretch, in case you're wondering."

"I'm not."

"Suze filled you in, huh?" said Dylan. "She's a sharp girl—or maybe you're hip to that already?" He paused, giving Bernie a sideways look; Bernie was silent. "The solution to the mystery," Dylan went on, "is that this great state ran into an overcrowding situation, and a judge had to let a couple hundred of us go before we all got asphyxiated."

I had trouble understanding that, gave up somewhere in the middle, just knew I wanted to bite him more than ever.

"Your lucky day," Suze said.

"You know me," said Dylan. He paused, maybe to let her say something, but she didn't. "Hope I'm not being nosy," he said, "but are you and, uh, Bernie here, an item?"

"None of your business," Suze said. "But the answer's no."

I checked on Bernie; he was looking at the ground.

Dylan smiled his big bright smile. "A thousand apologies," he said. "Any chance you could do me a little favor?"

"How did you even know I'd be here?" Suze said.

"Called the paper."

"And?"

"And they said you were working on a story about some private eye, gave me this address."

Bernie's head turned sharply toward Suze, something I didn't see often, a sign of surprise. I spotted a tennis ball near the tree and picked it up.

"Just like that?" Suze was saying. "They gave you the address?"

"Nice gal on the phone," Dylan said. "And maybe I let the situation seem a tad more urgent than it is, not on purpose, of course."

"What is the situation?" Suze said.

"I'm relocating," Dylan said.

"Where to?"

"L.A.," Dylan said. "Got a job waiting."

"Doing what?"

"Interesting stuff," Dylan said. "Flying out today. Thing is, I could use a ride to the airport."

Suzie glanced around. "How did you get here?"

"Buddy dropped me off."

Suzie opened her mouth to say something. I can tell when a human is about to say no, had plenty of experience with that, and "no" was coming. But at that moment a police cruiser appeared on our street, slowing down and parking in front of the house. Rick Torres, wearing his uniform, gun on his hip, stepped out.

"All right," Suzie said to Dylan. "Get in the car."

"You're a peach," he said.

The lemon-eating expression that I'd seen on Myron King's face now appeared on Suzie's. What with peaches and lemons, I got confused. "See you, Bernie," Suzie said.

"Yup," said Bernie.

They drove off. We all watched them—me, Bernie, Rick Torres.

"Who was that?" Rick said.

"Suzie Sanchez. She's a reporter for the *Tribune*."

"The one who did that piece on you?"

"Yeah."

"We all got a charge out of it, down at the station."

Bernie said nothing.

"But all the boys agreed she got one thing wrong—Robert Mitchum couldn't hold a candle to you."

"Knock it off."

Rick laughed. "Hey, Chet." He came over, patted my head. "Don't care for reporters," he said.

"No?" said Bernie.

"Always got some secret agenda—can't trust them, in my experience."

What was he saying? I trusted Suzie, for sure, one of the most reliable treat sources I'd ever met. I started to back away from Rick, but then he scratched at the base of one of my ears, a perfect spot. That planted me right where I was. Ah, this was the life, although maybe not for Bernie, who was gazing down the empty street, his face not happy. How come? My chances of getting to the bottom of that weren't good, not with this lovely scratching going on. Rick stopped—too soon, always too soon—and pulled an envelope from his pocket. I gave myself a good shake, unscrambled my head, leaving it all peaceful and quiet inside, actually kind of empty.

Rick handed the envelope to Bernie. Bernie took out a photo from inside and examined it.

"That's her," he said. "Madison Chambliss."

"Taken last night with a cell phone outside a movie theater in North Vegas, the Golden Palm Movie Palace. You can see the ticket window there in the background. Guy who snapped it—projectionist on his way to work—turns out to be a crime buff, saw the photo on some site, maybe ours, and recognized her. Didn't speak to her, evidently, but he did call the LVPD. They checked out the cell phone—time code's legit."

"She was by herself?"

"Looked that way, according to the projectionist. She came walking out of a showing as he was going in."

Bernie bit his lip. That was something I didn't see often. Good or bad? I couldn't tell. "Do her parents know?"

"Yup. I think the mom's already on her way up there."

"And the LVPD?"

"They put her on their runaway list." Rick shook his head, not the headshake meaning "no," but the one for "not much hope," a feeling I didn't understand. "That's a long one, up in Vegas," Rick said.

Rick dropped us off at the garage. The Porsche was in the lot, all washed and shiny. Bernie paid the bill, and then we were off to Vegas!

"Starter coil," Bernie said after a while, possibly not in a mood like mine. "Guess what that costs."

I had no idea, only knew it wasn't good or Bernie wouldn't be worrying. Our finances were a mess. Maybe I'd find a wallet somewhere. That had happened more than once, but they'd always been empty, although wallet leather tasted great. No other moneymaking ideas came to mind. And why was it so important? We ate like kings, had a roof over our heads and the coolest car in the whole Valley. Fresh breeze, warm sun, riding shotgun: My mood brightened again, although a treat would have been nice. I sniffed the air, smelled no treats, not even old moldy ones under the seat. We passed a horse trailer, and I caught a glimpse of a big horse eye through the side slats, got off a quick bark-bark-bark, machine-gun style. Did I spot a flicker of fear in that eye as we zoomed away? Horses were jumpy—what a fun fact!

After that I got sleepy and lay down. Just as I was nodding off,

Bernie muttered, "And we're not an item, that's for sure." Uh-oh: He was worried about all sorts of things. I slipped into dreamland, found myself chasing rabbits right away.

When I woke up, the sun hung low in the sky, and we were driving down a broad avenue lined with weird buildings, weird lights, weird people, weird everything.

"Vegas," Bernie said. "Welcome to the ninth circle."

Ninth circle? A new one on me. Back in the Charlie and Leda days, we'd been to a ranch called the Circle-Z. Talk about chasing rabbits! Although that rabbit episode hadn't turned out so well, led to a disagreement between Leda and Bernie and Bernie sleeping on the living-room couch for a long time, maybe even till she and Charlie moved away. Thoughts of the Circle-Z turned my mind in the direction of another ranch, but what one? A ranch . . . a ranch with a mine on the property, yes, and Madison's face high up in the barn window. Had to remember that: very important.

"What're you barking about, boy?"

I looked Bernie in the eye, barked and barked.

"C'mon, Chet, ease up."

I eased up.

Not long after that, we parked in front of a building with a marquee out front and a brightly lit golden palm tree on the roof. Marquees meant movie theaters, not welcoming places in my experience—had never been inside one, even though I'm a big movie buff.

"Better stay put, Chet," Bernie said, getting out.

Did I know that was coming? Sure, but it didn't help. I opened my mouth very wide, stretching it to the max, no idea why.

"Be right back." But Bernie had only taken a step or two when Damon Keefer got out of the car parked behind us; I knew it was him partly from the goatee but more from the sudden strong odor of Prince the cat. At the same time, Cynthia Chambliss, smelling of flowers, lemons, and a hint of human sweat, got out of another car, parked a few spaces ahead. They approached Bernie. He turned so he could face them both.

"Have you got her?" he said.

"No," said Keefer.

"Not yet," Cynthia said. "But soon—I'm so hopeful, now that we know what's going on."

"Which is?" said Bernie.

"Cynthia refers to the fact that this is clearly a runaway situation," Keefer said, "and not something worse."

"That's not clear to us," Bernie said.

"Us?" said Keefer. "Who is 'us'?"

"I told you before," Bernie said. "The Little Detective Agency."

"Why isn't it clear?" said Cynthia, her eyebrows pinching in together, sure sign of human anxiety. "Sergeant Torres said he spoke to you. Didn't he explain about the photograph?"

"It's suggestive," Bernie said, "but I'm still not satisfied."

"Doesn't matter whether you are or not," Keefer said. "Cynthia and I are in agreement that your services are no longer needed."

"Why is that?"

"I just told you," Keefer said. "She's a runaway."

"That was possible from the start," Bernie said. "Nothing's changed."

"Except the venue," Keefer said. "We've decided, Cynthia and myself, that if we choose to proceed with a private detective, we'll hire one from the Vegas area."

Bernie's face sometimes had a way of thinning out and going hard at the same time, as though turning to stone. When that happened, it was usually "Look out, perps and bad guys." But not this time. Bernie just said, "I can recommend a few people."

"That would be very ni—" Cynthia began.

Keefer cut her off. "Unnecessary," he said. "Just send the final bill at your convenience."

"You can add it to the stack," Bernie said.

"Huh?" Keefer said.

"Somewhere under the one from Myron King—wouldn't want to jump the line."

"What does he mean?" Cynthia said, turning to Keefer. The smell of her sweat was a little stronger now, actually quite pleasant. "Who's Myron King?"

"The waterfall man," Bernie said. He got in the car. Keefer's face looked dark and swollen; Cynthia was opening her mouth to ask him something else. We zoomed off. Bernie made the tires squeal. I loved that.

We drove for a few blocks, made some turns, stopped at a convenience store. Bernie went in, came out with cigarettes and chew strips. He moved the car into the shade of a huge billboard that showed coins pouring out of a slot machine. We sat there, smoking and chewing.

"Staying on a case when you're not getting paid," Bernie said. "How stupid is that?"

I didn't know. These chew strips were a new kind to me, saltier than I was used to but chewier, too, in a way that was hard to pin down. I tried another.

Bernie took a deep drag, blew the smoke out slowly. Smoke rings, please: I loved smoke rings, but Bernie didn't make any. "Know what else bothers me? Suzie never said she was doing another story. I thought she was just hanging out with us. You know—because she wanted to."

Missed that one. Suzie did hang out with us, and of course she wanted to: We had fun. And would keep having fun as long as she didn't forget who the partner was. Bernie flicked the cigarette outside.

"Tell you what, Chet. Let's go be stupid."

That was fine with me.

TWENTY

Pretty soon we were back in front of the Golden Palm Movie Palace; no sign of Keefer or Cynthia. The sun went down, and the sky turned dark pink. I'd never seen sky like that before. It made me uneasy. I twisted around on my seat, trying to get comfortable.

"Vegas," Bernie said. "Nothing you can do about it."

I settled down. Not long after that, a beat-up van parked nearby. A man got out, carrying round flat cans under one arm, kind of like Frisbees but bigger; in his free hand he held a paper bag.

"That's him," said Bernie. "The projectionist."

Projectionists, a new one on me, turned out to be little guys, very thin, with arm tattoos and spiky hair. As this particular one came closer, Bernie opened the door and stepped out.

"Got a moment?" he said. "I'm a detective working on the Madison Chambliss case."

The projectionist stopped, looked up at Bernie. "I already told you guys all I know," he said.

"Won't take long," Bernie said. "What's your name?"

"My name? I already told you guys."

"Tell me again."

"Anatoly," the projectionist said. "Anatoly Bulganin."

"Russian?"

"American," Anatoly said. "Born and bred in New York City, like I already told—"

Bernie held up his hand, palm out. "We're not those guys," he said.

"Huh?"

Bernie handed him our card. Anatoly gazed at it. "Private?" he said.

Bernie nodded. "Retained to look for the girl." Were we still retained? I got the feeling Bernie was pulling a fast one, couldn't put all the pieces together. But it didn't matter, because at that moment I caught a whiff of cooked beets. I straightened up in my seat. I knew beets because Leda had grown some, back when we'd had a vegetable garden. The smell was reminding me of something, but what? I sniffed the air.

Anatoly handed back the card. "Private—doesn't that mean I don't have to answer your questions?"

"You don't have to answer anyone's questions," Bernie said. "But in this case—a missing kid—wouldn't it be a bit strange?"

"The other guys—the LVPD—said she's a runaway."

"Still counts as missing in my book. Just go through it real quick for us."

Anatoly sighed, the kind of sigh humans make when they give in. Bernie was good at making people do that, and I was better. "Right about where I'm standing now was where I took the picture," Anatoly said. "I was on my way to work, and she was coming out." He raised the paper bag in the direction of the door to the theater. The beet smell got stronger. "I'm kind of a crime junkie, and I recognized her from this site I go to."

"What's the name?"

"Desert Mayhem dot com," Anatoly said.

"Did you talk to her?"

Anatoly shook his head. "I wasn't sure it was her till I went back to the site. And what could I do, anyway? I'm just a private citizen."

"Nothing to beat yourself up about, Anatoly. You did fine." Anatoly relaxed a little, his whole body changing. "How did she look?" Bernie said.

"How did she look?"

"Happy, sad, anxious, in a hurry?"

"Like an ordinary teenager, that was all I saw."

"Good enough," Bernie said. Anatoly turned to go. "One more thing," Bernie said. "What was playing last night?"

Anatoly motioned again with the paper bag, this time at the marquee. "Same as tonight. We change on Thursdays."

Bernie read the marquee aloud. "*Chainsaw Exorcist Two*."

"Even better than number one," Anatoly said.

"Hard to imagine," said Bernie.

Another wave of beet smell passed over me. It was coming from the bag, no question, but that wasn't the point. The point was I remembered where I'd smelled it before, who it reminded me of—Mr. Gulagov! I started barking. Anatoly jumped in his skin, a pleasant sight.

"Call off your dog! What the hell's going on?"

And not just barking: I seemed to have sprung out of the car, backed Anatoly against a parking meter.

"Easy there, Chet," Bernie said. I lowered the volume maybe a little bit. "He's K-9 trained. Packing some weed in that bag, Anatoly? No problem, as far as we're concerned."

"Weed?" said Anatoly. "No weed. This is my snack."

"Hash brownies, by any chance?"

"No hash brownies, no drugs of any kind. The body is the temple." Anatoly opened the bag so Bernie could see. "Borscht."

"What's that?" Bernie said.

"Soup," said Anatoly. "Russian soup, from beets."

Tell me something I don't know. I barked harder.

"Chet! For God's sake. It's soup."

Soup. I knew that, actually liked some soups, especially beef consommé, but this soup from beets reminded me of—

"Chet! Stop!"

I stopped, backed away.

"Sorry for the misunderstanding," Bernie said. "And thanks for your help."

"Yeah, sure, misunderstanding," said Anatoly, stooping to pick up those big flat cans, which seemed to have fallen to the sidewalk.

Bernie turned toward the car, paused. "Just thought of something."

Anatoly paused. "What?"

"Zlatoust," Bernie said. "Does that word mean anything to you?"

Anatoly shook his head.

"It's Russian," Bernie said. "Maybe I'm pronouncing it wrong."

"Maybe," said Anatoly. "But I wouldn't know—I don't speak Russian."

We drove around Vegas for a while, hit the Missing Persons bureau and a few youth shelters, came up with zip; then headed for home under a sky that soon looked normal, black and full of stars. Bernie smoked. I ate a Slim Jim we'd picked up somewhere along the way; loved Slim Jims, could have lived on them exclusively. It was nice, just eating Slim Jims, maybe more than one, and staring at the fiery end of Bernie's cigarette, which I couldn't stop doing for some reason. We listened to Billie Holiday. "Hear that?" Bernie said. "Roy Eldridge on trumpet. The great Roy Eldridge."

Of course I heard. Trumpets were my favorite, made the very best sound in the world. Bernie hit replay, and we listened to the same song again. And many more times. That was Bernie when he found something he liked. We had that in common, me and Bernie.

"They called him Little Jazz, don't know why."

Me, neither. Also, I didn't care.

After a while we pulled over for a pit stop. Bernie went against a mesquite tree; I chose a trash can. He gazed up at the sky; I listened to the two trickles—mine was better, on account of the drumming sound from the trash can.

"See the Milky Way?" he said.

Milky Way? What the hell was he talking about? Long drives never tired me, not a bit, but I knew it wasn't the same for Bernie. We got back in the car. Bernie started to turn the key, then paused.

"*Chainsaw Exorcist Two,*" he said. "Is that the kind of movie a kid like Madison would want to see?" I waited for the answer. "No way, Chet. I'd bet the house."

Please, not that.

By the time we got home, Bernie had raccoon eyes, which happened when he was really wiped out. Don't get me started on raccoons. I myself felt pretty peppy, having dozed off somewhere along the way. The message light was blinking, but Bernie didn't notice. He opened the cupboard over the kitchen sink and took out a bottle of bourbon. Bernie liked bourbon a lot, tried to stay away from it. He poured himself a glass, raised it to his lips, and saw the blinking light. Bernie went over and pressed a button.

First came the voice of Leda, Leda in a bad mood. "We've been invited on a cruise off Cabo this Saturday. I know it's your weekend, but I'm sure you wouldn't want Charlie to miss the opportunity."

Then the voice of a man I didn't know. "This is Robert Burk. I'm personal assistant to a financier here in the Valley. We're looking for someone to handle security on the Maui compound for two weeks starting the day after tomorrow. Lieutenant Stine of Metro PD recommended you. Last-minute, I know, but the pay is good—five thousand dollars. If interested, get back ASAP. That's five thousand per week."

Then Leda again. "And I can't believe you still haven't repaid Malcolm for covering the tuition."

Bernie sank into a chair, the glass held loosely in his fingers. Cabo? A cruise? No Charlie this weekend? And what was this about Maui? I went over to my water bowl and took a sip: flat and tasteless. I thought of heading into the bathroom in search of something fresher, instead circled around a bit and lay down.

Bernie rubbed his face. "Know what those messages were like, Chet? A three-act play."

Bernie, go to bed. Please.

"What the hell are we going to do? Ten grand. Why now?"

He took a long drink. I rose, walked over, sat on the floor beside him. Bernie brushed something off my back. What? Not another tick?

"See the problem?" he said. "Ten grand and soft duty on Maui versus zero for a case we're not even on anymore." I didn't know anything about Maui, but soft duty sounded nice. "And what if

Madison turns out to be a runaway after all?" Madison: I could
see her at the window. And hear her, too. She'd said, "Don't you
hurt that dog." At that moment I spotted Boris's knife lying on
the kitchen table. I went over and growled at it.

"Chet?"

I kept growling. She wasn't a runaway. I growled and
growled.

"What is it, boy, what's on your mind?" Bernie picked up the
knife, turned it over in his hands. "Something's bothering you."
He drummed his fingers on the arm of the chair, slowly downed
the bourbon. When the glass was empty, he called Robert Burk,
assistant to the financier, and turned down the job. Maui, whatever that was, would have to wait.

The phone rang, bright and early. I lay curled up on the floor at
the foot of the bed, comfortable beyond belief, my head all nice
and foggy. Up on the bed, Bernie crashed around, fumbling for
the phone. It fell on the floor. "Christ almighty," Bernie said.

"Hello? Hello?" Hey—Suzie's voice, tinny and distant: Bernie
must have hit the speakerphone button by mistake. "Hello?"

"Suzie?"

"Hi," she said. "Didn't wake you, did I?"

"Oh no, course not. Been up for hours."

After a slight pause, Suzie said, "I was just wondering if you
found her."

"No."

"Did you go to Vegas?"

"Yes."

"But she's a runaway after all?"

"Not sure about that."

"Oh? How come?"

I heard Bernie sit up. "I've got a question of my own," he said.

"Shoot."

"What's your interest in this?"

"My interest? I don't understand."

"Are you writing a story? Is that it?"

Another pause. "I hadn't decided."

"Were you planning to clue me in?"

"I'm sorry. I should have. But it wasn't my main motivation."

"What was your main motivation?"

Silence. And in that silence, another voice, a man's voice, came over the line. "Hey, babe," he said, "who's on the phone?" I recognized that voice, and so did Bernie—I could tell from his face. It was the voice of Dylan McKnight, ex-boyfriend, jailbird, loser. I rose, up on all fours.

"Gotta go," Bernie said.

"No, wait," said Suzie. "I'm— I'm out of town right now, but I had a thought about Keefer, based on our talk with Myron King. What bank handles his financing?"

"Thanks for the tip," Bernie said. "Bye."

"Bernie? Wait, I—"

Bernie hung up. He turned to me. "Went to L.A. with him," he said. His eyes were blank. I pressed my head against the side of his leg.

After a quick breakfast—bacon and eggs for Bernie, bacon and kibble for me—he opened the safe in the office and took out the watch. Bernie had a fancy watch, inherited from his grandfather, who'd once owned a big ranch where Mesquite Road and our whole neighborhood was now but lost everything, possibly because of a drinking problem, although the drinking problem might have come from some other story Bernie had told me, a story about another relative. But forget all that. The point is, Bernie never wore the watch, which stayed in the safe at all times, except for when we took it to Mr. Singh, the pawnbroker.

"Bernie! Chet!" said Mr. Singh. "How is our beautiful time-piece today?"

Bernie handed it over. We left, a big wad of cash in Bernie's pocket and a bite or two of curried goat kebab in my mouth. Mr. Singh was the bomb.

We drove over to Leda's. She and Malcolm, the boyfriend, had a big house in High Chaparral Estates, one of the nicest developments in the whole Valley; I'd heard Leda mention that more than once. Malcolm was a brilliant software developer, whatever that was, making money hand over fist; she'd mentioned that, too.

We parked and walked up to the front door. Leda and Malcolm had a big green lawn, and the path was lined with all kinds of flowering bushes. I lifted my leg a couple of times—I always save a little, just to be ready for situations like this. Bernie knocked on the door, and it opened right away. Malcolm looked out, talking on a cell phone, something about capturing residuals, a new one on me, although I was familiar with marsupials, had actually seen one, a possum, I think, captured by a fox on the Discovery Channel.

Malcolm, still talking on the phone, raised his eyebrows at Bernie.

"That money I owe you," Bernie said, his voice quiet, almost inaudible, very rare for Bernie.

"Have to call you back." Malcolm stuck the phone in his pocket. "Yes?" he said.

"Here," said Bernie, holding out some bills. His back straightened; I could feel the effort it took. "And thanks."

"Oh, ah, no problem," said Malcolm, pinching the money between his thumb and index finger, as though taking something smelly.

At that moment Charlie walked up behind Malcolm, a toothbrush in his hand. His eyes got big. "Dad?"

"Hi, Charlie."

"Dad, hi." Charlie stepped around Malcolm, hesitated. Bernie reached forward and picked him up.

Then Leda appeared. A quick back-and-forth went on, most of which I missed, except for something about why hadn't Bernie simply sent a check. But by then Charlie had spotted me.

"Chet the Jet!" He wriggled out of Bernie's arms, ran over, gave me a big kiss. I gave him one back. He jumped up on me, and I rode him around the lawn. Charlie laughed and laughed, holding on with his little hands. "Ride 'em, cowboy." I bucked a few times, not too hard. He made squealing sounds.

"For God's sake," Leda said. "Those are hydrangeas."

"Were," said Malcolm.

A minute or two later, we were on our way home. Bernie was silent almost all the way. Just as we turned onto Mesquite Road, he said, "Know how much water those hydrangeas need?"

Oh no. Water again.

Bernie sat down with his laptop. "Gotta think," he said. I gazed at the knife, lying beside him on the table. I tried growling at it again but Bernie didn't hear, probably on account of how hard he was thinking. After a while he said, "Suzie's probably right." About what? I had no idea, but I tried not to interrupt when one of these deep-thinking sessions was under way. Soon Bernie was on the phone, making call after call. On the last one, he said, "I understand your bank handles the financing for Pinnacle Peak Homes at Puma Wells." He listened and said, "Oh, when did that happen?" More listening, and then Bernie said goodbye. He turned to me. "Western Commerce Bank cut Keefer loose a few months ago, and this guy says he doubts there's another bank in the state crazy enough to take him on." Right over my head, all of that. But the knife on the table, Boris's knife, was a different story.

Bernie did some more tapping at the keyboard. Soon the printer was pumping out paper. Bernie waved a few sheets at me. "Look at this—all liens on Pinnacle Peak. It's a house of cards."

House of cards? One of my very favorite games. I always came in at the end, and always won. Bernie turned back to the keyboard. I went over to the table, growled at the knife, couldn't help it.

"C'mon, Chet, I'm trying to think."

The house grew quiet. Bernie's thoughts roamed around like faint breezes. I found a nice spot under the table, wedged between two chairs, and closed my eyes. Tap tap on the keyboard: a soothing sound. I had complete confidence in Bernie.

TWENTY-ONE

I woke up sometime after the end of the deep-thought session and caught Bernie patting the pockets of a pair of jeans in the laundry pile, obviously searching for a forgotten smoke. "Oh, hi, Chet," he said, tossing the pants aside in a casual way, like he'd actually been doing the laundry, "how about a walk?"

A walk? Never a bad choice, especially now—I could tell from Bernie's eyes, nonsparkling, that the deep-thought session hadn't led very far. Bernie did some of his best thinking on walks; my best thinking could come at any time—I was kind of unpredictable that way. In a moment we were out in sun and fresh air, on a nice long ramble up the canyon and back down Mesquite Road, passing Iggy's house. Iggy's house was smaller than ours and a little run-down, with tiles missing from the roof here and there and the trim faded colorless. At least it seemed colorless to me: Bernie always says I'm not good with colors, basing his opinion on who knows what. But back to Iggy's house: One other thing about it was its age, older-looking than all the other houses on Mesquite Road. That made sense, because the couple who lived there with Iggy—Mr. and Mrs. Parsons—were old, too, had possibly even known Bernie's grandfather back in ranchland days, or one of them had, the details foggy in my mind. The only up-to-date thing at Iggy's was the electric fence. The electric-fence dude had come to our place, too, after Iggy's was all set up, given Bernie a long spiel about lawsuits and liability, subjects that turned us off, me and Bernie. Bernie had interrupted him, taken Iggy's new collar in his hand, and walked right over the invisible line on Iggy's lawn, testing the shock on himself. Then Bernie turned to the electric-fence dude and shook his head. That was the end of that.

But Iggy's rambling days were over. At first he'd come out on the front lawn as usual, and I'd drop over to play, but when I left Iggy always tried to follow me, a little slow to get the electric-fence concept, ending up with a bad surprise every time. Now he hardly came to play out front anymore, doing his business in the backyard, separated from ours by the Parsons's garage.

I could see him as we went by at the end of our walk, watching out the window. Iggy's watching-out-the-window technique needed improvement. Sometimes, like now, he got his nose too close to the glass and fogged it up. That frustrated Iggy, and he started in on his yip-yip-yipping. I barked back. Iggy yipped. The window fogged up some more. Then: surprise. The front door opened, and old Mr. Parsons looked out. He wore long pants and a shirt buttoned to the neck, but his feet were bare. Why did that grab my attention? Couldn't tell you.

"Mr. Little?" he said.

We stopped. "Yes?" said Bernie.

"Spare a moment?" said Mr. Parsons; he had a high, thin voice.

"Sure." Bernie walked over. I followed.

"Amazing how he does that," said Mr. Parsons.

"Does what?"

"Stays right by you, even without a leash."

"Chet's not a fan of the leash," Bernie said.

Mr. Parsons laughed, a wheezy laugh that ended in a kind of gasping fit. I didn't know Mr. Parsons very well but was starting to like him—those bare feet were tough and wide, spread out all over the place, like he didn't wear shoes much. "Neither's ol' Iggy," he said, "but he don't follow like that, no way, no how. Fact is, Mrs. Parsons hasn't been feeling too well lately."

"Sorry to hear that."

"Thank you. Had a bit of a stroke, according to the doc. Which is why I haven't been taking Iggy on his walks—can't really be leaving Mrs. Parsons."

"I could take him if you want."

"Very kind," said Mr. Parsons, "but I wouldn't presume. Maybe Chet could come over once or twice, have a little play with Iggy out back."

"Sounds good," Bernie said. "How's right now?"

From inside the house came a banging noise: Iggy, for sure, throwing himself against some door that was keeping him from joining us.

"Right now wouldn't be the best," said Mr. Parsons. "I'm going to give Mrs. Parsons her pills, kind of complicated with how many there are, keeping track and all."

"Call when you'd like Chet to come over," Bernie said.

"Will do," said Mr. Parsons. "Nice to see Chet looking so well. Truth is, I was concerned after that other night."

"What other night?" said Bernie.

Mr. Parsons squinted, the way humans do when trying to see something far away. "Can't recall, exactly." He shook his head. "I'm on some pills myself," he said, "get them online, but they're supposed to work the same as the real ones. Interfere with my memory, which wasn't too good in the first place, not these days." He licked his lips. "And seeing him here like this probably means I got the whole thing wrong."

"What whole thing?"

"Happened real quick, in any case."

"Mr. Parsons? What did?"

More crashing sounds from deep inside the house. Mr. Parsons seemed not to hear them. "Now it's coming back to me, the particulars. Might even have been one of those nights you had a tent set up out back and a fire going. Always get a kick out of that—Mrs. Parsons can see down from the upstairs window, where we've got the rocker. Anyways, a little later—Mrs. Parsons might have been having some trouble getting comfortable that night—I was downstairs, happened to look out the kitchen window, thataways." Mr. Parsons pointed down the street. "What I thought I saw—hard to say on account of darkness, and how quick it happened, like I said, so don't hold me to it . . ." His voice trailed off and his eyes got blurry.

"I won't hold you to it, Mr. Parsons. What did you think you saw?"

"Hard to believe, really," said Mr. Parsons. "More like something in a dream. But a car was parked down there, outside that house on the other side of the street, the one with the for-sale sign, and two guys threw something in the trunk and drove off."

"What kind of something?" Bernie said.

"That's the dreamlike part," said Mr. Parsons. "More properly, might call it nightmare." He glanced down at me. I was thinking, You're going great, old buddy. Spit it out. "What it looked like to me," he went on, "was a dog. And not just any dog but this one here, namely Chet." He reached out, gave me a pat. His fingers, all gnarled and swollen, felt cold. "On the other hand, here he is in the flesh, so I must've been seeing things."

"I don't think so," Bernie said. His face had gone all hard. "What can you tell me about the two men?"

"Nothing," said Mr. Parsons. He closed his eyes. "One might have been bigger than the other. The blond one."

"One of the men was blond?" Bernie's voice sharpened. The hair on my back rose a bit.

Mr. Parsons opened his eyes. "The bigger one. His hair stood out in the night."

A woman called from inside, her voice weak. "Daniel? Daniel?"

"Sorry," said Mr. Parsons. "Must go." He closed the door. Iggy crashed into something one more time.

We crossed the street, over to the house with the for-sale sign.

"What happened here, boy?" Bernie said. "I get the feeling I've been pretty stupid."

Bernie? Stupid? No way. Bernie was always the smartest one in the room, except for maybe when he'd had too much bourbon. There was a night, for example, when he'd been stringing the Christmas-tree lights, a story I may get to later.

We gazed at the house with the for-sale sign. The shades were drawn, and some rolled-up newspapers lay in the driveway. I went and picked one up, was starting to run around with it when a woman came out of the house. She wore a business suit, carried a big briefcase, and had some kind of phone plugged in to her ear.

"You're early," she said. "It doesn't start till noon."

"What doesn't?" Bernie said.

"The walk-through. Aren't you an agent?"

"A neighbor."

"Oh? Which house is yours?"

Bernie pointed. The woman came forward. "Charming," she said. "And you don't need me to tell you what a great street you're on, with the canyon so near. Values are holding up nicely. If you ever think of selling . . ." She handed Bernie her card.

He took it, at the same time saying, "Chet?"

I dropped the paper, what was left of it, tried to look small.

Bernie examined the card. "This is your listing?"

"You're looking at the listing queen of the East Valley," the woman said. Then she spoke her name, missed by me, on account of an annoying scrap of newspaper turning up under my tongue. The woman and Bernie shook hands; she was one of those two-handed handshakers, holding on to Bernie's longer than necessary. Uh-oh. And the way she was standing changed, too: Had her chest been sticking out quite that far before? In certain situations, always with women, Bernie was helpless.

But now he didn't seem to notice. "How long has the house been empty?" he said.

"A couple months, except for some renters."

"The renters are still here?"

"No, they cleared out last week, hardly stayed more than a few days, even though they paid for a full three months up front."

"I don't remember seeing them around," Bernie said. "What did they look like?"

"I only met the one who signed the rental contract, a big guy, blond, might have been foreign—he had an accent. Swedish, maybe?"

"Did you get his name?"

"His name? It'll be on the contract, but I don't—"

"You'll have a photocopy of his license?"

"Of course, but—"

Bernie handed her our card. "I'd like to see it."

The woman eyed the card and then eyed Bernie. "What's going on? You said you were a neighbor."

"And that's true," Bernie said. "But we're also working on a case, and this blond guy is involved."

"I really don't—"

"A missing-persons case," Bernie said. "Her name is Madison Chambliss. She's fifteen years old."

The woman gave Bernie a long look, then started digging in her briefcase. She took out a sheaf of papers, stapled together, and gave them to Bernie. He leafed through.

"Cleon Maxwell, 14303 North Coronado, Rosa Vista," Bernie said.

Cleon Maxwell? But the perp's name was Boris. What sense did that make? Bernie angled a page so I could see the black-and-white photo of a driver's license.

"You're showing the picture to your dog?" the woman said, her eyes opening wide.

I didn't like her tone, but neither could I put her in her place. Truth is, I'm not too good with photos, even in black and white. The man in the photo had blond hair and kind of looked like how I remembered Boris, but I couldn't be sure. A different story, listing queen, if driver's licenses came with smell samples instead of pictures, you'd better believe it.

"He's K-9 trained," Bernie said.

Partially K-9 trained, as I might have mentioned. Why had that cat come along right in the middle of the final test, open-country tracking? My certificate was all made out, but I never got it.

"How did I miss this?" Bernie said as we drove to Rosa Vista. "They've been watching us almost from the moment we took the case." He banged the side of his fist against the steering wheel. That kind of thing didn't happen often. "I must be losing my mind, Chet." I hoped that wasn't true: Bernie's mind was one of our biggest assets, on a par with my nose. I laid a paw on his knee. He drove fast, even weaving in and out of traffic a bit, not like him at all. But fun, all that speed and weaving, no doubt about it. I stopped worrying and got in a very good mood.

We took a ramp off the freeway, headed toward the sun on a wide straight road. "Coronado," said Bernie. "Hate Coronado." Why? It looked like so many streets in the Valley, wide and straight and going on forever. "Know what he did to the Indians?" Bernie added after a while, losing me completely.

He slowed down, started reading off the numbers. "Fourteen-one, fourteen-two, here we go." We parked in front of a restaurant, and a good one. I didn't have to look, just knew from the smell. Bernie read the sign: "'Max's Memphis Ribs.'" A rib joint? I'd heard of rib joints, had never actually been in one. My mouth started watering right away, but then I remembered that a lot of restaurants weren't very welcoming when it came to my kind.

The front of the building was all glass. We walked to the door, hesitated. A man behind the counter inside saw us, pointed to me, then did a come-on-in fluttering of his fingers. One of my favorite human gestures, that finger flutter: almost made me wish for fingers of my own. Bernie opened the door, and we went in. Mercy. It smelled like heaven in Max's Memphis Ribs. We walked up to the counter, and Bernie said, "Looking for Cleon Maxwell."

"Found him," said the man. This was Cleon Maxwell? Pretty confusing: He didn't resemble Boris at all, was black, for one thing.

Bernie picked up the slack, not missing a beat; we were a

good team, me and Bernie, in case that's not clear yet. He handed Cleon Maxwell our card. "Working on a case," he said. "Any chance you've been a victim of identity theft?"

"Tell me about it. Russian gangsters, that's what the cops said. But I slapped a fraud alert on my credit report before too much damage got done."

"Good news," said Bernie. "Did they catch anyone yet?"

Cleon Maxwell shook his head. "They weren't too optimistic on that score." A phone rang, and then another. "Anything else I can help you with?"

"No," said Bernie. "Thanks for your time."

"Don't mention it," said Cleon Maxwell. "Nice-looking dog you've got there. He like ribs, by any chance?"

"Actually," said Bernie, "we both do."

"Take a seat," Cleon Maxwell said.

We sat in the car outside Max's Memphis Ribs, unable to move, either of us. Bernie burped once or twice. "Never eaten so much in my whole life," he said. "But was it good or what?"

Yes and yes! Plus we had two-for-one coupons, courtesy of Cleon Maxwell, possibly the greatest human being in the whole Valley, not counting Bernie, of course. Was there a better job than this? We just sat in the car and breathed, let the world spin. Bernie says the world spins, and if he wants to think that, fine, but I've never noticed it myself. People came and went at Max's Memphis Ribs, looking happy, every single one. After a while, Bernie said, "Rental contract's a dead end. Only one thing to do now, as far as I can see—we've got to go back to the night they grabbed you, pick up the trail."

Picking up the trail: my kind of thing. Energy started flowing back into me right away.

"That means starting at that animal shelter in Sierra Verde."

The animal shelter where Suzie found me? All of a sudden I didn't feel so good. Bernie reached over, gave me a pat. I smelled some of Max's Secret Sauce still on Bernie's hand and licked it off, but deep inside I still felt bad.

TWENTY-TWO

We drove across the Valley, away from the sun. The Valley went on and on. "Look at this," Bernie said at one point, waving his hand around. "All new since the last time I was here." And a little later, "Coronado wasn't the only one. They were all like that." What was this? We were still riding on Coronado? It looked more like a freeway to me. Not long after that, "See what I see? Home Depot. That means a whole new town is on the way." Soon after, he muttered something about Home Depot being the nucleus of some horrible atom. Bernie was losing me, but the breeze, almost hot for a long time, then cooling a bit as we climbed into the mountains, felt great. I could ride shotgun forever, keep going on and on, with some snacks along the way, of course, plus the odd pit stop. "Tell you one thing," Bernie said as we pulled over to gas up, "this is why I'm for Indian casinos, no matter what. They finally get their revenge, and in spades, pardon the pun." No problem—I could forgive Bernie for anything, including puns, whatever they might be. He had some trouble with the credit-card swiper and went inside to pay. Maybe he'd come out with a Slim Jim or two, or even—hey!—a box of bacon bits. Bacon bits: so long since I'd had bacon bits that I'd almost forgotten they existed.

Bernie came out, and I didn't spot Slim Jims or bacon bits, just a big bottle of water. That meant he still wasn't hungry, what with our little session at Max's Memphis Ribs—those coupons had to mean we were going back one day for sure; Bernie loved a bargain—and maybe I wasn't hungry, either, but snacks often happened when we were gassing up. Snacks taste better when you're hungry, but do they ever actually taste bad? I ask you.

Bernie poured water into my traveling bowl, held it out for me. I lapped some up—nice and frosty. Bernie tilted the bottle up to his mouth, gazed at the sky. "What if the monsoons don't come this summer?" he said.

I didn't know.

We drove up and up, angling back and forth in the mountains on a two-lane road, reaching wide-open country, traffic thinning out to mostly just us. I started smelling all kinds of wild smells and— What was that, moving fast up ahead by the side of the highway? A roadrunner? Yes! A real roadrunner. Would you get a load of that little bugger? Oh, how I'd always wanted to—

"Chet? Easy, now."

We flashed by the roadrunner, but not so fast that I didn't catch that tough-guy look in his beady eyes. He veered off, tore into the chaparral, and vanished. Real fast, but my money would be on me.

Not long after that, we climbed a pass at the top of the mountain and started down. The air was fresh, the sky clear, the land stretching on forever. "You can see all the way into New Mexico from here," Bernie said. Mexico: The word gave me a sudden bad feeling, but I didn't know why. Then, as we rolled into a dusty little town, I remembered how Mr. Gulagov had wanted to train me to fight down there, down in Mexico. Was that the same as New Mexico? No idea, but I had a message for Mr. Gulagov: Bernie is with me now, fella. I gave myself a good shake.

"Sierra Verde," Bernie said, slowing down. He glanced at me. "Anything look familiar?"

Nope. Oh, wait a minute. What about that bar back there with the neon martini glass in the window? Maybe—

"Doesn't matter," Bernie said. "We'll start up here." He turned a corner, climbed a side street lined by a few buildings, some boarded up, and parked in front of the last one. Bernie glanced at me from the corner of his eye. That last building, standing behind a tall gate at the end of stone path, a low building of no particular color, with a thin plume of white smoke rising behind it: I knew that building, oh yes; it looked way too familiar. I got down on the floor.

"Hey, boy, everything's okay."

I stayed where I was. A trembling began in my body, not a lot I could do about it.

"C'mon, Chet. Going to need your help."

I climbed back up on the seat.

"Thattaboy. Hop out."

Hopping out of the shotgun seat: I'd done it so many times, but now, maybe because of the trembling, I fell short, slipping back on the seat.

"It's all right, fella." Bernie's face was real hard, that stony look that happened when he was angry. Angry at me? Couldn't be, not with how gentle and soft his voice got when he said, "Take it easy. I'll be right back."

Nope. That was no good, either. I got my back legs under me and hopped out, barely making it. Bernie didn't say anything, just gave me a nice scratch between my ears. We walked up the stone path, side by side. Bernie opened the gate. I caught the scent of my guys, lots and lots of them—my nation, the nation inside a nation, as Bernie said—and it brought back everything about this bad place. I held my head up, and my tail, too, and kept going.

We entered the building, and there I was, back in the small reception room with the counter and lots more smells, including smoky ones I now understood. A man in a white coat stood behind the counter. Did I know him? Impossible to forget: the man who'd promised to have me out of that small building with the metal door and the brick chimney in no time. I hung back a bit.

"Hi, there," said the man in the white coat. "Brought in a stray?"

"No," said Bernie, his face as stony as I'd ever seen it. "Do you recognize him?"

"Who? The dog?"

"His name's Chet. He was in here last week."

The man in the white coat shook his head. "We run a busy place, lots of customers in and out, twenty-four-seven."

"This particular customer," Bernie said, "was claimed by a friend of mine named Suzie Sanchez. She's a reporter for the *Valley Tribune*. Jog your memory at all?"

The man's mouth opened. Pink patches appeared on his face, although I might have been wrong about the exact color. I stopped hanging back, stepped up beside Bernie.

"Suzie would be hard to forget," Bernie said. "Did she mention she's preparing a series on shelters?"

"Uh, it's coming back to me. This here's your dog, was that it? And the reporter, she, uh, happened to . . ."

He ran out of words. Bernie said nothing, just stared at the man.

A silly smile appeared on the man's face, up at one corner, down at the other. "Looks like things worked out in the end," he said.

Bernie didn't agree or disagree. "What I need from you," he said, "is all the information you've got concerning how Chet came to be here."

"'Fraid I wasn't on when—"

"But I'm sure you keep records."

"Oh yes, records, of course." The man moved to a computer, hit some keys. "Here we go." A printer made some machine sounds, very unpleasant to my ears. The man handed Bernie a sheet of paper. Paper was very important to human beings: They spent a lot of their time messing around with it. The appeal was lost on me.

Bernie's eyes moved back and forth over the page. That was reading; it always looked a little weird, in my opinion. He looked up. "All it gives is the date and time of arrival. I want to know who brought him in."

"Wasn't it some biker?"

"The name," said Bernie.

"Doreen was on the desk," the man said. "She might know— one sec." He went through the door at the back. "One sec" was probably a way of saying "stay put," a hint Bernie seemed to miss, because he walked right around the counter and followed the man. I followed Bernie. The man didn't seem to be aware of our presence.

We walked down a corridor I knew, with cells on both sides, chain-link fronts, and one of my guys in each. They all started barking. I didn't recognize a single one from before, but I did recognize the woman up ahead, writing on a clipboard. The man in the white coat raised his voice over all the excitement. "Hey, Do, there some ass—" The woman looked over, saw us. The man in the white coat followed her gaze, went silent. Bernie ignored him, approached the woman, but I missed whatever he said, because at that moment I heard a yip-yip-yip that reminded me of Iggy. Oh no. I turned to the nearest cell: not Iggy but a puppy that looked like Iggy in his younger days. He stuck his nose through one of those tiny squares between the chain links. I ducked down, gave him a bump with my own. He wanted out of there so bad; his soft brown eyes told me that. Did he think I could help? Poor puppy.

"C'mon, Chet, we're out of here," said Bernie.

And moments later we were outside, me and Bernie, back in lovely mountain air. I hopped up onto my seat, clearing the top of the door by plenty, maybe the highest leap ever for me, a personal best. Bernie turned the key and stepped on it, didn't speak till we were back on the main street. "Brrr," he said, as though very cold, actually giving himself a shake, not unlike one of mine. "Okay, Chet, what have we got?"

I waited to hear.

"A big biker, no name. Can you believe they don't even take the names? Plus, she says there's a bar where the bikers some-times hang out, supposed to be just about . . ." Bernie pulled over, parked in front of the bar with the neon martini glass. There were big motorcycles on both sides of us. "Don't even breathe on those hogs," Bernie said. "Not to mention any of your other tricks." Wouldn't dream of it: The bikers were my friends. And what a great name for motorcycles. I knew what hogs could do from my one visit, kind of unplanned, to a pig farm, wouldn't be forgetting that lesson anytime soon.

We went through swinging saloon doors, like the kind in old westerns. At one time we'd watched a lot of old westerns, me and Bernie, but Bernie had kept saying, "See? That's how it used to look." Over and over, until the fun went out of it for him and the westerns finally sank down to the bottom of the DVD pile and stayed there.

We stopped inside the swinging doors and looked around: a few tables and a small stage on one side, a long bar on the other, a pool table at the back, and sawdust on the floor. Sawdust on the floor: what a great idea! Right from the get-go I had to fight the urge to roll around in it.

And bikers, yes; some at the bar, two more playing pool—and one of the pool players was the huge dude. I recognized him right away from his size and wild white beard, but also I could smell him from where I was. Some of the bikers glanced at us, then went back to their beer: They seemed to like those long-neck bottles.

"Can I have your attention for a moment?" Bernie said in a loud, clear voice. Now they all turned. "Do any of you recognize Chet, here?" I felt so many eyes on me; they gave me a funny feeling. I tried twisting my head around almost backward to make it go away.

No one answered Bernie's question. What was going on? These were my bikers—I recognized others beside the huge guy, like the woman with the safety pin through her eyebrow and the short dude with upper arms that reminded me of a Christmas ham Leda had once served. I love Christmas, have I mentioned that already? Maybe I'll get a chance later to explain why. But right now I couldn't understand why my biker buddies—we'd sung together!—were acting so strange. I walked over to the pool table and stood before the huge guy, wagging my tail.

"Chet seems to know you, buddy," Bernie said, coming up to my side.

The huge biker—not many men made Bernie look small, but

this one did—stared down at us and said, "You smell like a cop to me. I'm not buddies with cops."

Hey! Did cops have a smell of their own? If so, I'd never picked it up. Was it possible this huge biker had a better sense of smell than I did? He rose in my estimation, and he was already up pretty high, what with that ride on his bike and all.

"I'm a private detective," Bernie said. "Not a cop."

"Private detective means cop to me," the huge biker said. "We don't like cops."

"Goes without saying," Bernie said. "You're bikers."

Uh-oh. Was that side of Bernie coming out? Why now?

The huge biker's hand tightened its grip on his pool cue. Now he was falling in my estimation, falling fast. "You the smart-ass type?" he said.

"Sure sounds like a fuckin' smart-ass to me," said the ham-arm biker, coming over from the bar. He had a chain dangling in his hand, big and heavy.

Bernie turned to him. "What I say and what you hear may not match up."

"Huh?" said the ham-arm biker.

"But there's no point going into that. I think you guys found Chet out in the desert, for which I'm very grateful. All I want to know is how and where it happened and then we'll be out of here and the fun can resume."

There was a silence. Then the ham-arm biker spoke in one of those mimicking voices, maybe the worst kind of human voice of all. "'The fun can resume,'" he said. And then in his normal voice, also pretty unpleasant: "I think he's a fag besides bein' a smart-ass."

"Well," said Bernie, "at least you're having thoughts. Now try to think back to when you first saw Chet."

"At least I'm what?" said the ham-arm biker, his whole face swelling up, kind of resembling his arms. "You son of a bitch." And he swung the chain at Bernie.

One thing about Bernie: He can really move. And another thing, maybe not too nice, is that some part of him, not often, doesn't mind getting in situations like this, maybe even wants to, separating Bernie from just about every other human I've ever met. Whatever the reason, the chain never landed on Bernie. Instead, it ended up in his own hands and somehow got wrapped around the ham-arm biker's thick neck, and then the ham-arm biker was sprawled at the base of the bar, his eyes rolling up, a sight that got me excited. I nipped at the first leg I saw. There was a grunt from up above, and the huge biker charged at Bernie, swinging the pool cue at Bernie's head. I remembered Bernie saying that swinging was not the way to fight with a pool cue—you had to poke with it—and knew this would be over soon. Bernie stepped inside, did that edge-of-the-hand-to-the-throat slashing thing to the huge biker, who dropped like a tree we'd once taken down.

All the bikers were roaring now and closing in, but Bernie didn't seem to be in a hurry. He knelt on the huge biker's back, grabbed him by the throat, and said, "Everybody calm down if you want him to live."

The bar went silent.

"Okay, big guy," Bernie said. "Let's have it."

In a gasping voice, the huge biker said, "He just come out of nowhere, into our camp, the fuckin' dog, and—"

"His name's Chet."

"Huh?"

"Say 'Chet' instead of 'the fuckin' dog.'"

"Chet," said huge biker.

I felt a breeze behind me, realized I was wagging my tail. Was this a good time for that? I tried to make it stop.

"Go on," said Bernie.

"That's it," said the huge biker. "The fu— Chet come into our camp out of—"

"Where was this?"

"Out on the Apache Wash, hard by the New Mexico line."

"Draw me a map."

"Huh?"

Bernie pointed at the floor. The biker reached out with his enormous hand, drew a map in the sawdust. Bernie gazed at the map, then released his hold on the biker and rose.

"Let's go, boy."

We started toward the swinging doors. None of the bikers said a thing. As he passed the bar, Bernie reached into his pocket and tossed some bills on it. "Next round's on us, ladies, gentlemen," he said. Oh, Bernie: Our finances were a mess; how come he couldn't remember that? But at that moment I didn't care. Was Bernie the best or what? I took a roll in the sawdust on my way out.

TWENTY-THREE

We drove across the desert, following a dirt track that disappeared from time to time, at least to my eyes. "Imagine being a scout in the old days," Bernie said. "Wouldn't that be cool? Like Kit Carson." He was in a very good mood. One of those strange buttes rose off to one side. "What a country! I just want to run over every inch of it, never stop." We rolled along for a bit, and in a lower voice, Bernie added, "Well, maybe not run." And later still: "Gotta get in shape." All of a sudden he looked sad. Why? I didn't get it. I opened my mouth as wide as I could, really stretching it out. Sometimes when I did that, like now, my lip got hooked over one of my teeth. Bernie noticed and smiled a little smile.

The going got bumpy, and Bernie slowed down, weaving around stones and low spiky bushes. After a while a funny look appeared on his face, and he sniffed the air. Don't get me started on the uselessness of the human nose. "Smell anything, Chet?" Bernie said. Where did he want me to start? "Like oil, maybe? Burning oil?" Well, of course. I always smelled burning oil when we were in the Porsche, never thought much about it. Bernie stopped the car, got out, opened the hood, gazed at the engine. I hopped out and trotted around, lifting my leg on some of those spiky bushes and a round rock with a flat rock sitting on top of it—couldn't ignore something like that. Next time I checked, Bernie was under the car, clanging around with one of his tools and grunting. The tools: uh-oh. Nothing good happened after the tools came out. I wandered around a barrel cactus, found an interesting hole in the ground. I stuck my nose in and detected a somewhat fishy smell, not as strong but sharper and more thinned out than the smell from a real fish. That smell meant one thing and one thing only: snake. I yanked my head back. Snakes scare the hell out of me. I'm not ashamed to admit it. But, and this might surprise you, I actually caught one once, fat and black, on a hike we took in high piney country somewhere. What got into me that day? We were walking along, me and Bernie, and all of a sudden—

"Chet? Looks like we're good to go."

I glanced over. Bernie, nose smudged with grease, was pouring some liquid into a funnel sticking out of the engine; we kept cans of this and that in the trunk. He closed the hood, and soon we were back on the road, all by ourselves in the great outdoors. I still smelled burning oil, but Bernie seemed happy. "This car's gonna last forever," he said. That was what I liked to hear.

We passed some weird rock formations, the shadows of everything—including the car and our own heads—growing longer and longer, reaching out ahead of us. A low, round hill appeared in the distance, stony and red—but don't take my word for it on the red part—and at its base I spotted a squarish shape, the kind of shape that meant humanity. We went by a squashed beer can, then another. "Getting there," Bernie said. He had a knowing look on his face, probably just like those long-ago scouts he'd been talking about. Had Kit Carson followed beer cans across the desert?

Not long after, the track crossed one of those dried-up stream-beds, rocky in the middle but with a few greenish dwarf-size trees along the sides. "The Apache Wash," Bernie said. "Water down there, and plenty of it—but for how long?" I looked and saw no water, not a drop. Sometimes I worried about Bernie. This water thing was driving him crazy. I rested my paw on his leg. "Hey, boy," he said, and we bumped up the other side of the wash. The track kind of petered out after that, but by then we were practi-cally at the base of the low hill, and I could see that the squarish shape was the falling-down shack by the bikers' old campfire.

We parked by the shack, got out, walked over to the black-ened fire pit. Bernie kicked at a bottle or two, picked up the butt end of a joint, peered into the shack. I dug up a charred burger piece and made quick work of it. Bernie turned. "Chet! What are you eating?"

Nothing. It was true. The eating part was over. I sniffed around at this and that, went into a quick trot, looked busy. Ber-nie returned to the car, took the binoculars from the glove box, trained them on some faraway hills, pinkish—I thought—in the fading light. I didn't like the binoculars, especially when he put them up to his face, almost plugging his eyes in to the thing. Humans were already a little too close to machines for my comfort.

"Chet. Ease up."

Was that me, making a sound not too distant from whining? I eased up. Bernie scanned the distance for a while, then lowered the binoculars. He sat on a rock, unfolded a map, laid it on his lap. I sat beside him. He patted his pockets in that familiar way, checking for cigarettes, even though, trying to quit, he never car-ried any. "You wandered into this campsite, Chet, but from what direction? Where did you start?"

I sat beside Bernie, waited for him to figure it out. Meanwhile, I was getting hungry. Any chance of more charred burgers lying around? I sniffed the air: buzzards, Bernie's aftershave, gasoline, burned mesquite, and yes, water, real free-running unbottled water, even with none to be seen, but no burgers. And also: that sharp, fishy smell. I shifted closer to Bernie.

He folded up the map, stuck it in his back pocket, turned to me. "Think you can remember, boy?" he said. "How you got here?" He scratched between my ears, found a spot that desperately needed scratching, even though I hadn't known. "We don't have a whole lot of options right now."

What was he asking? How we got here? Of course I remembered, of course I could lead the way!

"Easy, Chet, easy."

Oops. What was I doing, my front paws up on his shoulders like that? I settled back down on all fours. Bernie went to the car, came back with the flashlight and our .38 special, which he tucked into his belt. I loved that .38 special. Bernie was a crack shot. I'd seen him on the range—loved the range, too, but he'd only taken me there once, on account of the whole experience being a bit too exciting. Of course, I'd been younger then, would probably handle it much better now. I gazed at the .38 special. Take a potshot at something, Bernie. Anything! Coke bottles on a fence rail, for example. Smithereens! But the .38 special stayed in his belt.

"Want some water?" he said.

Good idea. I was thirsty, hadn't even realized it. Bernie filled my bowl. I drank.

"All set?" he said. "Lead the way."

I walked over to the campfire, pawed at the ashes, then circled around and headed into open country, away from the sun, my

shadow in front of me, a long, long Chet and getting longer. After
a while I sniffed the ground and changed direction. We angled
toward those pinkish hills, Bernie a few steps behind, my nose in
the air, but more often to the ground. I was searching for the most
familiar scent in the whole wide world, namely my own. Pick up
my own scent, follow it back to Mr. Gulagov's ranch with that terrible old mine, get my teeth on a pant leg or two, case closed.

But my scent: Where was it? I changed direction again, headed
toward a flat, barren stretch and a shriveled grayish plant, the only
living thing around. I sniffed at the base of the plant, stuck my
nose right against its leaves, if that was what they were, long waxy
things with, uh-oh: spines. Too late.

We took a short break while Bernie removed the spines. Then
I went right back to the plant.

"Chet, for God's sake."

I sniffed and sniffed, and maybe because I'd disturbed it some,
the plant gave up its secret: a faint, almost undetectable smell of
old leather, salt and pepper, mink coats, a soupçon of tomato; and
to be honest, a healthy dash of something male and funky. My
smell: yes sir. My smell and my smell only, undeniable evidence
that Chet the Jet had passed this way.

"Onto something, boy?"

Yup. I got my nose right down in the hard-packed dirt,
warmer than the air now—the heat of the day still caught in the
earth—and sniffed around for more traces of me. It took what
seemed like a long time, but then, near a rusty scrap of something
human-made but no longer identifiable, I caught another whiff,
even fainter than the first, almost not there. I turned toward those
pinkish hills, to the tallest one down at one end, went into a slow
trot, nose down. Another whiff? I thought so, and changed direction again. Then came a long spell with no more scent, and when

I looked up, those far-off hills were still far-off but no longer pink except at the very top of the tallest one; and our shadows no longer showed. Instead, shadow covered everything, and the sky was darkening.

"How you doin'?" Bernie said.

The wind rose, blowing from the distant hills. I raised my nose and tested it. How was I doing? Great. We could do this. But the truth was that the wind brought nothing, *nada,* zip, and that surprised me: The wind was usually my friend. I changed direction a bit, sniffed at some tumbleweed. Buzzard again—a snap to identify buzzard stink—and maybe some kind of lizard, but nothing of me. The wind blew harder, and the tumbleweed rolled away.

Night fell, an endless black sky full of stars, and soon the moon as well, round and white. Bernie had all these strange ideas about the moon—like it had no light of its own and had once been part of the earth—but all I knew was that it did things to me; hard to explain, but I felt my sharpest in moonlight. And this moonlight was the brightest I remembered. Bernie, whatever his beliefs about moonlight, didn't have to switch on the flash, not once.

We kept going, the only sound coming from the wind; Bernie and I knew how to move in silence. Once I spotted a gleam, hurried to it, sniffed at a shard of glass. Something there? Maybe, just maybe, a hint of mink, my minkness. I changed direction again, went into a slow zigzag, searching, searching. The moon moved across the sky. I picked up this and that—no more minkness, but the soupçon of tomato a couple times, and once the male funkiness, certainly mine—and changed direction and changed again, and maybe once more. Bernie walked along beside me. Sometimes, when I went into my trot, he had to jog, his heavy breathing breaking the silence. Time passed, maybe lots of it. He didn't say a word. I could feel his confidence. Bernie believed in me. That made me even stronger than my normal self. I could keep searching all night if I had to.

And then: at last! Up ahead I spotted a sign on a post, even though we were in the middle of nowhere: a sign I remembered, a sign I'd seen the night of my flight from Mr. Gulagov's. I ran to it, Bernie following. Now he did use the flash, shining it on the sign. I could see how worn it was, the letters faded almost all away. Bernie brushed his hand lightly over the wood and said, "'Ghost' something or other, it looks like. 'Five miles.'" He turned to me. "'Ghost Town,' most likely—lots of them around. Were you here, Chet?" "Ghost Town" didn't mean anything to me, but was I here? Oh yes. I took a step or two closer to the sign and suddenly got hit by my smell, the most potent shot of it so far. I took off.

"Chet! Chet! Slow down."

I tried to slow down but had a hard time, what with the way the smell kept getting stronger and stronger. I trotted ahead, ran back, circled Bernie, kept going. We went on and on like that, but I didn't get tired at all, hardly noticed when the moon sank from sight, the stars dimmed, the sky paled. We were on track, following that scent, no doubt about it, every component in place: old leather, salt and pepper, mink coats, soupçon of tomato, plus the funky part. This was it! I started running, couldn't hold back. For a while I heard Bernie running behind me, but then he stopped. I turned back to look. He wasn't running, in fact had ramped down to a slow walk. Bernie! Come on! I turned, charged ahead, my scent everywhere, and was reaching full speed when—

What was this? Beer cans? The remains of a fire? A falling-down shack? Oh no. We were back at the biker's campsite? How could that be? We'd searched all night. I froze, one front paw poised in the air.

Bernie came up beside me. "Looks like we've gone in circles, boy," he said quietly. I lowered my paw, lowered my head, too.

Daylight spread across the desert, revealing how dusty we were, me and Bernie. Dusty because of the wind that had risen during the night? I didn't know. In the light, I could also see that Bernie had raccoon eyes again. "Sure is pretty," he said, "the desert at dawn." Not to me, not at that moment: I felt so bad about my failure I couldn't look at Bernie's face. We got in the car, crossed over the Apache Wash, found the track, drove back up into the mountains and back into Sierra Verde. I lay on my seat, tired; but allowing myself to sleep? No way.

"Hungry, boy?" he said.

I was, but allowing myself to eat? No way. Bernie stopped the car. I sat up. We were parked in front of a convenience store. Bernie took the .38 special from his belt, tucked it in the back of the glove box, and was reaching for his door handle when out of the convenience store came a man carrying a bag of groceries. A little dude, very thin, with arm tattoos and spiky hair.

Bernie went still. "Don't move a muscle," he said, so quietly I almost couldn't hear.

I didn't move a muscle, didn't even breathe. This little spiky-haired tattooed dude? We knew him, me and Bernie, oh yeah: Anatoly Bulganin, projectionist at the Golden Palm Movie Palace in Las Vegas. We were far from Vegas: I knew that very well. And I knew Bernie. Right now Bernie would be thinking: What's the little dude doing here? I perked right up.

TWENTY-FOUR

Anatoly Bulganin, spiky-haired projectionist, walked across the parking lot, popped the trunk of a car, and lowered the groceries inside, not looking once in our direction. Had Bernie told me what a projectionist did? Couldn't remember, but I knew it was something no good, just from the sound.

"Bingo," Bernie said, voice lowered.

Bingo? Why bingo? Wasn't that some strange game Bernie had played one night at the Patrolmen's Benevolent Association fund-raiser, a game he might have won except for an unfortunate incident involving my tail and his card with the little markers?

"See that car?" Bernie said. "Blue BMW." He got out of the Porsche. Anatoly, closing the trunk of the BMW, turned and saw Bernie. Anatoly's face did funny things. "Hi, Anatoly," Bernie said. "A little far from home, are we not?"

"I, uh," said Anatoly. Then, surprisingly quick, he raced around to the driver's door of the BMW and flung it open, not even taking the time to fully close the trunk, which sprang back up. By then I was springing, too. I landed on the pavement, bounded past Bernie, and launched myself at Anatoly. An instant too late: The driver's door slammed shut with him inside, and I hit the hard steel with a thump that sent me somersaulting backward. The next thing I knew, the BMW was peeling out of the lot, missing me by not much.

"Chet? You all right?"

I rolled over, rose, unsteady at first, but then fine. Fine and just a bit mad.

"Let's roll."

I was more than ready. We hopped in the Porsche and took off after Anatoly the projectionist. He was doomed, just didn't know it.

The Beemer roared down the main street, passed the bar with the neon martini glass in the window—no hogs parked outside, but it was still early—and swung up a side street, tires smoking. Bernie didn't drive nearly as fast—he wouldn't do that in a populated place—so when we got to the side street, there was no sign of Anatoly. We rumbled up the side street, past the last houses and into open country, and then Bernie floored it. Almost right away the pavement ended; the Beemer was still out of sight, but Anatoly's dust hung in the air, telltale dust and plenty of it. Our engine made a deep throaty sound, like some powerful beast. Was a car a kind of machine? Couldn't be. Machines I had problems with, but cars I loved.

The road—getting narrower and bumpier—twisted up and up into the mountains. Bernie was a great driver—have I mentioned that already? We skidded around corners, zooming, but the nose of the Porsche always kept pointing straight ahead. And the look on Bernie's face? The best, the look of the hunter with the prey in view. Maybe not quite in view yet, but message to Anatoly: You're toast. I'd been in a few car chases like this—one of the very best perks in our line of work, car chases—and they always ended the same way, with some perp's pant leg between my teeth.

The road took us higher and higher, steep rocky slopes looming on one side, a sheer cliff dropping off on the other. Bernie geared down—I loved gearing down, especially how the revving went up at the same time, pushing me back in my seat—Bernie was a master! What was more fun than this? Huh? I ask you.

But where was I?

On Anatoly's heels, with Bernie gearing down. We leaned in to a sharp curve, a curve where the drop-off side jutted way out, and from there we could see another curve like it up ahead, and rounding that curve, trailed by clouds of dust: the blue BMW, its still-open trunk bobbing up and down. Only a matter of time: a favorite human expression, although not of mine—anything about time had a way of sliding away from me, like a bar of soap I'd once tried to corral on the bathroom floor. But I knew the expression was right for a moment like this, and I started salivating the way I always did when we were about to snap up the perp.

The Beemer disappeared around the bend. Bernie changed gears, and we bombed down a short straightaway, then hit the next bend, the same bend where we'd seen Anatoly moments before. Around the bend, the road narrowed and roughened, rising on another long curving stretch, the Beemer not even halfway up. We were gaining, and gaining fast. Some spiky-headed little piddler was going to outdrive Bernie? Dream on.

We closed in, Bernie downshifting, upshifting, hands and feet doing maneuvers, making adjustments nonstop. Now I could see Anatoly's head through the back window of the BMW. His head changed angles, maybe because he was checking the rearview mirror. Scary sight, was it not, buddy boy, the Little Detective Agency in hot pursuit? The Beemer sped up, then started fishtailing, the back end whipping more and more wildly, the whole car skidding closer and closer to the cliff edge, and at the point where it was about to shoot off into the air—did I mention there was no barrier of any kind?—it suddenly straightened, groceries flying out of the trunk, and kept going. An apple soared up into the blue; I had a crazy urge to retrieve it. What was that about? Bad idea, I knew that, but I couldn't help wondering: Could it be done?

With all that back-and-forthing, Anatoly had lost a lot more ground. We closed in fast, everything flashing by—curve after curve; the rocky slopes on one side; dust boiling up from the wheels of the Beemer; and the drop-off on the other side—as though we were skirting the edge of the sky itself. I was sitting straight up, even straighter than straight up—in fact, I had my front paws on top of the windshield frame—ready, able, willing. Anatoly checked the rearview mirror again—now I could even see his eyes, open wide in fear, and I could smell his fear, too—and Bernie held up his hand palm out in the sign that meant stop. But Anatoly didn't stop, even sped up as he took another bend, the Beemer's rear end losing traction, sliding, sliding; and at that moment Bernie did the most amazing thing: He turned the wheel hard, downshifting at the same time, and shot past the Beemer on the rocky-slope side.

Now we were in front, and Anatoly was eating our dust! How perfect was that? "Next we slow this little caravan down," said Bernie. One word for Bernie: genius. "And then we ticket him for littering," he added. Littering? I didn't get that, was still turning it over in my mind when— Boom! Something went wrong. First an actual boom that seemed to come from right under us—oh no, car trouble now?—and then a black cloud, thick and wet, erupted from under the hood and splashed over the windshield, blinding us.

Things happened fast after that. We started spinning, round and round on the narrow road, spinning and skidding at the same time, skimming the rocky base of the steep slope, sparks flying everywhere, then veering the other way, one wheel spraying loose gravel off the very edge, the rubber maybe even slipping a little bit over, out into nothing, and the whole time Bernie's face didn't change at all as he shifted, braked, twisted the wheel this way and that. But we couldn't see, not through the blackened windshield. And still, all the time, spinning and spinning. Did the Beemer flash by, ahead of us once more? I thought so. But I couldn't be sure, and at that moment I had other things to think about, like the way we were colliding with the base of the rocky slope again, harder this time, so hard I shot up and out of my seat.

Then came a horrible moment when I soared through open sky—I've had nightmares like that—up and up and suddenly down. I landed hard but on all fours. Oh, so good to have all fours. I wasn't on them for long, flipping over and over, coming to rest at last in the middle of the road, breathless but unhurt. I gave myself a good shake, saw the Porsche up ahead, straightening out, slowing down, Bernie back in control: We were going to be okay. But then—what was that? A huge rock came tumbling down from the steep slope and thudded onto the road, right in front of Bernie. Nothing he could do: The Porsche hit the rock dead on, bounced end over end, took off into the air, and hurtled over the drop-off on the other side of the road, vanishing from view.

Bernie!

The next thing I knew, I was standing at the edge, peering down. Way, way below, the Porsche spun through emptiness, down, down, down, finally crashing on a wide, rocky ledge and exploding in flames. Then it was very quiet, the only sound my own breathing.

Bernie!

"Chet?"

I looked down. There, clinging with one hand to a tiny out-crop in the cliff, was Bernie, face all bloody, almost in my reach. Our eyes met. The muscles in his arm popped out like thick cables as he tried to pull himself up to the edge. But he couldn't do it, not with one hand, and there was no place for his other hand to grip, the cliff face so sheer. I leaned over the edge.

"No, boy."

Didn't hear that. I leaned over the edge some more, front paws digging down into the cliff face, back paws anchored with all my strength on the road. Then I lowered my head, stretching out as far as I could, but it wasn't far enough. I couldn't quite reach Bernie.

"Back off, boy."

Out of the question. We stayed like that, heads almost in touching distance, the muscles in Bernie's arm straining. Then he got an idea. I saw it in his eyes, had seen that look many times. He reached down with his free hand, unbuckled his belt, slipped it off, got a good grip on one end, then flipped the buckle end up to me. I caught it in my mouth, clamped down with a force that couldn't be broken.

"On two," Bernie said. I got ready. "One, two."

I hauled back with all my might. Bernie held on to the belt, at the same time pulling with his other hand, the one with a grip on that single outcrop in the cliff face. He rose, slow, so slow, but up, and up a little bit more. My muscles—down my neck, down my back, into my legs—were on fire. Up and up came Bernie, eyes now level with the edge. Did he look afraid? Not at all, not to me. He let go of the outcrop and reached out—for one moment held up only by the belt—and got his free hand on flat ground, pressing down hard. At that same instant I hauled once more with everything I had, and he was up, first his upper body flopping on the road and then all of him wriggling to safety!

He hugged me. "It's okay, Chet, you can let go."

I tried to let go of the belt buckle, but it was caught between my teeth. Bernie got it loose. I licked his face, tasting his blood and sweat. He held my head in his hands, gave it a squeeze.

"Gotta lose ten pounds," he said. "Maybe fifteen." I wasn't sure how much that was, and anyway, Bernie looked fine to me; at the same time, I couldn't help thinking that a little reduction on his part would make the hauling easier if we ever had to do this again.

The whole world was still, except for the faint hum of a far-off engine. We followed the sound and, on a distant road part way up another mountain, saw a moving blue dot. "At least I got the plate number." That was Bernie, right there, way ahead of the other guy. He stroked my back. I laid my ears down flat. "I owe you, boy, big-time," he said.

A ridiculous suggestion. We were partners.

We got up, went to the edge, gazed down at the smoking remains of the Porsche. "It was on its last legs anyway," Bernie said. "We'll get another one." Last legs? What was he talking about? And where would we get another one as good, the coolest car on the road? Impossible. Plus, there was the question of money. Our finances were a mess. Bernie was a genius, so why couldn't he remember that and accept that we would have to make do with the crummy old pickup? "Nevada plate on that Beemer," said. He smiled at me. "C3P 2Z9—hang on to that." Impossible to be mad at Bernie. We started walking.

Back at home, tired, hungry, and thirsty. Bernie paid off the taxi driver—we'd also hitched rides with a trucker and a missionary, and ridden on two public buses—and we went inside. The message light was flashing. I went over to my water bowl and drank it dry. Bernie grabbed the bourbon bottle from the cupboard over the sink, pressed a button on the message machine.

"Cynthia Chambliss here." She sounded excited. "I've had a call from Madison. She's fine, says she's coming home soon—just working out a few things. We shouldn't worry, she says, and please don't waste a lot of time and money looking for her. Um, thought you should know. Have you sent your bill to Damon yet? I want to tell you how grateful—"

Bernie picked up the phone, dialed a number. "Hello, Cynthia? Bernie Little. I got your message and—" He paused. I could hear her voice on the other end, high and kind of strange. "I'm fine," Bernie said. "Why wouldn't I be?" Another pause. "Who told you that?" Bernie said, putting the bourbon bottle down on the counter, unopened. "Cynthia?" he said. "Any chance you taped that call with Madison?" He listened. "That was smart. I'd like to hear it." He paused again. I heard silence on the other end. "Won't take long," Bernie said. "We'll be right over." Cynthia started to say something that sounded like the beginning of "no," but Bernie hung up.

He turned to me. "Damon told her I'd been killed in a wreck." He reached for the pickup keys, hanging on a hook by the fridge. "What would make him think something like that?"

No clue. Did we have to get to the bottom of it now? What about dinner?

TWENTY-FIVE

"Light my fire," said Cap'n Crunch in that horrible croak of his. Oh, brother, if only I could, like right under your scaly yellow feet. He stood on his perch—the cage on Cynthia's kitchen counter now, not in Madison's bedroom—and stared at me with his wicked little eyes. His weird spiky comb seemed to have grown since the last time I'd seen him, looked the size of his whole head or even bigger. He didn't like me, was anything more obvious? Right back at ya, amigo.

"Coffee?" said Cynthia. She'd changed, too, looked older, thinner, more pinched up, with lines on her face I hadn't noticed before; but humans, especially the females, were tricky that way—maybe I was noticing because she had her hair pulled back in a ponytail and wore no makeup.

"I'd like to get right to the call," Bernie said.

"Of course," Cynthia said, moving to a phone. "I can't tell you how wonderful it was to hear her voice. We can get past this."

"Past what?" said Bernie.

"Why, whatever's troubling her," said Cynthia. She bit her

lip—I'm always on the lookout for that one—and added, "Maddy was at such a vulnerable age—I see that now."

"When was this?" Bernie said.

The pinched-up grooves between Cynthia's eyes deepened. "When Damon and I got divorced. At the time she didn't seem too affected—so many of her friends come from brok— from blended families, that kind of thing. But now I see—even though divorce is better for kids than a bad marriage, maybe for a girl like Maddy, so bright and sensitive . . ." She looked at the floor, her voice trailing off.

"How bad a marriage was it?" Bernie said.

"You don't agree?" she said. "About divorce being better for kids than a bad marriage?"

A muscle jumped in the side of Bernie's face. "I'm not agreeing or disagreeing," he said. "I'm just asking about the marriage."

Cynthia's eyes went blurry. "Does it matter now?"

"I don't know," Bernie said. "I'm trying to put things together. We've got a lot of loose ends."

"What do you mean?" Cynthia said.

We had nothing but loose ends, as far as I was concerned.

"We can get to that," Bernie said. "First the call."

Cynthia's finger hovered over the buttons on the phone cradle. "It happened yesterday. So lucky not to miss it—I was halfway out the door, literally." She pressed one of the buttons.

"Hello? Hello? Mom?"

I knew that voice, a voice I liked very much: Madison's voice. She'd said, "Don't you hurt that dog." Hard to forget something like that, and I never would. You can take it to the bank, whatever that means.

"Mom? Are you there? It's me, Maddy."

Bernie's face was very still. He had his head tilted a bit to one side. I realized that I did, too.

Then came a click, and in a breathless voice, Cynthia said, "Maddy? Maddy? Is that you?"

"Hi, Mom, it's me."

"Maddy! Sweetheart, oh my God! Are you all right? Where are—"

"I'm fine, Mom, just . . ." There was a pause, and in that pause I thought I heard her choking up, the way humans did when they were about to cry, but then she seemed to take a deep breath and went on. ". . . just working some things out, that's all."

"What kind of things? I've been worried sick. We've been looking all over, the police, a private detective, everybody. Where are—"

"Don't worry, Mom. I'm fine. That's why I called. Don't worry—and don't waste a lot of time and money looking for me. I'll be home soon, Mom."

"How soon?"

"Soon."

"But when?"

"Soon, Mom. And you know what?"

"What?"

"I've been thinking it might be nice to get a dog."

"A dog?"

"A big funny-looking dog, maybe like one I saw the other day, with mismatched ears. Is there a ghost of a chance we could do that?"

Bernie's face went pale, all the color draining out of it. Had I even seen that before?

"Of course, we can get a dog, but when—"

"Got to go, Mom. Love you."

Click.

Bernie looked at Cynthia, then at me. His body was very still, a stillness I could feel. I knew he was thinking fast; about what, I had no idea. I had a thought of my own: Are mismatched ears necessarily a bad thing?

Bernie went to the machine, hit a button or two. Funny sounds of people talking way too fast started up, then slowed, and I heard again: "A big funny-looking dog, maybe like one I saw the other day, with mismatched ears. Is there a ghost of a chance we could do that?"

"We never had any fights about having a dog, if that's what you're thinking," Cynthia said.

"I wasn't," Bernie said.

Cynthia didn't seem to hear. "I mean, she wanted Cap'n Crunch, and I said yes right away."

Big, big mistake.

Cap'n Crunch raised his wings in a way that reminded me of Count Dracula and said, "Make it a double."

"Is a dog some sort of replacement?" Cynthia said. "Is that where you're going with this—a consolation prize for the parents splitting up?"

Hard to follow, but "consolation prize" sounded offensive to me. And funny-looking? Where did that come from?

"That's not where I'm going with this," Bernie said. Color returned to his face, and he looked more like himself; for a moment or two I'd been worried.

"Then explain," said Cynthia.

"Your daughter's a very smart girl."

Cynthia nodded. "But what's that got to do with the call?" Bernie didn't answer right away. He had a hard look on his face, a look Cynthia couldn't miss. "She's telling the truth, isn't she?" Cynthia said.

"About what?" Bernie said.

"About coming home soon. You agree on that, don't you? Sergeant Torres does."

"You played it for him?"

"He was here a couple hours ago. He agrees. She's coming home."

Bernie nodded, a nod Cynthia probably took for his own agreement, but I knew better: That slight nod of Bernie's could mean anything, all part of his interviewing skill.

"Good," said Cynthia. "Because why else would she call? She doesn't want me to worry, even though I've been worried half to death." Her eyes filled with tears; they overflowed and ran down her face.

"Um," said Bernie, looking uncomfortable. "Uh." He patted his pockets, hoping to find who knew what. Cynthia walked quickly from the room. Bernie turned to me. "You saw Madison, didn't you, boy? You nailed the whole thing, and I didn't even know."

I wagged my tail. What else could I do? But had I nailed it, cracked the case? No, because we didn't have her. So maybe I'd actually screwed up. My tail went still.

"Good work, boy," Bernie said. "The best. But whatever you're planning with this bird? Forget it."

Whoa. What was that supposed to mean? Sure, the distance from me to the birdcage seemed to have shrunk quite a bit somehow; I was actually nearing striking range, if anything like that had been on my mind, instead of the furthest thing from it, which was the honest truth and nothing but.

"Chet?"

I sidled away from the counter, sat with my back to Cap'n Crunch. Cynthia returned, dabbing her face with a tissue. "My apologies," she said.

"Nothing to apologize about," said Bernie. "I'm assuming Damon knows about this call."

"Oh yes. I told him right away."

"Did he come over to listen to it?"

"No. But I gave him a description. We don't have an especially good relationship, even for exes after all this time, but we trust each other in this one area."

"What area is that?" Bernie said.

"Maddy and her welfare. She's the best thing either of us has ever done. Non-parents might not understand that. Sorry, I don't remember if you have kids."

Bernie had that hard look again.

Did Cynthia seem a little scared? I'd seen Bernie do that to clients before. "That, uh, cut on your face seems to be bleeding a little," she said.

"Dull razor," said Bernie, dabbing at the cut with his sleeve. Dull razor? True, Bernie did get shaving cuts, plenty of times, but a shaving cut on the forehead? I realized he was deliberately saying nothing about our adventures on that high mountain road out of Sierra Verde. How come? No idea. I eased myself the tiniest bit closer to Cap'n Crunch. The Cap'n shifted nervously on his perch. "I'd like to get the time line straight," Bernie said.

"What time line?"

"One," said Bernie, "exactly when this call came through. Two—when you called Damon. Three—when you called me. Four—when Damon told you about my supposed death."

Uh-oh. At times like this, when Bernie got going with one of those rapid-fire numbered lists of his, I couldn't focus. Cynthia gave some kind of answer. Bernie came back at her with more questions, this time counting them off on his fingers. The words all mushed together, became background noise, not particularly unpleasant. I found myself inching over toward the Cap'n, possibly entering bumping-the-cage territory. Cynthia's countertop was kind of high. If I could just get my nose above the—

"Up yours," Cap'n Crunch cried out in his wretched squawk, at the same time rising off his perch a bit, wings in the Dracula spread again. Up yours? I thought he could only say: Make it a double, light my fire, Madison rocks. Now he'd added "up yours"? Infuriating. I wanted to—

"Chet?"

I tried to look innocent, not so easy with one paw up on the counter. I lowered it in a subtle way. Bernie gave me a nice pat; at least that was what I thought, until I realized he had a good grip on my collar.

"One last thing," he said. "Where did Damon get this idea I'd been killed in an accident?"

"He told me he'd heard it," Cynthia said.

"Where?"

"He didn't say."

"Do me a favor," Bernie said. "Let him keep thinking it's true."

"Too late," Cynthia said. "I already told him. Did I do wrong?"

"No," Bernie said.

"And why wouldn't you want Damon to know? What's going on?"

"I'll explain later," Bernie said. "Got to go."

"I don't understand," Cynthia said.

Me, neither, but it didn't bother me: I was much more used to Bernie and his ways.

---

* * *

"What happened to you?" said Rick Torres.

"Dull razor," said Bernie.

"Uh-huh," said Rick.

We were in the Donut Heaven lot, parked cop-style, driver door to driver door. Bernie bit into a chocolate-glazed doughnut; Rick and I were working on crullers with a nice dusting of powdered sugar.

"You heard the tape?" Bernie said.

"Yup."

"Pretty smart of Cynthia, thinking to record the call."

"Your point?" said Rick.

"No point. Showed presence of mind, that's all."

"Your point?"

"No point."

"Hey, Chet," Rick said, looking past Bernie. "Got an extra cruller here, big guy."

Yes, please. Regular meals didn't seem to be happening lately, and I was famished.

"Empty calories," Bernie said, holding up his hand. The extra cruller stayed in the cruiser. He stirred his coffee with his finger. "The tape."

"Seemed kosher to me," Rick said.

Kosher: I knew that word; it had something to do with chicken, specifically, the best chicken I'd ever tasted, at the celebration dinner after the final stakeout in the Teitelbaum divorce. I waited to hear how chickens were coming into the case.

"The girl just ran off to get her head straight?" Bernie said.

"Happens all the time."

"With kids like her?"

"Who knows what she's really like?" said Rick. Hey, I did: She was great. "But first we get a photo of her walking alone out of some theater in Vegas," Rick went on, "and now this call. Plus—no ransom demand, the biggest marker of all in my book. So, since I understand you're off the case anyway, and pro bono work in the private-eye sector was unheard of till you came along, why not wait, see if she turns up in the next few days?"

"What about you?" Bernie said. "Are you off the case?"

"There is no case, Bernie. That's what I'm trying to tell you."

Bernie's voice sharpened. "Did you at least run a trace on that call?"

"Don't take your frustration out on me," Rick said. Bernie was silent. "Yeah," Rick went on, "we ran a trace, or tried to. But the call came from a pay phone, could have been anywhere."

"What does that show you?" Bernie said.

"Shows me the girl used a pay phone."

"Where does anybody find a pay phone these days?" Bernie said.

Rick pointed. A pay phone stood in the far corner of the Donut Heaven lot.

"I meant," said Bernie, "why go to the trouble of finding one if you're coming home anyway?"

"There you go again."

"Where?"

"Reading too much into things."

"I don't."

"You do, always have. Not everything adds up. There's randomness, disorder, pieces that don't fit."

"Only because we're not smart enough to make them fit."

They went back and forth like that. I got sleepy.

"How's this for a piece?" Bernie was saying. "We found that blue Beemer."

Rick gazed at Bernie, then flipped open a notebook, leafed through. "The one with a supposed blond driver?"

"He wasn't in it," Bernie said. "But the movie-theater projectionist was."

"From Vegas?"

"Name's Anatoly Bulganin."

"Where was this?"

"Up in Sierra Verde."

"What's his story?"

"We never got that close."

Rick's eyes went to the cut on Bernie's forehead. "The plate?"

"Nevada," Bernie said. "C3P 2Z9."

"I'll run it," Rick said. "But don't be surprised if it adds up to even less than we've got now." He licked powdered sugar off his lips. I did the same.

TWENTY-SIX

"Clues in plain sight," Bernie said, more of a muttering, really. "Ain't that always the way?" He'd been doing a lot of muttering on the drive from Donut Heaven to wherever we were going. I didn't care—riding shotgun to any place was fine with me. All in all, I preferred the Porsche, but the nice thing about riding shotgun in the pickup was how high we were. Looking down into all those cars added a lot to the fun; why, I didn't know. I stuck my head out the window. The air was starting to heat up—summer on the way, according to Bernie—but we were the windows-open, AC-off type; the type, he sometimes said, that won the West.

"Here's a way of analyzing it," Bernie said. Uh-oh. Analyzing—probably not my strength. "Let's begin by asking one simple question. Of everybody we've met on this whole case, from the moment Cynthia Chambliss came driving up the street, who's the least trustworthy?"

Hey. Analyzing turned out to be a snap. The answer to the least trustworthy question was obviously Cap'n Crunch; one glimpse of his tiny wicked eyes and you knew that. But then where were we? Cap'n Crunch lived in a cage, and even supposing he managed to get out at night, say, and fly around, where could he possibly—

"Only one answer," Bernie said. "Damon Keefer."

Damon Keefer? Damon Keefer over Cap'n Crunch? Wasn't so sure, myself. But then I remembered how Keefer smelled of cat, and also remembered that specific cat of his, Prince, with his snooty ways; and I got on board. Bernie was right, as usual. Down in a passing car, a woman behind the wheel was talking on a cell phone while a member of my tribe in the backseat had her head in a grocery bag, corkscrew tail wagging wildly. I kind of liked that corkscrew tail, was starting to wonder about—

"And what do we do when we find a weak link?" Bernie said.

I tucked my head back inside the cab. No idea about the answer to Bernie's question, but that word "link" reminded me right away of the choke chain and Mr. Gulagov. He'd tried to change my name to Stalin! My name was Chet.

Bernie glanced at me. "Exactly right," he said, and only then did I realize I was growling. "When we find a weak link, we apply the pressure and keep it there till something gives. All set?"

No need to ask.

We tracked down Damon Keefer at his house, the huge house with walls around it and that strange fire-hydrant sculpture on the lawn. The sculpture wasn't actually on the lawn at the moment; a lush green lawn—I didn't have to look at Bernie to know he was frowning. Instead, the sculpture was up in the air, dangling from a hook on a crane mounted on a big truck. Exciting stuff, and I couldn't wait to get out of the pickup to see if I could jump up and touch the thing, but we just sat there while Bernie watched. Soon the crane swung the sculpture onto the bed of the truck, and the truck drove off. The men at the controls were vague shapes behind the windows of their cabs. The machines almost could have been doing all the work by themselves. That gave me a bad feeling. I nipped at a tuft on my coat and felt better.

Time for some action? Nope; we kept waiting, don't ask me why. But if Bernie thought waiting was best, we waited. We had our MO, me and Bernie. After a while Damon Keefer came out of the house, barefoot and wearing a bathrobe. He walked around the empty spot where the sculpture had stood. I noticed white flecks in his goatee, a new development, matching those new lines on Cynthia's face in a way I couldn't explain. Were we getting out now? I glanced at Bernie: yes.

I smelled booze on Keefer's breath the moment my first paw touched down. Hard to believe, maybe, from all the way across the lawn, but my sense of smell is probably better than yours—or have I mentioned that already?

Keefer looked up and saw us. "What the hell are you doing here?" he said. I remembered that way he had of saying unpleasant things in a low, quiet voice, and didn't like it any better.

"Where'd the sculpture go?" Bernie said.

"What's that got to do with you?" said Keefer.

"I kind of liked it," Bernie said. "But I'm no art expert."

"Are you an expert at anything?"

"We're going to find out," Bernie said.

Keefer's chin rose, one of those signs of human aggression, kind of strange on account of how it exposed the chin to a good hard smack, and I'd seen what a good hard smack on the human chin could do, plenty of times. "We're not finding out shit," he said. "Didn't I fire your ass? How come you don't stay fired?"

Bernie walked toward him. I was right alongside. The booze smell grew stronger, mixed with Prince's; one of the worst combos I'd ever come across, like the opposite of perfume. "No hard feelings," Bernie said. Keefer looked confused, opened his mouth to speak, but before any words came out, Bernie said, "How much did you get for the sculpture?"

"What makes you think I sold it?" Keefer said.

"My mistake," Bernie said. "Didn't know they had repo men in the art world."

I followed that, no problem: A buddy of mine named Bomber worked in the repo business, a pretty good gig, if not quite up there with mine.

"You've got a fine sense of humor," Keefer said; a bit puzzling, since he didn't seem at all amused. He reached into the pocket of his robe, took out cigarettes, lit one up. I sensed a change in Bernie's whole body: He wanted a cigarette bad. Keefer took a deep drag, and when he spoke again, his voice sounded more confident, like somehow the cigarette had lit a fire inside him. "I sold it," he said, "not that it's any of your business."

"How come?" said Bernie.

"Began to bore me," said Keefer. "Like you're doing now."

"I'm boring you?" Bernie said. "That comes as a surprise."

Keefer took another drag, watched Bernie from behind a smoke cloud, didn't speak.

"Here I was," said Bernie, "thinking you'd be glad to see me."

"Why is that?"

"Cynthia says you thought I'd died in a wreck—and now here I am, like a miracle, yet you don't seem pleased."

A miracle, yes! We'd pulled off a miracle out on that cliff, me and Bernie. This line of work—you can't beat it. But I could tell from the expression on Keefer's face that Bernie was right: Keefer wasn't happy to see us, miracle or no miracle.

"I'll be honest with you," he said. "I never liked your tone, right from the start. And now that it's clear from Maddy's call that she's coming home anytime now, no harm done, I can't think of a single reason I have to talk to you for one more second." He tossed his cigarette butt onto the dead grass where the sculpture had stood and stalked off toward the house.

We caught up with him in a step or two, Bernie on one side, me on the other. "Walking off in a huff won't work," Bernie said. "Too much at stake for that."

Keefer stopped and turned on him. "Get off my property or I'll call the cops," he said. "Does that work?"

Bernie nodded. "Works for me," he said. "Call the cops."

Keefer's face, even his whole body, seemed to swell up. I thought he might take a swing at Bernie. Yes, do it, do it! But maybe because his robe started to open and he had to tug it back in place, nothing happened, not of the violent kind. My mind flashed back to the bikers and all that ruckus and lovely sawdust. This was the life for me.

Now Keefer, face and body, was deflating, like a basketball I'd once gotten hold of after it came bouncing out of a school yard. "What is it you want from me? Money? Is this a shakedown?"

"What would I be shaking you down about?"

"Search me," Keefer said. "You guys have a reputation."

"What guys do you mean?"

"Private detectives. Word gets around."

"Let us in on it—what's the word?"

"Blackmail," Keefer said.

"Blackmail?"

"You start working for a client, worm yourselves into their lives, find the dirt."

"What's the dirt on you, Damon? Save us some time."

Keefer's eyes shifted to Bernie, then away.

"How deep in debt are you?" Bernie said. "How far gone?"

"You're way off," said Keefer. "I have normal business debts, balanced by revenues, as per the master plan."

"What master plan?"

"For Pinnacle Peak Homes at Puma Wells, of course," said Keefer. "A top-ten development of the year, according to *Valley* magazine—in case you're interested in actual facts."

At that moment cat smell came rolling down on me, enough to make me dizzy. I looked up and saw Prince on a balcony over the front door. And what was he toying with? A dead bird? Or maybe not quite dead yet? Disgusting, that kind of behavior, completely unimaginable to me; plus, I'd never caught a bird in my whole life. Why was that?

"What about your other investments?" Bernie said.

"What other investments?" said Keefer.

"In the movie business, maybe."

"Lost me."

"You don't have an ownership stake in any movie theaters?" Bernie said. "Up in Vegas, for example?"

Keefer seemed to deflate a little more. "You make no sense."

"I've even got a specific theater in mind," Bernie said. "The Golden Palm Movie Palace."

Keefer's face had gone all bony, reminding me of an investigation we'd once done in an old folks' home, something about a rigged canasta game, the details never clear in my mind. "What are you saying?" he said.

"I'm just asking the question: Are you an owner of the Golden Palm Movie Palace?"

"A ridiculous question, and the answer is no. I'd never even heard of the place till the police called."

"Any idea who does own it?"

Keefer sagged slightly, as though hit by a strong gust. "How would I know something like that?"

"Just asking," Bernie said. "I'm trying to get your daughter back."

"What the hell is wrong with you?" Keefer said. All of a sudden he was inflating again, his face flushing. I didn't understand him at all. "Are you stupid? You're off the goddamn case. There is no goddamn case—she went away to get her head straight and now she's coming home. You listened to the call, didn't you? Can't you understand simple English? We don't need your services. You got your money, way more than you deserved. Now vanish." Keefer, all flushed and inflated, still didn't raise his voice, keeping it low and nasty, which was even worse somehow. Bernie stupid? That was a new one. Below the hem of his robe, Keefer turned out to be one of those dudes with skinny calves, not much to sink your teeth into, but I got ready anyway.

"I did listen to the tape," Bernie said. "Why didn't you?"

"Huh?"

"If it had been me, I'd have driven over to Cynthia's first thing and listened to that tape for myself."

"You're not me, thank Christ," Keefer said. "Cynthia gave me a complete report."

"That's one explanation," Bernie said. "Doesn't do it for me, seems a little detached."

"Detached?" said Keefer. "Look who's talking. You have no idea what this is like." And now what was this? Bernie deflating a little? Had Keefer gotten to him in some way? I didn't know. "You're a son of a bitch, you know that?" Keefer said.

"Maybe," said Bernie. "So here's the son-of-a-bitch theory. You didn't need to listen to the call because you already knew what she'd say."

"You're insane," Keefer said. "You think Madison and I are in some sort of collusion?"

"That would be the best-case scenario," Bernie said.

There was a pause, maybe while Keefer absorbed Bernie's words. I didn't absorb them at all, kept my eyes on Keefer's skinny calves, saw them tense. I glanced up real quick: Keefer was taking a big swing at Bernie. Bernie hardly moved, just shifted his head a bit, and Keefer's fist shot harmlessly by. At that moment I lunged, snapped at one of Keefer's legs, ended up snapping nothing but air. Why? Because Bernie had already grabbed Keefer and lifted him right off the ground, shoving his back against the door.

"What's the real scenario, Damon?" Bernie said. "Fill us in."

"Let go of me."

"First the truth."

"The truth is on that tape. I don't know any more than you." And then Keefer started to cry, fat tears with even some sobbing: a revolting spectacle, to my mind, and probably Bernie's, too. He let go of Keefer. Keefer's feet hit the ground. He staggered, almost fell. A feather floated down from the balcony.

Bernie gazed at Keefer. Keefer looked away, dabbed his eyes with the sleeve of his robe. "Last chance to get on the good side, Damon," Bernie said. "What made you think I'd been killed in an accident? Take your time—a lot is riding on your answer, whether you know it or not."

I went and stood right beside Bernie. I had no clue what he was talking about, but I knew mastery when I saw it.

Keefer's mouth opened, closed, opened again. He licked his lips and said, "I got an anonymous call." Up on the balcony, Prince was licking a paw with his pointy little tongue.

We turned and walked away. Keefer was on the bad side. I'd known that the first time I'd caught a whiff of him, of course. Sometimes I was ahead of Bernie, mastery or no.

TWENTY-SEVEN

Nixon Panero was one of our best sources, kind of strange because we'd put him away for a year or two. He had an auto-body shop at the end of a long line of auto-body shops in a flat, treeless part of town where guys slouched on every corner, up to no good. My old buddy Spike was slouching, too—sprawled, in fact, with splayed-out paws—by Nixon's gate when we drove in. He saw me and raised his tail. Spike was one scary-looking dude, part Rottweiler, part pit bull, part unknown, and had been in many scraps, including one with me the night we'd taken Nixon down, but he was getting on now, less belligerent, his warrior face turning white.

Nixon was sitting in a chair in the yard, watching one of his workers spray-painting flames on a black fender. The air filled with paint smells, sweet and harsh at the same time. "Hey, boys, been a while," Nixon said. "Where's the Porsche?"

Bernie shook his head.

"Finally crapped out on you, huh?" said Nixon, sounding happy about it. His eyes were too close together, even for a human, always a disturbing sight for me.

"Something like that," Bernie said.

Nixon spat in the dirt. "I can get you another one, even more beat up."

"Yeah?" said Bernie. "How much?"

"Don't have it yet," said Nixon. "I'm just saying the possibility's out there."

Or something like that. I wasn't really listening, on account of Nixon being a tobacco chewer, which made his spit pretty interesting. I went over and sniffed at the dirt where the glob had landed. It smelled like Bernie's breath in the morning, if he'd been smoking the night before and hadn't brushed his teeth yet, but even stronger, with an added bitterness. Normally at a moment like this, I'd move on to an experimental lick or two. Not this time, amigo.

"Supposing," Bernie was saying, "a guy had to borrow some money."

"No need—us two, me and you, we got a history," Nixon said, and started laughing, a laugh that went on too long, got a little crazy, ended in hacking, and then another glob horking out, splatting down nearby. "You can pay me by the week, the month, whatever."

"I'm talking hundreds of thousands," Bernie said. "Maybe even more."

"For a thirty-year-old Porsche?"

"This isn't about the Porsche." Bernie pulled up an overturned trash can and sat down; I sat, too. "This is about a developer type in the middle of a big project who gets cut off by the banks and has no other resources, at least that I can find."

"We're not talkin' about you?"

"Do I look like a developer type?"

Nixon's close-together eyes examined Bernie. "Maybe with

some cleanin' up, haircut, new shoes. Shoes tell the tale, Bernie—can't believe you don't know that by now." He opened a flat can, stuck another plug of dip in his mouth. "So this developer type goes huntin' for street money?"

"That's my theory," Bernie said. "I want to find the lender, whoever it is."

The second glob was bigger than the first and had an even stronger smell. I went over and was lowering my head for another sniff when something bumped me from behind. I turned and there was Spike. He bumped me again, away from the glob, and gave it a sniff himself. I bumped him back, barely moved him at all—Spike was so heavy, and still strong. But it was my turn at the glob, so I bumped him again, harder this time. Spike faced me, showed his teeth, all yellow and brown now, and growled. I showed my teeth and growled back.

"Hey, knock it off," Nixon said.

What was this? Spike actually knocking it off just because Nixon said so? Spike walked around in a circle and lay down in the shade of Nixon's tow truck, his white face much more visible than the rest of him; for some reason, that made me sad. I backed away from the glob.

"More orange at the tips of those flames," Nixon said. "Make a fuckin' statement." The painter nodded, sprayed more orange. Nixon turned to Bernie. "This developer of yours got a name?"

"Damon Keefer."

"Don't know him," Nixon said. "He's into some shylock for mid–six figures?"

"Educated guesswork on the exact amount," Bernie said. Nixon scratched his head. Mine got itchy right away, so I scratched it, first with a front paw, then harder with a back paw, which always did the trick.

"Serious green," Nixon said. "Kind of narrows the list." He took a pencil stub and a grimy spiral notebook from his chest pocket and began writing. "We got the Spirelli brothers down in Modena." He licked the pencil; all of a sudden I wanted to lick it, too, so bad. "Then there's Albie Rose, but they say he's close to retirement now, maybe wouldn't want to mess with something like this. You know Albie?"

"Heard of him," Bernie said.

"Been married eight times."

"Didn't know that."

"All showgirls from Vegas, each and every one, three of them named Tiffany."

"Vegas keeps coming up in this case."

"Then maybe you should try Albie. He does some business in Vegas."

"Any chance he owns a movie theater up there?"

"Wouldn't put it past him—he's the cultured type."

Bernie gave Nixon a look.

"An intellectual, is what I'm saying," Nixon said.

"Heard of them," said Bernie. "Anyone else?"

Nixon scrunched up his face. Some humans did that when they were trying to squeeze out a thought; I wished they didn't. "There's Marcellus Clay in Sunshine City, kind of diversified these days—aliens, coke, identity theft—but he's always got money on the street." Nixon opened his eyes, blinked a couple times, wrote in the notebook, stuck the pencil behind his ear. Was there any way to grab it? "That's pretty much the list," Nixon said. He tore off a sheet of paper, handed it to Bernie.

"Any Russians?" Bernie said.

"Don't know no Russians," said Nixon. "Don't know and don't wanna know. Do I start checkin' out old Porsches?"

"Depends on the price," Bernie said.

"Money, money, money," Nixon said. "Stickin' my nose in, I know, but maybe you should raise your fees."

"I'll think about it," Bernie said.

Please do. Right now we were charging zero. What kind of business plan was that?

Albie Rose lived in the biggest house I'd ever seen, more like a palace, surrounded by high walls. A guy with big shoulders and a gun on his hip led us across vast green lawns to a huge swimming pool. On a deck chair by the pool lay a fat old man in a tiny bathing suit. His skin was oiled and deeply tanned, just about the color and texture of a turkey Leda had left too long in the oven one Thanksgiving. I tried not to look.

"Mr. Rose?" said the guy with the gun.

The old man opened his eyes, hard eyes I didn't like at all. "You Bernie Little?" he said.

Bernie nodded.

Albie Rose waved the guy with the gun away. He strolled to the end of the pool and stood by the diving board, probably way too hot in his all-black outfit. I was pretty hot myself; the pool looked inviting.

"Did some checking up," Albie Rose said, still flat on his back. "You have an interesting reputation."

Bernie nodded again.

Albie Rose glanced over at me. "Not one of those trained attack dogs, is it?"

"Not trained, no," said Bernie.

An it? I was an it? I moved a little closer to poolside.

"I don't like violence," Albie Rose said.

"Me, either, Mr. Rose," said Bernie.

"Call me Albie. Only my wives called me Mr. Rose. But as for violence, sometimes there's no other way—am I right, Foster?"

"Yes sir," said the man with the gun.

"I'm sure this isn't one of those times," Bernie said.

"Take a seat," said Albie.

Bernie pulled up another deck chair, sat on the end. "I understand you're a kind of financier."

"Not kind of," Albie said. "How much are you looking for?"

"None," said Bernie. "I'm just trying to find out how the business works."

"Why?"

"To better serve my clientele," Bernie said.

Albie gave Bernie a long look, then sat up. "Foster," he called. Foster came over, raised the back of Albie Rose's deck chair, returned to his post by the diving board. The old man wiped some sweat off his flabby chest, flicked it away with the edge of his hand. It smelled like this old cheese Bernie had brought home once. For a few moments I could smell nothing but old cheese, rising off Albie in waves. "Go on," Albie said.

"Suppose someone came to you for money, five hundred grand, just to name a figure—what happens next?" Bernie said.

"I say yes or no."

"Based on what?"

"Could be anything."

"Like?"

Albie shrugged. "Won't look me in the eye, or looks me in the eye too much. A crier—don't lend to criers. Or he's not wearing a tie."

"Not wearing a tie?"

"Come to me for money you wear a tie. I'm old-school."

"What about the purpose of the loan—is that a factor?"

"Purpose of the loan?"

"What the money's for."

"Survival," said Albie. "They come to me for survival. It's always the same."

"Suppose you say yes to the five hundred grand," Bernie said, "and the borrower turns out to be slow making the payments."

"That would be stressful," Albie said. "I don't get involved. Handling stress is Foster's department."

Foster stood motionless by the diving board.

"What's his approach?" Bernie said.

"Foster was a promising baseball player at one time," Albie said. "Drafted in the sixth round by the Dodgers. He still has his bat."

"Louisville Slugger," Foster said. He spoke in a normal voice, but it carried across the pool.

"Had one myself," Bernie said. "Any stressful situations recently?"

"Nah," said Albie. "Not for years. Man of Foster's talent— word gets out."

Foster made a little bow. "But it's more the philosophy that keeps things running smooth, boss," he said. "You don't mind my saying."

"Philosophy?" said Bernie.

"In five words," said Albie. "Deal with cash businesses only."

"For example?"

"Dentists," said Albie. "I love dentists. They make good money, look around for investments, always pick wrong, get buried."

"What about real estate developers?" Bernie said.

"Wouldn't touch 'em."

"Why not?"

"What I just said—cash business. Developers got no cash flow at all. Dreamers, sure, I rely on dreamers, but what's the one thing they gotta have besides their big stupid dreams?"

"Cash flow," Bernie said.

"Now you're cooking," said Albie. "No charge for the lesson."

Bernie made one of his nods that could have meant anything. Albie's hard eyes watched him closely.

"I got a question of my own," Albie said. "What developer's paying you?"

"I'm not working for any developer," Bernie said. "There's a developer in the case."

"Name?"

"Damon Keefer—he's got a big project going up at Puma Wells."

"Puma Wells," said Albie. "My wife—one of 'em, Tiffany, it might have been, or that other Tiffany, with the tits—used to ride up there, ride for miles, nothing but open country. You ever think about shit like that?"

"Every day," said Bernie.

Albie nodded. "Too many goddamn dreamers," he said. "That's what's wrong with the American dream. As for your guy, never heard of him."

Way down at the bottom of the pool I saw a shiny ring, plastic or rubber, one of those pool toys. I liked pool toys. Have I mentioned I'm a pretty good diver?

"Are all your competitors like you?" Bernie said. "Philosophically, I mean."

"What competitors?"

"The Spirelli brothers. Marcellus Clay."

"The Spirelli brothers? Marcellus Clay? Now you insult me."

"Not intentionally," said Bernie. "But would they do business with developers?"

"The Spirellis, never. That's not where they go wrong. Marcellus Clay's capable of anything."

Bernie rose. "Thanks for your time," he said.

"Headed out to Sunshine City?" Albie said. "I'd be— Hey! What the hell's he doing in the pool?"

Bernie looked over at me. "The dog paddle," he said. "It's his only stroke."

And there might have been more back-and-forth, but I missed it, hearing nothing but bubbles streaming past my ears as I dove down through lovely cool water and snagged the shiny ring. Rubber: I gave it a good squeeze and swam—swimming is like a fast trot, only in the water, nothing to it—to the surface.

Albie was laughing at something Bernie must have said. "You're a funny guy," he said. "Funny guys are smart. I like having them around, if you get my meaning."

"I have a job," said Bernie.

"The dog's kind of funny, too," Albie said. "What's his name?"

"Chet."

"Good name. How much do you want for him?"

"You're funny, too," said Bernie.

I got out of the pool, shook myself off, water spraying everywhere, the very best part of swimming.

"Drop it," Bernie said.

Aw, did I have to?

"He can keep it," said Albie.

I dropped the shiny rubber ring by the side of the pool. Albie gazed at it for a moment, then looked at me, and finally at Bernie. "There's maybe one other guy," he said. "Kind of a newcomer, don't know him at all. Name of Gulagov."

Gulagov? I barked, good and loud. No one seemed to hear. I tried again.

"He wants that toy," Albie said.

"He's got lots of toys," Bernie said.

The toy? I wasn't barking about the toy. This was the kind of moment when humans let out a sigh of frustration, but my sighs are all about contentment, so that was that.

"Russian?" Bernie was saying.

"We got Russians now," Albie said. "Whole wide world's coming to the Valley, in case you don't know."

"I know," Bernie said.

"Could use someone like you," Albie said.

"No, thanks," said Bernie.

We began walking away.

"Ninety grand to start, plus benefits and a nice Christmas bonus," Albie called after us. "Think about it."

From the look on Bernie's face, I could tell he wasn't thinking about it. Me either, despite the messiness of our finances. Coming to work every day and seeing Albie in that tiny bathing suit? Plus the constant smell of old cheese? Count me out.

TWENTY-EIGHT

Back at the office, a little room next door to Charlie's bedroom, at the side of the house facing old man Heydrich's fence. A basket of kids' blocks lay in one corner—the room was meant for a sister or brother who never came along; sometimes I played with the blocks myself. The rest of the office was mostly Bernie's books—on shelves, in stacks here and there, sometimes scattered on the floor; plus the desk, with phone and computer; the two client chairs; and a nice soft rug with a pattern of circus elephants—kind of like my own personal cubicle, just without walls, very cozy, although even the idea of elephants got me nervous.

"Russian connections, Chet," Bernie said, tapping away at the keyboard.

I lay on my stomach on the elephant rug, front paws stretched out, working on a chew strip, my mind drifting to thoughts of Max's Memphis Ribs. Those two-for-one coupons—I hoped Bernie remembered.

He got up, went to the whiteboard hanging on the wall. "Start with Anatoly Bulganin," he said, writing on the board. "Then there's the knife, made in Zlatoust." He drew a picture of a knife, not very good. "Plus Ms. Larapova, suddenly, after our visit, no longer working in the office at Pinnacle Peak." He drew a picture of a woman with a tennis racquet, also not very good. "What am I leaving out? Oh yeah—Cleon Maxwell, ID stolen by Russian gangsters." More drawing: Was that supposed to be a pig? Please don't forget those coupons, Bernie, that's all I'm asking. "And now we've got a Russki moneylender, name of Gulagov." Bernie made a funny-looking mark on the board—a mark I'd often seen and might have been the sign for money—and beside it added a kind of hook with a round dot at the bottom.

He went back to the desk, starting tapping again. "Anatoly Bulganin, projectionist in Las Vegas, happened to snap the picture of Madison that seemed to show she was free and on her own, just another teenage runaway. *Happened* to snap the picture that *seemed* to show—see where I'm going with this, Chet?"

What was the question? Seemed to show, blah blah blah. One thing about the so-called gift of so-called speech: Too often it just went on and on. Besides, I already knew damn well Maddy wasn't a runaway, had known practically from the start. Bernie, get on the stick.

Tap, tap, tap. "Why don't we return to the question that came up with Albie Rose—who owns the Golden Palm Movie Palace?"

Oh, sure, and how about where they get their popcorn while we're at it? Not a big fan of popcorn myself: mostly air, except for those unpopped kernels that get stuck between my teeth, sometimes for days. Even now I could feel a little something caught back there. When was my next appointment with the groomer? She always brushed my teeth, one of my favorite things in the whole world. I got my chew strip way back in my mouth, maneuvered it around, trying to get rid of whatever was bugging me.

Tap tap. "Here we go, Chet—looks like the Golden Palm Movie Palace is owned by the Rasputin Environmental Investments Group. Get it? Rasputin?"

I did not.

"Interesting choice." He drew a wild-looking bearded man on the whiteboard. "Why not Chekhov or Tchaikovsky or any number of—"

The phone rang and Bernie answered it. "Little Detective Agency," he said. Then came a pause, and in a very different sort of voice, he said, "Charlie. Hey. Since when are you making phone calls?" He listened and laughed; he was sitting forward now, holding the phone in both hands. "Yeah," he said, "that button's the speed dial." More listening, then: "There's no actual slow-dial button . . . How come there's no slow-dial button? Good question, Charlie. It's like why there's no giant ants—who needs 'em?" Didn't have a clue what Bernie was talking about, but I heard Charlie's little laugh on the other end. I myself was pretty good at making Charlie laugh—licking his face worked every time. The laughter of human children—there was never too much of that. "Now you know how," Bernie was saying, "you can call anytime you . . . Charlie? You still—" Quietly, Bernie said, "Bye," and hung up. He stared out the window. Bernie had a kind of stare where his eyes went blank. He was doing it now. What did he see at times like this? I didn't know. After a while he swiveled his chair around and looked down at me. "We've got to find the girl, Chet," he said. "Got to find her soon."

He went back to the computer and tapped away, sometimes getting up and adding something new on the whiteboard. I closed my eyes, sleep on the way. I'd had some lovely naps on the elephant rug, soft but also with a nubby texture that felt so nice. Sleep on the way, but for some reason it didn't close in, not completely.

Fine with me: A very pleasant fog settled over the elephant rug, nothing penetrating it but Bernie's voice and that tap-tap, both soft and far away.

"Russians," he said. And later: "Rasputin Environmental— what else do they own, I wonder." Tap tap. "And Keefer stinks, no doubt about that." I couldn't have agreed more—he stank of that horrible cat, Prince; a bit of a surprise that Bernie had picked this up, scents being my department, although at times our duties overlapped—but I lacked the energy at the moment to thump my tail in support. "Patterns, patterns—first the sighting outside the Golden Palm, then the call. Both setups, of course, and not only that, but Maddy tried to clue us in—what a kid! So they're feel- ing pressure. Got to be pressure from us, boy, meaning we must be getting close, our activities influencing theirs. Kind of like Heisenberg's uncertainty principle, Chet—the very act of doing the experiment influences the results, so we can never be sure of them—how's that for irony?—even if . . . or was it Max Planck?" He muttered on for a bit. Sometimes, like now, I got anxious about Bernie knowing a little too much about everything. Maybe if he just stuck to basics, like our finances and those two-for-one coupons at Max's Memphis Ribs, we'd be better off.

Tap tap. "Gulagov. Did we get a first name? Here's one— Dmitri. And Yevgeny . . . Anton . . . Ruslan . . . any chance one of them's connected to Rasputin Environmental, which would hook him in to the Golden Palm setup and then—"

The doorbell rang. Bernie got up to answer it. I rose, too, shaking off the fog in an instant—anything about the door was a security issue, my territory. We opened up, and surprise! It was Janie. Janie was my groomer, the best groomer in the whole Valley. She had a great business with a great business plan: "Janie's Pet Grooming Service—We Pick Up and Deliver." And there, right out front, was Janie's truck, silver and sparkling in the sunshine.

"All set," said Janie. She was a strong woman with a broad face, big hands, and dirty fingernails. I loved Janie.

"We had an appointment for today?" Bernie said.

Janie whipped out some device with a tiny screen, held it so Bernie could see.

"Guess I forgot," Bernie said.

"Rain check?" she said, which I didn't get at all. No point checking—it never rained in the Valley.

"No," Bernie said. "Looks like he wants to go."

I got back down on all fours.

"I'll have him back in two hours," Janie said. Amazing, you might say, how I'd just been thinking about a nice grooming session and now here we were, but it's not: That kind of thing happens to me all the time. "Chet, easy there, big guy," Janie said on the way to the truck. She was almost as tall as Bernie, and I had to jump pretty high to lick her face, but I could do it, no problem. She laughed, just like Charlie, a high little laugh, kind of strange in a woman her size. But it sounded great to me. Was this the life or what? I couldn't wait for the toothbrush.

Janie had a nice setup in a strip mall not far away. First came the tub room, which was mostly a big steel tub filled with sudsy water. Janie scrubbed and scrubbed. I pushed back against the brush; wish I could tell you how good it felt.

"Where've you been, Chet?" Janie said. "Brought the whole desert in with you."

I thought of Mr. Gulagov's ranch, and crawling through the horrible old mine; but only briefly—wouldn't want to spoil a visit to Janie's with stuff like that.

We moved on to the shower, a smaller steel tub where all the suds got washed away. Janie jumped back just in time, hardly getting sprayed when I shook off—we knew each other pretty well. I hopped out of the small tub by myself, trotted into the drying room, rolled on my back.

Janie laughed again. "Got it down to a T, don't you, Chet?"

Whatever that meant. Let's just get going. I liked the drying part, first getting rubbed down with towels, but even more when the hair dryer came out and Janie ran it back and forth over me, at the same time drawing a big stiff comb through my coat, drawing it nice and slow, slow, slow. Ah, bliss. Did Janie do that two-for-one-coupon thing?

"Looks like you need a trim," Janie said.

Trim away.

Janie got out the scissors and did some trimming. After that she did some clipping and buffing of my nails. And then, finally, the toothbrush. Janie always sang a song while she brushed my teeth.

"Brush your teeth with Colgate
Colgate dental cream
It cleans your breath
What a toothpaste
While it cleans your teeth."

Loved that song, one of my very favorites. I raised my head and did some of that woo-woo-woo vocalizing I'd learned by the campfire. Janie laughed, her eyes shining, and gave me a pat. Some humans had a soft spot for us and some did not; Janie was the first kind. Pat pat, and then the laughter faded and her hand slowed somewhere in the middle of my back, felt around, moved off, returned, felt around some more. "Got a bit of a lump there, Chet?" she said.

Not that I knew of. Lump? What was that, anyway? Something Janie could comb out? I waited for her to get the comb again, but she did not. Lump. I thought of a perp named Lumpy Flanagan we'd once put away, but didn't dwell on him for long—an ugly brute, with an overbite and no chin—and then forgot the whole thing.

"Okay, Chet, we're done." Janie and I went out to the parking lot, climbed into her truck. I felt great. A female of my tribe passing by on a leash had to be tugged away. Who could blame her?

We drove up Mesquite Road and parked in my driveway behind the van. Janie let me out the back—I didn't get to ride shotgun in her truck, something about insurance. Insurance was one of those things I didn't understand, just knew that humans worried about it a lot and that we didn't have much, me and Bernie, on account of our finances. I glanced next door, and there was Iggy at his window. He saw me, too, and started barking, a screechy yip-yip-yip that didn't stop. I let out a bark of my own, just saying hi. His barking got wilder; he jumped up and down, raced back and forth behind the window.

"Your buddy's sure trying to tell you something," Janie said. She knocked at our door.

No answer.

She pressed the button that rang the bell. No answer, but the bell didn't always work, something about a fuse. Replacing it was on the list. Bernie kept a list in the bottom drawer of his desk, added to it from time to time; the bourbon often came out after those listing sessions.

Janie knocked again, harder. Iggy was still barking. Janie called, "Bernie?" She raised her voice and tried again, knocking on the door—pretty much pounding—with her big fist. "Bernie?

Bernie?" She listened. I listened, too, heard nothing. Janie looked around. "Where's the Porsche?" she said. And then, "He must've stepped out." Her face squeezed in toward the middle a bit, one of those signs of human annoyance. She put her hand on the knob and turned it. Hey. The door opened. Bad security: but that was Bernie.

Janie looked in. "Bernie? Bernie?"

The house was silent. I went into the front hall, sniffed Bernie's jogging shoes, lapped some water from one of my bowls, picked up my squeaky ball, squeaked it a couple times. It sounded fine.

"Guess he left it unlocked for us," Janie said. "Think it's okay to leave you by yourself?"

I squeaked the squeaky ball at her. Of course it was okay: I lived here.

"I'll write a quick note, then, get him to call me about your . . ." Her voice trailed off in the middle of whatever she was planning to say. That often happened when some human and I were alone together, always leaving me with the feeling that the talking kept on inside their heads, no silence ever. Between you and me, and no offense, but I really wouldn't want to be human.

Janie wrote on a Post-it note—Bernie used to paper the office with them before the whiteboard came along—and stuck it on the inside of the door. "Okay, Chet." She gave me a nice pat, soft and gentle. "Take good care of yourself, now." Janie closed the door and went away. I heard her truck start up, and then the sound of it faded away. Iggy was still barking.

I trotted around the corner toward the kitchen. After grooming, I often got hungry, mealtime or not. I was wondering whether I'd left anything in my breakfast bowl—had that ever happened, even once?—when I caught the smell of strangers. And not just any strangers, but strangers who smelled partly of cooked beets. I let out a bark that echoed through the house, came back to me sounding so savage it scared me. I did it again, even louder. After that I ran from room to room, barking the whole time, feeling the hair standing rigid all down my back.

Everything looked normal: kitchen, food bowl empty; dining room that never got used; living room with the big TV where we watched movies, me and Bernie; the big bedroom, very messy, as usual; Charlie's room, neat as a pin, whatever that meant—I'd stuck myself with a pin once, seen nothing neat about it at all. But normal, that was the point, everything normal. Then I went into the office.

Something was wrong; and not just the odor of the beet strangers, by far the strongest of anywhere in the house. What was it, what was wrong? I ran around in circles, sniffing and barking. It took me a long time, but then I saw: Where the whiteboard always hung on the wall was now empty space, the paint brighter than in the rest of the room. I sniffed some more, sniffed Bernie's smell, of course, but almost overwhelmed by the smell of the beet strangers.

Oh no. Bernie was gone.

I raced through the house, barking and barking. All the doors were closed, and all the windows, too, with the AC finally on, now that the real heat was coming. I couldn't get out! Bernie! I threw myself against the front door. I'd seen Bernie bash a door down once, but ours didn't budge, didn't even make a cracking sound. I tried again with all my strength. All that did was knock Janie's Post-it note off the door. It fluttered sideways and disappeared behind the recycling bin.

Bernie!

TWENTY-NINE

Night. I was beside myself. I hurried through the house, checking and rechecking all the rooms over and over, stopping only when I heard something, or thought I heard something, and if I really did hear something it always turned out to be a car driving by, or a plane high overhead, or Iggy barking again. Worse, I hadn't been able to hang on any longer, although I'd tried and tried, and ended up shaming myself by the toilet in the hall bathroom.

Bernie. Where are you? Something bad had happened—I felt it through and through. The beet strangers had come, and now Bernie was gone, and the whiteboard, too. Bernie gone—gone and maybe in trouble—and I couldn't get out, couldn't go find him. Me, in charge of security. I found myself back at the front door, throwing myself at it again and again, with no results. Bernie had been talking about results not long ago, while we worked in the office. What had he said? I had no idea. I barked and barked, savage barking that filled the house, but did no good at all. Then— What was that? I went still, ears perking right up.

But it was only Iggy: yip yip yip. I didn't even bark back.

What could poor old Iggy do? My only hope was—what? What was it? Then I knew: My hope was Bernie coming back, coming through the door. Maybe now? I watched the door, didn't take my eyes off it, got ready to jump all over him. The door didn't open. After a while a car came up the street, a loud car that sounded a bit like the Porsche. But we didn't have the Porsche anymore, did we? I could still see it sailing off that mountain road and burning in the gully far below. This was confusing. Could that be Bernie outside, somehow driving up in the Porsche anyway? The loud car kept going, the engine noise fading, fading, gone. I rose up, started clawing at the door. I was clawing so hard I almost didn't hear the phone ringing.

I ran down the hall and into the office, stood in front of the desk, watched the phone ring. Ring, ring, and then a voice, a voice I knew and liked. "Bernie? It's Suzie. If you're there, please pick up. I'd really like to talk to you. Um. Uh. I've made a mistake, Bernie, and I just hope that, um . . . Well, please give me a call if you can. Bye."

I leaped up, knocked the phone off the desk. The whole thing—cradle part, speaking part, wires—went tumbling onto the floor, landing behind the desk. And from down there, I heard Suzie.

"Bernie? Are you there? Is that you?"

I let out a bark.

"Chet?"

I barked and barked. Suzie! Suzie!

"Chet? You all right?"

I kept barking. After a moment or so, there was a click, and no more Suzie. I squeezed down under the desk, wriggled on my belly toward the glowing phone lights. Another woman spoke, not Suzie, her voice unfriendly, not a fan of my kind, I could tell right away. "If you'd like to make a call, please hang up and dial again." I barked at her. "If you'd like to make a call, please hang up and dial again." I barked louder. She said it a few more times, all about dialing again, and I got angrier and angrier. Then the phone started beeping, quick and harsh, hurting my ears. I poked at the phone with my paw, but it kept beeping, on and on, unbearable.

I left the office, started hurrying through the house again, a dark house with no lights on. I couldn't get calm, not with that beet smell in the air, and the constant beeping. In the laundry room, I found an old leather sandal of Bernie's and chewed it to bits. I barked some more, thought I heard something beside the beeping, went still. Was that a siren? Yes, a siren, far off. I waited for it to get louder, but it did not, got quieter instead, and then came silence, except the beeping, and Iggy once or twice. Soon he went silent, too. Iggy was my buddy. He wanted to help me, just couldn't. Poor old Iggy. I rose up and clawed again at the front door. What else could I do? I clawed and clawed, getting nowhere. Then a vague memory came to me, a memory of a movie we'd watched, me and Bernie, maybe of Rin Tin Tin, where Rinty opens a doorknob all by himself. Had Bernie even said, "We should learn that sometime"?

But we hadn't. How did Rinty do it? I slid my front paws down from where they'd been clawing at the door until they bumped against the knob; it gleamed faintly from the streetlight down the block. I pawed at the knob, first with one paw, then the other. Nothing happened. Knobs were supposed to turn; I'd seen them turn so many times, but this one would not. I pawed and pawed, faster and faster, heard a growling sound that startled me for an instant before I realized it was me. After a while I dropped down on all fours, took a little rest, and was just about to rise up and try again when I heard a car on the street.

It came closer and closer. I heard the squeak cars sometimes make when they stop. Then came a moment or two of engine noise—did I recognize that particular engine sound?—and after that, silence. But only for a moment; a car door opened and closed, and footsteps came up the walk. Did I recognize those footsteps? I thought so.

Someone knocked on the door. "Bernie? Are you there?" It was Suzie.

I barked.

"Chet?"

The knob turned. The door opened. There was Suzie, her face all worried. I bolted outside, right by her, round and round the front yard. A hot dry breeze was blowing up the canyon, carrying all kinds of city smells—grease, tar, car exhaust, especially car exhaust, lots and lots of that—masking what I needed, which was beets and Bernie. At last I picked up a trace of beet scent, followed it across the yard and past our trees to the road, where it died out.

"Chet?" Suzie called. "Maybe you'd better come here." I paused, glanced over at her. She'd turned on the front-door light. Her face looked pale, her eyes huge and dark. Come there? I forgot about that immediately, trotted in bigger and bigger circles around the place where the beet scent had petered out, finally finding it again. Now it led me back across the yard, not through the trees this time but around them and along the narrow paved alley by the house, old man Heydrich's fence on the other side. A faint current of Bernie came mixing in. Have I mentioned Bernie's smell? A very nice one, my second favorite, in fact—apples, bourbon, salt and pepper. Beets and Bernie: The mixed-together scent trail took me to the office window and ended right there.

"Chet?" Suzie came up beside me. "What's wrong?"

I sniffed around, found a trace of the head-clearing smell from the markers Bernie used on the whiteboard, but then Suzie stepped in front of me and her scent—soap and lemons—obliterated it.

"Come on, Chet," she said. "Let's go inside."

I didn't want to go inside; I wanted to find Bernie, that was all. The next thing I knew, I was hurrying back to the road—where the scent died out as before—then doubling back to the office window.

"Chet? What is it? What's going on?" Suzie put her hands on the window frame, pushed. The window slid up. "Not locked," she said. "Is that normal?"

Of course not. Nothing was normal, not with Bernie gone. I gazed up at her.

"How long were you alone in there?" she said.

I started to pant, just a little.

"Let's get some water," Suzie said. She stroked between my ears. We walked around to the front door and entered the house. Suzie snapped on more lights. I drank from the bowl in the front hall, all at once very thirsty, then caught up with Suzie as she went from room to room, looking around, checking the closets, even peering under the two beds, Charlie's and Bernie's. In the office, she found the phone and cradle on the floor, set it all back on the desk, and the horrible beeping stopped at last. After a pause, Suzie took out her cell phone and dialed some numbers. Almost right away a phone started ringing, not the big one on the desk, but close by. Suzie opened the top drawer and took out Bernie's cell phone, easy to identify from the duct tape wrapped around it. Bernie's cell phone rang and rang. Suzie pressed a button and listened for a few moments; I listened, too, heard Bernie's voice, something about leaving a message. Was Bernie there? I didn't understand. The duct-taped cell phone was here, meaning *there* was *here*. Machines were bad for humans, no doubt at all about that in my mind. I crawled under the desk. Suzie said, "If somehow you get this message, Bernie, please call. It's Suzie. I'm at your place right now—the door was unlocked, and I think Chet's been on his own here for some time. So if . . . Just call."

From under the desk, I could see Suzie raising the window and peering out—even sniffing the air, which humans sometimes did, although to no effect, in my experience. "Did something happen here, Chet? What did you see?"

Not a thing, but something happened, all right, something bad, had to be bad if those beet-smelling people, Mr. Gulagov and his—

The desk phone rang, right above my head. It rang and rang, vibrating the desktop, and then came a voice I knew: "Yo, Bernie, Nixon Panero here. Maybe got a replacement for your Porsche what got trashed. Gimme a call." Click.

Suzie said, "The Porsche got trashed?" I came out from under the desk. "Meaning what?" Suzie's eyes were even bigger and darker now. "It's no longer on the road? Bernie's not out driving somewhere?" I circled for a bit, then stopped and barked in front of the empty space where the whiteboard had hung. Suzie gazed at me. I could feel her thinking, thinking hard. "I'm calling the cops," she said.

We waited in the kitchen. Suzie poured some kibble in my bowl, but I didn't eat. Not long after, Rick Torres arrived, wearing jeans, a T-shirt, and bowling shoes—I'd gone bowling once with Bernie but it hadn't ended well—followed by a cop in uniform. "Hey, Chet," Rick said, and gave me a pat. He was smiling, didn't look worried at all. Suzie started talking to him, real fast and complicated, hard for me to catch on. She led the men through the house, going from room to room. I followed. We entered the office last.

"How do you explain the window being unlocked?" Suzie said. "And the front door, too?"

"The thing is," Rick said, "Bernie can be unpredictable at times." A quick smile crossed the uniformed man's face.

"I haven't found that," Suzie said. "Not at all. I think he's extremely reliable."

"Couldn't agree more," Rick said. "In all the big things. But every now and then, since the divorce, that is, he kicks his heels up a bit."

"What do you mean?" Suzie said.

"Like that night at the Red Onion, right, Rick?" said the uniformed cop. "Wasn't he the one with that gal who played the ukulele? The gal with the ginormous—" Rick made a slight chopping motion with his hand, and the uniformed man went silent.

"No matter what," Suzie said, "he'd never leave Chet alone in the house for such a long time."

"I believe that's happened once or twice, in fact," Rick said. "Hasn't it, big guy?" The answer was yes; but I forgave Bernie—things like that could happen. I stood motionless, giving nothing away.

"Even if that's true," Suzie said, "which I highly doubt, why wouldn't he take his cell phone?" She held it up.

"That's easy," Rick said. "He hates his cell phone, hates technology in general."

"But isn't he working on a case?" Suzie said. "Suppose an important call came through."

"What case?" said Rick.

"That missing girl, Madison Chambliss."

Rick shook his head. "There is no case. The girl's been seen having fun times in Vegas, also called her mom to say she'd be home soon."

"Does Bernie know that?"

"He does. Whether he's totally absorbed it yet is another question."

"Meaning?"

"Bernie can be stubborn—one of the things that makes him so good at his job, and also such a pain at times."

Suzie gave Rick a quick glance, not friendly. "Maybe he's working on other cases," she said. "I think we should check his computer."

"For what?"

"Any notes he might have made, something to lead us to him."

"Uh-uh," said Rick.

"Why not?"

"Why not? Because he could be coming through the door any second, and I wouldn't want to have to explain why I was snooping around in his files."

"It's not snooping. We're only trying to help. And where's his laptop? Doesn't he have a laptop, too?"

"Probably took it," Rick said. "And Bernie doesn't need help. Not when it comes to taking care of himself. Don't know how well you know him, but Bernie's as tough as they come."

"Bernie?"

"Guess you haven't seen him in action," Rick said. Suzie gazed at him, said nothing. "And he's only been gone— What? A matter of hours? He's probably strumming some ukulele as we speak."

"He doesn't play the ukulele," said Suzie.

"Actually, he does," said Rick. "He's pretty good."

Better than that—he was great, although I hadn't heard him play in a long time. Suzie and Rick were eyeing each other; the uniformed cop yawned, and I yawned, too, even though I wasn't the least bit tired.

"I'm staying with Chet," Suzie said.

"Up to you," said Rick. "When he finally rolls around, tell him I ran that plate he asked about. Registered to some kind of environmental investment outfit, it turns out—the baddest of the bad."

We were alone in the kitchen, me and Suzie. "What does he do for coffee?" she said. On the road, Bernie picked up a paper cup of coffee at any convenience store, but things were less simple at home, with bags of beans in the freezer, a grinder that only worked if pressed on not too hard or too soft, and a coffeemaker that leaked if he put too much water in it. Suzie got the system all figured out after a while, and fresh coffee smell—one of my favorites, although I didn't care for the taste at all—filled the air. She sat at the counter, sipping coffee, staring at nothing. All of a sudden she checked her watch, startling me a bit, then turned in my direction. "Why did I go to L.A.?" she said. "What's wrong with me?"

Nothing that I knew.

She poured another cup. "Don't you like your kibble?"

Not particularly, was the true answer. Steak, if available, was always my first choice, and there were many others in front of kibble. But just to be nice, I went to my bowl and scarfed up a mouthful or two. I was still at it when Suzie put down her cup, hard enough so coffee slopped over the side. She mopped it up with her elbow and said, "I can't stand this, doing nothing." She rose, walked to the office, me at her heels, and flicked on the computer. Except it didn't start up; the screen stayed black. Suzie bent down, checked the plug, tried the switch a few more times. "Is something wrong with the computer?" she said.

How would I know? At that moment I caught a whiff—very faint, almost not there at all—of the head-clearing marker scent, the marker Bernie used on the whiteboard. I followed it, the thinnest ribbon of a trail, to the window. I barked.

"You want out, Chet?"

I did.

Suzie let me out the front door. I ran around to the side of the house, back down the alley between our place and old man Heydrich's. Almost right away I found the marker scent, followed it a few steps past the office window to the coiled-up garden hose, never used because of water issues. And there, behind the hose, in a pool of light from the office window, lay a jagged piece, not very big, of the whiteboard, Bernie's drawing of the wild-looking bearded man in one corner and some writing below that. I picked up the piece of whiteboard and turned.

"What've you got there, Chet?" Suzie said, standing nearby. I went to her, offered it up. She held it to the light. "'Rasputin'?" she said, squinting at the writing. "'Ghost Mine'? 'S.V.'?" She turned the scrap over in her hands; nothing on the back. "Rasputin? Ghost Mine? S.V.?"

Ghost Mine? I barked. And barked some more. From next door came old man Heydrich's angry voice. "Do something about that dog, God damn it!" I growled. Did I need old man Heydrich right now?

"C'mon, Chet," Suzie said, her voice gentle.

We went inside. Suzie sat at Bernie's desk, gazing at the remains of the whiteboard. "S.V.," she said. "S.V." She tried the computer again, with no result. Then she took a Swiss army knife from her bag—we'd given Charlie one just like it for his birthday, although Leda hadn't let him keep it—and took the back off the computer. She stared at the insides, empty-looking to my eyes.

Was that all there was to a computer, empty insides? "Mother-board's gone," Suzie said. Way out of my territory, whatever that was. "And I can think of only one thing S.V. might stand for." I waited. "That town where I found you, Chet—Sierra Verde." I wagged my tail. Sierra Verde: We were back in my territory. "S.V.—what else could it stand for?"

Asking the wrong party, sweetheart. Suzie reached for her car keys. I was already on my way to the door.

THIRTY

We drove through the night. I smelled biscuits, remembered that Suzie kept a whole box in her car, but didn't want one. My stomach felt funny, all closed up. Suzie leaned forward, hands squeezing the wheel, her face tense in the lights of oncoming traffic.

She said things like "I don't believe in fate." And "How could I ever let Dylan suck me back into . . ." I remembered Dylan: pretty boy, jailbird, loser. He couldn't have sucked me into anything, not on his best day. The truth was that humans didn't turn out to be the best judges of other humans. We, meaning me and my kind, were much better. Once in a while they tricked us; some humans got up to a lot of trickery, strangely like foxes, but usually we were on to that type from sniff one.

After a while traffic thinned out, and Suzie's face was mostly in darkness. We left the freeway, started up into the mountains, curves tightening and tightening. From time to time a car came the other way, and I saw the wetness in Suzie's eyes. I put a paw on her knee. She gave me a pat. "Does he really play the ukulele?" she said. "I'd love to hear that." An empty stretch of road went by. "I just hope . . ." She went silent. Was this hoping of hers about the ukulele or something else? Bernie really did play it, back in earlier days, knew all kinds of songs like "Up a Lazy River," "When It's Sleepy Time Down South," "Jambalaya," and my favorite, "Hey, Bo Diddley." Bernie's own favorite was "Rock the Casbah." I usually took my bathroom break when that one rolled around.

"I'm smart, that's the ironic thing," Suzie said. "Fourteen hundred on my SATs, graduated cum laude—so how can I be so stupid?" Couldn't follow her on that one. "And I'm getting so sick of irony I want to puke." Uh-oh. I shifted away from her, closer to the door.

But no puking took place; maybe Suzie's stomach settled down. That sometimes happened—I remembered an adventure with anchovies that could have turned out much worse than it did. The night went streaking by. Once I caught a golden flash of cat's eyes, only much bigger. The hair on my back stiffened up. I knew what was out there.

"Is it true—that he's as tough as they come?" Suzie said. "I've known a few tough men—they never made me laugh. Or played the ukulele. On the other hand, there's the whole West Point thing, his combat experience . . . Oh God." She started chewing at one of her knuckles, a sign of extreme human worry; I had a few moves like that myself. "If only we could see around corners," she said. I liked Suzie, even if she sometimes had trouble making sense. Seeing around corners, for example: Who needed it? Smelling around corners was a piece of cake, told me all I needed to know. And say a piece of cake was actually lying around the corner, well, then I could . . . I got a bit lost in my own head, and curled up on the seat for a while. Bernie was tough. I'd seen him do amazing things, like with the bikers. Nothing bad could happen to Bernie. My eyes closed.

I woke up on the main street in Sierra Verde. The bar with the neon martini glass went by, the glass lit up but only darkness behind it, and no hogs parked out front. From not too far away came a nervous, high-pitched bark, the kind my guys sometimes make in the middle of a bad sleep; and I thought of that place up the next side street, with all the cages and the plume of white smoke. Suzie didn't turn up the side street, kept going for a few blocks, reached the convenience store where we'd seen Anatoly Bulganin step out with a bag of groceries. No cars outside, but the lights were on and a man sat slumped behind the counter. Suzie pulled over, took out her cell phone.

"Hi," she said. "Lou? Busy night?" She listened; I heard a man's voice on the other end. "If you get a chance," Suzie went on, "I'd like you to run a search for 'Rasputin' with 'Ghost Mine.'" More listening. "Like the crazy Russian monk," she said. The man on the other end had a loud voice, but I couldn't make out the words. "No," Suzie said, "he died a long time ago, and that's not the point—it has nothing to do with him or the czar. Just a name, Lou. R-A-S-P-U-T-I-N . . . yeah, like Putin, only with 'Ras' at the beginning . . . yeah, you're right—Rastafari is a different kettle of fish." She clicked off, turned to me. "My dream was getting a job at the *Washington Post*, like Woodward and Bernstein." Suzie's dream skimmed by, missed completely on my part. My own dreams were all about hunting in the canyon, chasing down perps, and sometimes dining on steaks smeared with A.1. sauce. I especially liked when Bernie grilled crosshatched patterns on the meat, couldn't tell you why.

Suzie slid down the windows. Desert air rolled in, cool and fresh, meaning morning was on the way. Suzie hugged herself and shivered, as though it were really cold. "I had a dog when I was a kid," she said. "When my parents got divorced, he went to the pound."

I gazed at her in the light that spilled from the convenience store. A sad story, I knew that—and sure as hell wouldn't want to end up in any pound myself—but still, I loved . . . well, just about everything, the whole deal.

"You're a good boy, Chet," she said, opening her door. "I'm grabbing a cup of coffee." She got out, went into the convenience store. My stomach still felt all closed up, but I knew they had Slim Jims in there. I could possibly manage a Slim Jim.

Headlights shone in the rearview mirror. I looked back and saw a pickup approaching, not fast. As it came closer, I could see the driver's face, a pale circle behind the windshield. Very pale, with long shadows cast by big sticking-out cheekbones; and tiny ears; and light-colored hair, almost white even though he wasn't old: Boris! I knew Boris, all right, wasn't going to forget someone who'd knifed me, not ever. I sat up high on my seat, almost let out a bark. But I knew that would be bad, knew that Bernie would want me to keep my mouth shut at a moment like this, would have made a little motion with his hand, just between us. Easy, Chet, let's take 'em down nice and easy.

The pickup—light-colored, not as big as ours—drew closer. As it came alongside me, I saw Boris's face clearly, lit by the green glow of his dashboard lights. He was smiling. That green smile enraged me. I didn't think—that was Bernie's department, and he could have it—just sprang out the window, landing on the road behind the pickup. The pickup turned out to be going much faster than I'd judged from inside Suzie's car. I chased after it, sprinting now, caught up as Boris reached the only stoplight in town. Red, but he drove on through, even stepping on it. Last chance. I gathered myself and leaped, a tremendous leap, one of my very best, up and over the tailgate and down into the bed of the truck, a soft, silent landing.

Or maybe not: Through the narrow back window I saw Boris suddenly turn his head, the pickup slowing. I ducked down, completely still, one more shadow. The pickup sped up again. I raised my head, saw Boris facing front. We rolled through the silent town. From my angle, down low, I could see the tops of the buildings and above them the starry sky, a few clouds moving fast, so wispy the stars shone through them. Then all at once, no more buildings: We headed out of Sierra Verde, down the mountain road and on to the desert plain, the desert plain that stretched all the way to New Mexico.

I lay on a tarp, my back against some coiled rope. I smelled gasoline and gunpowder; and very faintly, my second favorite combo: apples, bourbon, plus that hint of salt and pepper that made it a bit like my own smell. Bernie had been here, right in this very truck bed! A feeling comes to me and my kind when we know we're on the right track, a sort of tamped-down excitement. I felt it now; the tamping-down part maybe still waiting to kick in.

We were on the dirt track I knew, the bumpy one where Bernie had thought about the old days and Kit Carson, and other Bernie-type things I couldn't remember. I kept an eye on Boris's head through the narrow window, a big head, too big for even a thick neck like his. The headlights shone on passing sights I remembered—a tall two-armed cactus like a giant person, spiky bushes I'd marked, a flat rock sitting on a round rock. Later came the dried-up streambed, the low hill, the falling-down shack, and the track fading to nothing. Boris stopped by the remains of the bikers' campfire and got out. I lay low, maybe not as low as I could, with my head poking over the edge of the tailgate, but I had to see out, didn't I?

Boris walked toward the blackened firepit, kicked a beer can once or twice, whistled an unpleasant tune. Then came a zipper sound and soft splashing in the dirt. Men were vulnerable at moments like this. I could take him down right now, no problem. But after that? I didn't know. Boris zipped up, and the moment passed. He looked up, his gaze suddenly right on me! And then sliding by; his vision—like every human I'd come across—just about useless at night. I sometimes felt sorry for humans, what with their obvious shortcomings, but not for Boris. Boris was bad, and soon he'd be living up at Central State, wearing an orange jumpsuit and breaking rocks in the hot sun.

Boris got back behind the wheel, still whistling. Won't be whistling soon, buddy boy. From this same spot, with no more track to follow, Bernie and I had set out on foot, in the direction of those distant mountains, pinkish then, invisible now. Boris didn't go the same way; instead making a long curve past the firepit and toward a jumble of shadowy rocks, the desert floor rough and uneven. We bumped along, Boris twisting the wheel from side to side, lumps of muscle sticking out in his neck, lumpy to begin with. The bumps got bigger, the pickup lurching back and forth. I went sliding off the tarp, thumped against the side of the truck bed. Boris started to glance back, but at that moment we hit an even bigger bump, the whole truck seeming to rise off the ground. He fought with the wheel. I rose up on all fours, went sliding the other way, panting now. Bernie's smell rose around me. I calmed down, and not long after, the ride got smooth again. I stuck my head out the side, peered ahead, saw we were on a track, long and straight. And not too far ahead rose the mountains that had been pink when Bernie and I had seen them before, but were now a dark band beneath a sky no longer quite as dark. My heart beat faster. Calm, Chet, have to stay calm. I crouched down behind the coiled rope.

* * *

Up above, the stars grew dim and slowly vanished. We were making a lot of turns now, the motor sounding like it was working hard. I rose and saw we were in the mountains, still dark, except for the very tops, outlined in milky white. The milky whiteness spread, pouring slowly over the land, a very beautiful sight. It was morning. We rounded a bend, passed some huge rusted-out machine of a type I didn't know, and there, up ahead, stood some run-down buildings—a long, low house, a barn, sheds, and, across from them, a steep slope with a big round hole at its base: Mr. Gulagov's mine.

Boris parked beside a car I knew, the blue BMW, all dusty now, and went inside the barn. I looked around, saw nobody, and hopped out. I sniffed at the BMW, at the barn door, and along the side of the barn, picking up a trace of my own scent. It led me to one of the sheds, and behind the shed, I found the cage where Mr. Gulagov had kept me. Stay calm, boy. But I growled, couldn't help myself.

Beyond the shed stood the house. I went to an open window, saw a kitchen. Mr. Gulagov sat at a table, sideways to me, piling up stacks of wadded bills. Ms. Larapova came into view, carrying a coffeepot. They were so close! In an instant I could be in there, showing Mr. Gulagov what was what. But would that be the right move? I waited, and while I waited, Mr. Gulagov said, "Is Boris back yet?"

"I'll check," said Ms. Larapova. She poured coffee for him and left the room.

Uh-oh. I backed away from the window. Maybe the best move would be—

A door opened right beside me—how had I missed that?—and Ms. Larapova came out of the house. One slight turn of her head and she'd have seen me, and then what? But Ms. Larapova did not turn her head. Instead, she went the other way, toward the barn, her hair in a long ponytail, swinging back and forth. From somewhere nearby I heard a radio and then a man clearing his throat. Any moment now people were going to be all over the place. I backed away, backed away some more, waiting for some idea to hit me, and all at once, by a low spiny plant growing all by itself between the house and the mine, caught the slightest whiff of Bernie.

I sped up, hurrying this way and that, sniffing, sniffing. Another trace, by a broken shovel; another, near an overturned mine car; and one more, by the railroad tracks that led into the mine. Bernie's scent grew stronger, much stronger. I followed it through the big round hole and into the shadows.

And there, with his back to a support beam, not very far inside the mine, sat Bernie! His eyes were closed. Was he sleeping? I was so happy to see him that at first I didn't notice that his feet were roped together; that his hands were bound behind him to the beam; that a choke chain, hooked to the roof of the mine, had him around the neck.

THIRTY-ONE

I moved closer to Bernie. Was he sleeping, or something else, something much worse? I could always smell that much worse thing, didn't smell it now. His chest rose and fell, filling up with air and letting it out, just like mine did. I heard a whimpering sound, realized it was me. Bernie's eyes opened. For a moment their expression was one I'd never seen in Bernie's eyes and never wanted to see again, an expression of—I don't even want to say it—defeat. But then he saw me, and his eyes changed. I won't forget that look anytime soon, although really it was just Bernie getting back to his old self.

"Good to see you, boy," he said, his voice low and tired. "I let them get the jump on me." His head was level with mine or a bit below. I went to lick his face but stopped when I saw the bruises and cuts. Bernie looked past me, toward the entrance to the mine. "All by yourself, Chet? How did that happen?"

A complicated story; I actually couldn't remember most of it. I wagged my tail.

Bernie smiled; just for a moment, but I saw that one of his front teeth was chipped. "Better go get help, Chet," he said. "There's not much time."

I didn't move.

"But how, right?" Bernie said. "Is that what's on your mind? You're way ahead of me."

Impossible. No one was smarter than Bernie. And even if I knew how to get help, there was no way I'd leave him like this. Nothing else was on my mind. I moved around the support beam, had a look at the ropes binding Bernie's arms to it—low down, around his wrists—and started gnawing.

I've done a lot of gnawing in my life—there was a purse of Leda's, for example, leather, despite its green color, and not just any leather but Italian leather, which I hadn't even known existed and yet turned out to be the best I'd ever tasted. Plus all kinds of other things—clothing, furniture, toys, garden tools—gnawed to bits, going way back to my earliest days. So some plain old rope, even fairly thick rope like this, wasn't going to be a problem. Have I mentioned the sharpness of my teeth? Like daggers, and not much smaller.

I worked fast, digging in between the strands, tugging and chewing, hardly even taking the time to enjoy what I was doing. The rope started fraying almost at once, fibers breaking and untwisting in my mouth. From time to time Bernie wriggled his wrists or strained against the rope, once so hard that the beam creaked. Good to see he had his strength, but he wasn't helping, more slowing me down, if anything. A thick strand parted, then another. The rope slackened. Wouldn't be long now. And then— watch out. I dug a tooth deep into what was left, pulled back with a side-to-side motion that always—

"Chet." Bernie spoke very low. "Get back."

I paused, looked up, saw two people framed in the entrance to the mine. One, carrying a water bottle, was the big woman named Olga, hair in a tight bun, the woman I'd seen once before, pulling Madison away from the barn window. The other person was Harold the driver, that single heavy eyebrow somehow making him a bit monkeyish. According to Bernie, humans came from monkeys, while me and my kind came from wolves: all you need to know. Harold carried a gun, smaller than our .38 special; it dangled loosely in his hand. I backed into the shadows, went still.

Olga and Harold approached Bernie. I could see him working his wrists, twisting and turning. Rope fibers frayed and frayed but didn't give. "How's the patient this morning?" Harold said.

Bernie gazed up at him, said nothing.

"Patient?" Olga said. "What is this 'patient'?"

"That's just a funny thing we say," said Harold.

"Who?" said Olga.

"Us," said Harold. "Americans."

"What is funny?" Olga said. She unscrewed the cap from the water bottle and held it out to Bernie, starting to tip it toward his mouth. He shook his head. At the same time he kept working his wrists; and now had the fingers of one hand working, too. "Drink—orders of Mr. Gulagov," Olga said. "You must live a little longer."

"I don't take orders from Gulagov," Bernie said. Behind his back, the remains of the rope fell away. I crouched down, gathered strength in my hind legs.

Harold came forward, stood over Bernie, the gun still loose in his hand. "Pour," he said.

Olga started pouring the water all over Bernie's face. I hated that.

"Drink, you son of a bitch," Harold said.

"After I work up a thirst," said Bernie.

"Huh?" Harold said.

A muscle flexed in Bernie's back and then his arms shot forward. Bernie was quick, the quickest human I knew, but maybe not today, maybe not this time. He swiped at the gun and missed. Olga's eyes opened wide. She dropped the bottle, just stood there, frozen for a moment. But not Harold—he started backing up right away, the gun rising. I sprang.

Possibly not quite on target: I slammed into Olga, knocking her flat, but made a correction in midair, twisting around back on myself and, as I came down, opening wide and sinking my teeth into Harold's wrist. He cried out. The gun went flying, landed between the train tracks. Olga scrambled toward it. I leaped over her, grabbed the gun, came to a skidding stop, wheeled around, and raced back to Bernie. He took the gun from my mouth, pointed it at Harold, then at Olga, back to Harold. "I don't want to kill anyone," he said. And then: "Actually, I do." That froze them. With his free hand, Bernie loosened the choke chain, got it off his neck, went to work on the rope around his ankles.

Soon the choke chain was around Harold's neck, and he was tying up Olga with the remains of the rope under Bernie's supervision. "I'm bleeding," Harold said.

"Tighten that knot," Bernie said.

Harold smelled of urine now. So did Olga. I felt good about that. When Olga's hands and feet were bound, Bernie freed the choke chain from the hook above and tied Harold to the beam with it. That meant putting the gun down. I stood right behind Harold, possibly nudging the back of his leg once or twice. He didn't try any tricks.

Bernie picked up the gun. "Not a sound," he said.

* * *

We waited, I wasn't sure for what. Olga lay on her side between the tracks, watching us with hateful eyes. Harold sat where Bernie had been, against the beam, wincing once or twice. Too bad for him. Bernie and I moved around behind him, stood in darkness. Bernie picked up the water bottle, poured some of what was left into a bucket for me, drank the rest himself. Not long after that we heard a voice.

"Harold? Olga?" It was Boris. Bernie made a tiny motion with his finger, side to side. "Harold? Olga?" We could see Boris coming toward us from the barn, a rifle in one hand. "Harold, moron, where the hell are you?" He reached the entrance to the mine, peered in. "Harold? Is that you? What—" The rifle came up, now in both hands.

Bernie stepped out from behind the beam. "Drop it," he said. But Boris didn't drop it, pulled the trigger instead. A bullet pinged off the rock wall behind us, pinged again deeper in the mine. Bernie fired, the muzzle flash—always exciting, although gunplay had a way of quickly becoming too much of a good thing, in my experience—lighting up the mine. Boris grunted in pain and staggered, clutching his leg. He fired another round, one-handed this time. It thwacked into the support beam, not far above Harold's head.

"Oh my God," said Harold.

Bernie fired again, hit Boris in the shoulder. He spun around, fell, dropped the rifle, reached for it. Bernie fired once more, kicking up dust between the rifle and Boris's hand. Boris crawled away, leaving the rifle behind, got to his feet, and limped toward the barn. A few steps from the barn, he fell again and lay there, raising his head toward the door once or twice and calling out, words that didn't carry back to the mine. I ran out, got the rifle— a big one, but it felt like nothing—and took it back to Bernie.

Now he had a gun in each hand. We usually ended up doing well in situations like that.

Silence. Then Olga, still lying between the tracks, turned to Harold and said, "Is all your fault for not tying him right."

"My fault, you stupid bitch?" said Harold. "I tied him fine. If you're looking for someone to blame, blame Stalin here."

I turned on Harold, barked in his face, making him flinch. That wasn't my name.

"Stalin?" said Bernie.

Harold licked his lips. "I can explain," he said. "I can explain a lot of things if you'll just let me go. I'll drive away, won't look back, you'll never see me again."

"What kind of things?" said Bernie.

"Shut up, you coward," Olga said.

"Why should I?" said Harold. "It's over."

"You do not know Mr. Gulagov," Olga said.

"I'm sick of Gulagov," said Harold. His voice was getting whiny, grating on my ears. "Sick of this whole business."

"What whole business?" Bernie said.

Harold's eyes narrowed in what I knew was the shrewd look. Bernie said that whenever you saw someone with the shrewd look, you knew they weren't. Went right by me, but I loved when Bernie said things like that. "I walk away from this?" Harold said.

"Anything's possible," Bernie said. "But I need to know more."

"Shut up," said Olga.

"Olga?" said Bernie. She looked at him. He put the barrel of the handgun across his lips, like the finger signal for "shhh" but stronger. Olga turned away.

"Suppose I told you," Harold said, "that this asshole Keefer got in to Gulagov for close to a mil. And stopped paying the vig, which was twelve grand a week. Which is how come Gulagov snatched the girl—as a hostage till her old man coughs up the dough."

"Tell me something I don't know," Bernie said.

Bernie knew all that? Wow. I glanced out at Boris, leaning on the barn door now, pulling himself up. Security was my responsibility.

"How about this?" said Harold. "There's been other hostages—that's how they do it in Russia. It always ended okay, money paid back, hostage let go, except for this one time."

"You will regret," Olga said.

Bernie tore off a strip of his shirt, pretty torn up already, went over to Olga, and gagged her. He could be harsh when necessary; me, too.

"Go on," Bernie said. "About the time it didn't end okay."

Harold shot a glance at Olga—now her eyes were flat, with no expression at all, but somehow scarier than before—and looked away. "Couple of years ago, up in Vegas. The money didn't get paid back."

"And the hostage?"

Harold shook his head.

"Buried?" Bernie said.

Harold nodded.

"In here?" said Bernie. "In the mine?"

Harold nodded again. "I can show you," he said. "What would that be worth?"

"Something," Bernie said.

"Me walking out?"

"We'll see."

Harold walking out? He'd Tased me! Do I forget things like that? Never. I stuck my face up close to Harold's, showed him some teeth.

"Do something about that animal," Harold said.

"His name," said Bernie, "is Chet. He doesn't seem to like you—why is that?"

"Um," said Harold. But we didn't get to hear his answer because at that moment the barn door opened, knocking Boris back down in the dirt, and Mr. Gulagov, half his face white with shaving cream, came out, pushing Madison ahead of him with one hand. With his other hand, he held a straight razor to her neck. Maddy's eyes were wide open. I saw red, whether I can see red or not.

Boris raised his hand. "Boss," he said.

Mr. Gulagov stepped around him, shoving Maddy forward. They came closer, crossing the patch of dirt separating the mine from the buildings. A few steps from the entrance, Mr. Gulagov halted, pulling Maddy up short. Olga sat up, eyes shining; Harold looked confused.

"This is a simple situation," Mr. Gulagov said. "Put down your guns and untie Olga."

"Just Olga?" Harold said. "What about me?"

Mr. Gulagov did not reply. His eyes never left Bernie. Bernie started moving toward the mine entrance, slow and easy. I walked beside him the same way.

"Not another step," Mr. Gulagov said. He shifted the razor slightly, now had the blade against Maddy's throat, actually touching. Tears overflowed both her eyes and dampened her face, but she didn't make a sound. Bernie halted, almost outside, a man length or a little more from Maddy and Mr. Gulagov. I halted, too. "Drop the guns," Mr. Gulagov said.

"Everything you're doing now will only make it worse for you in the end," Bernie said.

"I have no need for the like of you to do my thinking," Mr. Gulagov said. "I hope you are smart enough to know I always take the necessary action, take it quickly and with no regret." A drop of blood appeared on Maddy's neck.

Bernie dropped the guns.

"Now free Olga," said Mr. Gulagov.

Bernie turned and, as he turned, shot me a quick look. Mr. Gulagov's eyes were still on Bernie, hadn't left him. Bernie took a step back into the mine and, in a low voice, almost inaudible even to me, said, "Go."

Did I hesitate? That wouldn't have been me. I took a huge spring, my hugest ever, leaping right over Maddy's head. Mr. Gulagov's gaze, a bit late, swung over from Bernie to me, and filled with fear. Yes, he was scared of me and my kind—I'd known that all along—and his fear took over. He forgot about Maddy, thought only of survival, and slashed at me with the razor. I felt the blade rip through the tip of my ear, and then I was on him, knocking him backward to the ground, the razor falling from his hand. After that came a cloud of dust, me rolling in the dirt, Mr. Gulagov fumbling for the razor. He got a grip on the handle. I got ready to lunge. And then Bernie stepped in front of me, in one motion sweeping up Maddy and stamping on Mr. Gulagov's hand. I heard a cracking sound, and Mr. Gulagov cried out in pain. That confused look I'd seen in Harold's eyes? Now Mr. Gulagov's had it, too. Bernie kicked the razor away.

At that moment I became aware that Ms. Larapova had run out of the house. She jumped in the BMW and started driving away. Cars were coming from the other direction, one of them Suzie's, the rest with flashing lights on top. With all that going on, and Maddy sobbing in his arms, Bernie took his eye off Mr. Gulagov. That was where partnership came in. Mr. Gulagov began to wriggle away, toward the mine. What was he planning now? No idea. I grabbed him by the pant leg. Case closed.

* * *

The worst thing that happened after that was on the ride back, when Maddy begged Bernie to keep her father out of the story and Bernie had to tell her no. The best thing was seeing Cynthia's face when we brought her daughter home—seeing both their faces, actually. The second best thing was the box of high-end treats Simon Berg, Cynthia's boyfriend, sent from Rover and Company. Two UPS guys could barely carry it up to our door. Also good was the big check Simon cut, big enough for Bernie to buy the Porsche from Nixon Panero—even older and more beat up than the one we'd lost, muddy brown in color, except for the doors, which were yellow—and still have some left over for straightening out our finances, at least a bit. Rick Torres brought Bernie a bottle of bourbon and said he was sorry. He and Bernie emptied the whole thing in one sitting. When it got to looking like they were about to crack open another and maybe even start into a bit of arm wrestling, I went to bed.

What else? Metro PD collared most of Gulagov's gang. Anatoly Bulganin got picked up at the airport, trying to catch a flight to Russia. Boris spent time in the hospital on his way to jail. The DA slapped conspiracy charges on Damon Keefer, and no one went his bail. Keefer broke down in front of the judge, said he hadn't realized the kind of people he was dealing with, loved Maddy more than anything, had tried his hardest to raise the money to pay back Gulagov, had only needed a little more time. The judge was not impressed. Then there was Harold. Harold cut a deal and walked. Bernie let him know that remaining in the state or ever returning would be bad ideas. We dropped in on Mr. Singh for the watch and some curried lamb. I lost the tip of one ear, but mismatched ears are no big deal, in my opinion—have I mentioned that already? We took a long walk together, me and Bernie.

The monsoons came—I'd forgotten all about them!—and put Bernie in a very good mood. One night we went camping, backyard-style: me, Bernie, Charlie, and Suzie. She came over quite a bit, but don't ask me exactly what was going on with that. At times when she was around, I caught a careful look in Bernie's eyes; other times something else. On this particular night, we built a fire, roasted hot dogs—Hebrew National, my favorite—and Bernie brought out the ukulele. He taught Charlie to play it a little. More than a little, in my mind—the kid was a musical genius. They sang "Up a Lazy River" and "When It's Sleepy Time Down South." I joined in on "Hey, Bo Diddley." Soon after that, Suzie left, and Bernie said, "'Night, big guy," and Charlie gave me a pat, and they went into the tent to sleep.

I lay by the fire, watching it slowly die. I could watch fires forever. The night grew quiet, quiet as it ever gets in the Valley. I was falling asleep myself when all at once I heard the she-bark. And not just the she-bark but the she-bark sounding closer than before, much closer. Was that wishful thinking—an expression I'd heard Bernie use from time to time—on my part? Couldn't tell you. It was just the way I think, that's all. I rose, ran to the back fence, and leaped over, soaring into the night.

ACKNOWLEDGMENTS

Many thanks to my editor, Peter Borland, and my agent, Molly Friedrich.

Turn the page for a sneak peek at
Spencer Quinn's newest novel, the sequel to *Dog on It:*

THEREBY HANGS A TAIL

A Chet and Bernie Mystery

Available January 2010 from Atria Books

ONE

The perp looked around—what nasty little eyes he had!—and saw there was nowhere to go. We were in some kind of warehouse, big and shadowy, with a few grimy high-up windows and tall stacks of machine parts. I couldn't remember how the warehouse fit in, exactly, or even what the whole case was all about; only knew beyond a doubt, from those nasty eyes and that sour end-of-the-line smell, a bit like those kosher pickles Bernie had with his BLTs—I'd tried one; once was enough for the kosher pickles, although I always had time for a BLT—that this guy was the perp. I lunged forward and grabbed him by the pant leg. Case closed.

The perp cried out in pain, a horrible, high-pitched sound that made me want to cover my ears. Too bad I can't do that, but no complaints—I'm happy the way I am (even if my ears don't match, something I found out about a while back but can't get into right now). The perp's noises went on and on and finally it hit me that maybe I had more than just his pant leg. That happened sometimes: my teeth are probably longer than yours and sharper, too. What was that? Yes, the taste of blood. My mistake, but a very exciting one all the same.

"Call him off!" the perp screamed. "I give up."

Bernie came running up from behind. "Good work, Chet," he said, huffing and puffing. Poor Bernie—he was trying to give up smoking again but not having much luck.

"Get him off! He's biting me!"

"Chet wouldn't bite," Bernie said. "Not deliberately."

"Not deliberately? What are you—"

"On the other hand, round about now he usually likes to hear a confession."

"Huh? He's a goddamn dog."

"Language," said Bernie.

Those nasty eyes shifted around, looking wild now. "But he's a dog."

"True," Bernie said.

I wagged my tail. And maybe, on account of the good mood I was in—what was better than a job well done?—shook my head from side to side a bit.

"Aaiieeee! I confess! I confess!"

"To what?"

"To what? The El Camino jewel heist, for Christ sake."

"El Camino jewel heist?" said Bernie. "We're here about the Bar J Guest Ranch arson."

"That, too," said the perp. "Just get him offa me."

"Chet?" Bernie said. "Chet?"

Oh, all right, but how about that taste, human blood? Addictive or what?

Hours later we had two checks, one for the arson, one for the jewel heist, and a good thing, too, because our finances were a mess—alimony, child support, a bad investment in some company with plans to make Hawaiian pants just like the Hawaiian shirts Bernie wears on special occasions, and not much work lately except for divorce cases, never any fun. We run a detective agency, me and Bernie, called the Little Detective Agency on account of Little being Bernie's last name. My name's Chet, pure and simple. Headquarters is our house on Mesquite Road, a nice place with a big tree out front, perfect for napping under, and the whole canyon easily accessible out back, if it just so happens someone left the gate open. And then, up in the canyon—well, say no more.

"This calls for a celebration," Bernie said. "How about a chew strip?" Was that a serious question? Who says no to a chew strip? He opened the cupboard over the sink, where the chew strips were kept; at one time, a very nice time, they'd been on an open shelf, lower down. "And while we're at it . . ." Uh-oh. Bernie reached for the bottle of bourbon, standing by the chew strip box.

We sat out back, watching the light change on the far side of the canyon as the sun went down, Bernie at the table sipping bourbon, me under it, trying to take my time with the chew strip. This wasn't any chew strip, but a high-end bacon-flavored rawhide chew from Rover and Company, an outfit owned by our buddy Simon something or other, whom we'd met on a missing-persons case, our specialty. Bacon smell—the best there is—rose all around me, like a dense cloud. I glanced up at Bernie through the glass tabletop. Could he smell it? Probably not. The puniness of his sense of smell—and the sense of smell of humans in general—was something I've never gotten used to.

He looked down at me. "What's on your mind, boy? Ten to one you're thinking about how you chased that guy down." Wrong, but at that moment he reached over and scratched between my ears, right on a spot I hadn't even realized was desperate for scratching, so I gave my tail a thump. Bernie laughed. "Read your mind," he said. Not close, but I didn't care—he could believe whatever he wanted as long as he kept up this scratching, digging his nails in just so, an expert. He stopped—too soon, always too soon—and said, "How about Dry Gulch? Hell, we earned it."

I was on my feet, gulping down what was left of the chew strip. The Dry Gulch Steakhouse and Saloon was one of our favorites. They had a big wooden cowboy out front—I'd lifted my leg against him once, not good, I know, but just too tempting—and a patio bar in back where my guys were welcome. We went in the Porsche—an old topless one that had replaced our even older topless one after it shot off a cliff on a day I'll never forget, although I've actually forgotten most of it already—brown with yellow doors, Bernie driving, me riding shotgun. Loved riding shotgun: what was better than this? I stuck my head way up, into the wind: smells went by faster than I could sort them out, a kind of nose feast that I'm afraid you'll never—

"Hey, Chet, a little space, buddy."

Oops. Way over on Bernie's side. I shifted closer to my door.

"And ease up on the drooling."

Drooling? Me? I moved over as far as I could and sat stiffly the rest of the way, back straight, eyes forward, aloof. I wasn't alone in the drooling department, had seen Bernie drooling in his sleep more than once, and Leda, too, Bernie's ex-wife, meaning humans drooled, big time. But had I ever made the slightest fuss about it, or thought less of them? You tell me.

We sat in the patio bar at the Dry Gulch Steakhouse and Saloon, Bernie on the end stool, me on the floor. The big summer heat—not just heat but pressure, like a heavy blanket is always weighing down on you—was over, but it was still plenty hot and the cool tiles felt good. Bernie pointed across the street with his chin. "What's that?"

"What's what?" said the bartender.

"That hole in the ground."

"Condos," the bartender said. "Ten stories? Fifteen maybe?"

Bernie has dark, prominent eyebrows with a language all their own. Sometimes, like now, they grew jagged and his whole face, normally such a nice sight, darkened. "And when the aquifer runs dry, what then?" he said.

"Aquifer?" said the bartender.

"Any idea of the current population of the Valley?" Bernie said.

"The whole valley?" said the bartender. "Gotta be up there." Bernie gave him a long look, then ordered a double.

A waitress in a cowboy hat came by. "Is that Chet? Haven't seen you in a while." She knelt down, gave me a pat. "Still like steak tips?" Why would that ever change? "Hey, easy, boy."

Bernie had a burger and another bourbon; steak tips and water for me. His face returned to normal. Whew. Bernie worried about the aquifer a lot and sometimes when he got going couldn't stop. All our water came from the aquifer—I'd heard him say that over and over, although I'd never laid eyes on this aquifer, whatever it was. I didn't get it at all: there was plenty of water in the Valley—how else to explain all that spraying on the golf courses, morning and evening, and those beautiful little rainbows the sprinklers made? We had water out the yingyang. I got up and pressed my head against Bernie's leg. He did some light scratching in that space between my eyes, impossible for me to get to. Ah, bliss. I spotted a French fry under the stool next to Bernie's and snapped it up.

A bourbon or two later, Lieutenant Stine of the Metro PD—a trim little guy in a dark suit—walked in. Bernie had worked for him sometime in the distant past, before my adventures in K-9 school (washing out on the very last day, a long story, but it's no secret that a cat was involved), and had played some role in Bernie and me getting together, the exact details a bit foggy.

"Hear you cleared the El Camino case," Lieutenant Stine said. "Nice job."

"Luck, mostly," Bernie said.

"And a full confession to boot."

"Chet's doing."

Lieutenant Stine glanced down, saw me. He had a thin face and thin lips, didn't smile much in my experience, but he smiled now, somehow ended up looking a little dangerous. "He's a good interrogator," he said.

"The best," said Bernie.

I thumped my tail.

"Understand a tidy reward went along with that," the lieutenant said. A few stools down the row, a guy in a Hawaiian shirt glanced over.

"No complaints," Bernie said to Lieutenant Stine. "What are you drinking?"

A minute or two later, Bernie and the lieutenant were clinking glasses. I'd lost count of Bernie's bourbons by now; counting isn't my strength, not past two.

"Glad I ran into you," Lieutenant Stine said. "There's a little something that might be up your alley."

"Like what?" Bernie said.

Lieutenant Stine glanced down at me. "Up your alley for sure, come to think of it," he said. "And potentially lucrative besides."

"You have our attention," said Bernie.

Lieutenant Stine lowered his voice, but nowhere near out of my range. Have I mentioned the sharpness of my hearing yet, or was that just about my teeth? At that very moment, for example, I could hear a woman huddled over a cell phone at a table clear across the room saying "They're upping my medication." That sounded so interesting, I missed the beginning of the lieutenant's remark, tuning in in time to catch ". . . Great Western Dog Show."

"Never heard of it," Bernie said.

"I'm surprised," said the lieutenant. "There's been a lot of publicity." Bernie shrugged. I loved that shrug of his. If only I could do that! I gave it a try, but all that happened was the hair on my back stood up on end. ". . . coming to the Arena end of next week," the lieutenant was saying. "Used to be in Denver, but the mayor lured them here."

"Why?"

"For the money it'll bring into the Valley, what else?"

"What money?"

"Hotel bookings, food and drink, all the tourist shit," said Lieutenant Stine. "The flowers alone come to a quarter mill."

"Flowers?" Bernie said.

"Exactly," said the lieutenant. "The Great Western crowd is a certain class of people—happens to be the mayor's favorite class, actually."

"I thought he was the reform guy."

"You're not alone."

"So what does he want me to do?" Bernie said, knocking back more bourbon. "Give the welcoming address?"

Lieutenant Stine laughed. There was something metallic in the sound; it gave me a bad feeling, deep inside my ears. "Not quite," he said. "In fact, he didn't single you out per se—it's even possible he's never heard of you, believe it or not—he just wants someone like you."

"To do what?"

The lieutenant lowered his voice some more. "Bodyguard duty."

"Nope."

"Nope? Just like that?"

"We don't do bodyguard duty."

"What about the Junior Ramirez case?"

"That's why."

"This is different. First, it pays two grand a day. Second, next to a psychotic like Junior Ramirez, this client's a walk in the park." Lieutenant Stine laughed that metallic laugh again. "Just about literally," he said.

"Two grand?" Bernie said.

"And a bonus at the end wouldn't be a stretch."

"Who's the client?" Bernie said. And, despite my memories of guarding Junior Ramirez—especially that incident with the ice cream and the razor blade—I was glad. Our finances were a mess, and two grand was two grand, and a whole week of two grands was . . . well, I'll leave that to you.

Lieutenant Stine reached into his jacket pocket, took out a photo.

"What's this?" Bernie said.

"That's her long name on the back," the lieutenant said. "'Kingsbury's First Lady Belle.' But for every day I think they call her Princess."

"The client is a dog?"

I sat up. Bernie was gazing at the photo. I could see it, too. One of my guys was in the picture? Where? And then I spotted her: a tiny fluffball with huge dark eyes, reclining on a satin pillow. I knew satin pillows on account of Leda having had one, although it got chewed up in a kind of frenzy, the details of the episode not too clear in my mind. But that satin taste: so strange and interesting, a vivid memory. I glanced around the Dry Gulch bar: no satin in view.

"Not just any dog," said Lieutenant Stine. "Princess is one of the top dogs in the country. She won best in show at Balmoral."

"What's that?"

"You don't know Balmoral? It's on ESPN2 every year, Bernie—the biggest dog show in the country."

"Never heard of it," Bernie said.

Lieutenant Stine gave Bernie a sideways look. I'd seen other friends of Bernie's do the same thing, Sergeant Torres at Missing Persons, for example, or Otis DeWayne, our weapons guy—but didn't know what it meant. "So you don't want the job?" the lieutenant said.

Job? What job? Making sure that a fluffball on a satin pillow stayed out of trouble? That was free money, not a job. Come on, Bernie.

"Who's the owner?" Bernie said.

"Woman name of Adelina Borghese."

"Where from?"

"Italy, I think. But she owns a spread over in Rio Loco."

"Rio Loco?" Bernie said. "I'll talk to her."

The lieutenant nodded. "Knew you wouldn't say no to that kind of green."

The Hawaiian shirt man glanced over again.

Bernie's eyebrows went a little jagged. "I'll talk to her, that's all. I can still say no."

Lieutenant Stine went away. I polished off my steak tips, stretched out on those cool tiles, chilled out. What a life! The final chase through the warehouse ran pleasantly through my mind. And then again. After a while, I grew aware that the Hawaiian shirt guy had moved next to Bernie and struck up a conversation, at first about Hawaiian shirts, then about something else.

"What I run," he was saying, "is what you might call a hedge fund for the little guy."

"Little guy?" said Bernie.

"Not little in terms of intelligence or ability," the Hawaiian shirt man added quickly. "But for one reason or another, men of distinction who don't happen to be Wall Street insiders. I've had some nice play in commodities lately. You're familiar with the basics of tin futures?"

Bernie motioned for another drink, overturning the salt and pepper. "Can't be that complicated," he said.

"Exactly," replied the Hawaiian shirt man. And to the bartender when Bernie's drink came: "I'll get that." Then came a lot of back and forth about tin, puts, calls, Bolivia, and other mysteries. My eyelids got heavy, way too heavy to keep open. I let them close, drifted off. Harmless talk was all it was. As long as the checkbook didn't come out of Bernie's pocket, we were in good shape.

Sometime later I awoke, feeling tip-top. I got up, gave myself a good shake, looked around. The bar was empty except for me, the bartender, the man in the Hawaiian shirt, and Bernie. The only completely sober one was me. Then came the bartender, the man in the Hawaiian shirt, and Bernie, dead last. Also, the checkbook was coming out.